PIRATE GOLD AND MURDER

Book Thirteen: The Fiona Fleming Cozy Mysteries

PATTI LARSEN

Cover design by Christina Gaudet
www.castlekeepcreations.com

Thanks, Kirstin!

ISBN-13: 978-1-988700-74-8

CHAPTER ONE

I could honestly say there was nothing more incredible than opening my eyes to find a pair of gorgeous blue ones staring right back at me. I'd been enjoying this particular view for the last six months, with many, many more mornings to come. The rest of our lives together, to be exact, minus a few the delicious man I'd married was out of town.

How lucky could I possibly get?

Crew's crooked smile, the sexy one that actually made me secretly happy I no longer ran a demanding and time-consuming bed and breakfast on a daily basis spread to that brilliant gaze, the corners crinkling, sunlight from the parted curtains making his eyes sparkle. Literally sparkle. Like an angel or some kind of make-believe, Hollywood-created tall, dark and luscious hunk of manhood who couldn't possibly exist in real life.

Except he did. And he was in bed with me.

Growl.

If I still had Petunia's? I'd be up and at 'em, 6AM, with only rare opportunities to take in the yummy view of how his muscles tensed and bunched when he reached for me, how the heat of his skin made my whole body tingle when he tugged me close, the scent of him eliminating my ability to think straight for the few moments I inhaled him and let the world disappear.

How did I know? I'd had experience, right? While we dated. And though we'd been mostly well behaved, I'd had enough early mornings forced to drag myself away from him I now and would forevermore fully appreciate the fact I no longer had to put my happiness and my time and energy into other people's tourist experience. As much as I'd loved Petunia's, as much as I still missed the beautiful old house and the memories I'd made there, I loved Crew Turner more.

Bliss was sleeping in until 7:30 beside the man of my dreams.

I knew moving would wake the pug at our feet. Petunia had taken a few weeks to adjust to her new home at Crew's house, the poor, portly creature rather discombobulated by the change in her routine. She had, after all, spent the last eight years of her life in my grandmother's—and then my—home, woken every morning like clockwork far too early but just fine with her, spending her days surrounded by people and dropping food and tidbits handed over by guests who could read the DO NOT FEED THE DOG signs posted everywhere. While my previous six months had been a rather delightful descent into a job with more regular hours and the chance to spend time with the man I loved, Petunia's existence had taken a turn for the confusing.

She snorted when she joined us, her still rotund body heavy as she gracelessly tromped her way into our personal space and plopped her fat butt down on Crew's chest. He laughed and scratched her ear, making her yawn and cat-meow her approval. I offered my own caress, though I'd been starting to consider kicking her off the bed again since she was rather an uncomfortable third wheel when I wanted some private time with my husband.

My. *Husband.* Never got old.

"I think she's finally settling in." Crew worried about her as much as I did, bless him. It wasn't lost on me she'd been out of sorts not just because of the loss of Petunia's, but thanks to the poisoning she'd (barely) survived just before the wedding, not to mention the blow to the head she'd taken to knock her out the night that fire devoured the house that bore her name. I still owed Ruth and Peggy for that. I wasn't about to disagree with my darling former FBI agent turned former sheriff turned private investigator extraordinaire, though. While she might still have been acting quirky and nervous from all the changes, the pug had managed to maintain her sweetness, at least.

Maybe I was being hasty about kicking her off the bed.

Crew stretched with Petunia still on his broad chest, making her scramble for balance and finally hop over me to settle with her bulging brown eyes glaring at both of us like we'd insulted her somehow. Another long, warm hug and we were up and out of bed, a routine that felt like I'd spent my whole life designing it settling around us in a happy fog.

I caught myself humming most mornings as I made the bed, brushed my teeth with my hip pressed to Crew's while he shaved, while I poured our coffee and shared crispy bacon and medium eggs from a single plate, orange juice from a shared glass.

So this was what domestic bliss felt like. Yes, please.

"Did you want to drop Petunia off at the annex before we head to the club?" Crew glanced at his watch, a boyish grin tugging at his lips.

I grinned back with a start, realizing in the magical morning I'd almost forgotten what today was. Almost. "Mom will love to have her," I said, still feeling a bit guilty over dumping the annex on her and Daisy, though neither of them protested all that much. I helped out when they needed me, kind of a giant role reversal. But since the loss of Petunia's and my new daily endeavors at Fleming Investigations had taken over my time, I'd let the three-way partnership turn mostly into Mom and Day.

"I'll call MC when we're ready to go." Crew's

growing excitement was contagious as he tapped his fingers on the counter, one knee bobbing. He took the last two bites of his eggs a bit too fast, swallowing hard, gulping coffee. "I really want a chance to get a look at the bottom of the lake today."

And there it was, the bubble of anxious delight and nervous thrill that I'd been shoving down as hard as I could the last few weeks. Since my gorgeous husband, his jaw set and his determination winning us all over, told the Reading Hoard Crew (as we'd come to call ourselves) since Rosebert clearly knew about the truth of the treasure, there was only one thing to do.

Go public. And did we ever.

"She said the equipment arrived last night?" I cleared the dishes away while Crew transferred the last of his coffee to a travel mug, and one for me, while Petunia shuffled back and forth from one foot to the other, licking her chops before he handed her a little pile of blueberries he'd saved for her. She snorfled them down with suitable enthusiasm while he answered.

"Should be loaded on the boat and ready when we get there." His tone was calm, even, as much as mine was. A lie, both of us doing our best to uphold this charade of not caring one way or another if we found anything today. While my heart pounded, and I had to distract myself with loading the dishwasher to keep from shrieking out loud.

"Can we really cover the whole lake in one day?" I finally turned to him, my worry emerging. This was a huge endeavor, after all. One that, when we'd called a town hall meeting and actually revealed to the gathered residents of Reading what we'd found and what we were doing, had resulted in the kind of uproar that was usually reserved for visiting royalty.

I shoved that memory aside, too, of the cheering and the following minor protests and the national media we'd sidestepped, all the while wondering and worrying still about my missing friend. Pamela Shard might have assured me in an email she was okay, and in a way that proved it was her who'd sent it. But it had been six more months without a sign of her and there had been one other notable woman who'd vanished from Reading due to the Patterson family, so there was precedence to be concerned.

Nope. Not thinking about Fiona Doyle today. Not.

Crew handed me my coffee when I straightened from harnessing Petunia. "MC seems to think so," he said. "And my experience with side-scan sonar fits her assessment. As long as we stick to the pattern we planned on. Or." He paused then, grinned.

Or. Find the good captain's brigantine ship, the *Darkling Dragon*, sunk and waiting for us somewhere under there.

Ack. Stop it, brain. No jumping ahead of yourself today.

It was hard, though. Hard to maintain a normal tone of voice as Crew locked the front door of his little house, when he climbed into the front seat of his new SUV, me behind the wheel of my car to follow, while he drove up the street to the annex so I could drop off the squirming pug in my lap. So hard not to demand he double (okay, triple, yeah, make that quadruple) check the credentials of the treasure hunting team Liz recommended. Of course, I'd looked into MC Tortuga and her people. I now knew intimately (thank you, private investigation training) every dive they'd undertaken, their specialty underwater searches, each of her crew talented, passionate about their work and experienced enough I should have been reassured that Chantal Laniel, Anja Härle and MC herself would get the job done if anyone could.

Except. Well. Control freak much?

I glanced in the rearview mirror of my car and suppressed the frown that always fought for ownership of my face at the sight of the black sedan following me at what felt like a less-than-discrete distance. Not that I didn't like Darius Smith (surely his real last name, right? Right), mind you. The giant bully—sorry, bodyguard—who used to protect Malcolm Murray with such quiet composure and now did the same for me—from outside my house, firmly and without compromise outside my house— was a good person as far as criminal heavyweights who did the kind of work he did went. I even kind of enjoyed his sense of humor when I got the chance to actually talk to him. But having him hover over me, lingering in the background, making me uncomfortable and look over my shoulder endlessly? That got old fast.

Protesting to Malcolm ended in nada. And asking Darius to stop doing what his boss required of him? Like telling a brick wall to just freaking stop being a wall already.

Frustrated? Who, me?

And if I was annoyed and out of sorts, Crew was all kinds of put out and irritated. Though, to his credit, my gorgeous husband creature didn't show it often. Just enough I knew it lingered with him like a toothache. Every once in a while, the vein in his forehead would pulse, the cord in his neck standing out and even the old tic under his eye would fire up and I'd have to distract him to keep him from doing something we'd both regret. Yes, he carried a gun, but so did Darius and the behemoth of a giant in a suit and tie and plastic earpiece outweighed even the solid strength of the man I loved by six inches and over fifty pounds.

I bit back a sigh and purposely looked away from the sedan in the mirror. While Darius's presence reminded me constantly that Peggy Munroe and her grandniece, Ruth Wilkins, were still out there and gunning for me, it wasn't reassuring to know he was there. Instead, it made it impossible to sink back into the full and blatant ignorance I'd cultivated the bulk of my mostly happy existence. I missed it.

Daisy accepted the grunting, farting pug with a beaming smile and a kiss for my cheek. "Good luck, keep us posted!"

I hugged her as I left again, knowing I was hurrying now, the excitement too much for me and it wasn't until I climbed back into my car and followed the SUV, I realized I forgot to hug Mom. Bad daughter. She'd understand, though. She'd been there, Dad, too, when MC had agreed to help, when she and her crew, excited themselves when presented the evidence we'd gathered, agreed to join the search. Even offered to foot the bill for the hunt.

"Part of the job," the treasure hunter, her dark hair in a ponytail, blue-green eyes lit with something I recognized in myself as the lust to know, just know the truth, said in her low, calm voice. Like she'd done this a million times before despite the impish grin she'd flashed when she'd handled the doubloon I'd found in Grandmother Iris's music box. She had been much better at containing her excitement than I'd ever be. "And our financial backers love this kind of evidence. For a cut of the treasure."

I had the insurance money from Petunia's and enough saved up from how busy I'd been I could have funded the project. But I was happy to not have to dip into that cash, and since this really wasn't about getting rich (shiver, giggle, meep) but figuring out the mystery behind the treasure itself (keep telling yourself that, Fee), I didn't mind sharing.

With MC and Tortuga Divers. But as I drove past the sheriff's office and the male half of Rosebert climbed out of his cruiser to glare at us on the way by? Yeah, you can bet my generosity died a quick and painful death.

Because despite the fact they still had a piece of the map and there was a possibility we'd never find the treasure without it? The piles of whatever the old privateer had or hadn't hidden away could stay lost forever if that was the case.

One thing was absolutely, utterly and completely certain. I'd be sharing the hoard with my hated cousin and his little snip of a girlfriend over Captain Reading's dead body.

CHAPTER TWO

Cutter Lake's smooth surface flashed past the end of the dock as Crew pulled into the parking lot and stopped on the far side of the large, white pickup truck, the cap bearing the Tortuga Divers logo. I parked beside him, waving at Chantal where she leaned against the passenger's door, talking intently with Anja, instant concern tightening the already tense line running up the center of my back to my now aching shoulders at the sight of their grim expressions. A million worries woke, including the nervous anxiety tied to the fact we'd been wasting their time after all, and they were pissed to discover the treasure wasn't real. But as I exited my car, hurrying to them while Crew beat me to it, I could tell their anger wasn't aimed at me, at us.

"Something's wrong." My husband wasn't big on preamble and, frankly, neither was I.

Chantal's shoulders shrugged in a sharp up and down, her green eyes narrowed, normally kind and sweet nature clearly on edge. I'd started thinking of her as the easy-going, happy-go-lucky member of the group that put everyone at ease with her kind smile and ability to explain basics without judgment, even to a rank newbie like me. Not that Anja with her tall, willowy beauty wasn't lovely, or MC, for that matter. But I'd taken to thinking of them as three parts of a puzzle who each complimented the task at hand—the leader with her instant decisions, the teacher and her kind patience and the adventurous youngest member with her enthusiasm and fresh ideas.

Concerning to see these two suddenly uptight and upset. Gave me reason to worry, I guess.

"You could say that." Chantal exhaled deeply, slowly, like she fought her temper while Anja, arms crossed over her chest, looked away, lips in a line, bangs low and straight in a dark shadow over her brown eyes.

"The equipment?" Crew's obsessiveness over safety and the gear we were using was understandable. His commercial diver training—a massive leap ahead from fresh-from-her-beginner diving course me who was still trying not to panic I'd forget everything once under the water—made him uber cautious. A good thing, as far as I was concerned, and hadn't met any objections from the team.

But Anja's tight headshake, her long, dark hair shivering down her back as she denied his question, was joined by Chantal's echoing, "No." They both glanced past the front of the team truck toward the dock and, for the first time, I noticed MC stood near the gear shed, almost to the end of the wooden floats, where the boat we'd hired waited, bobbing ever so lightly on the shining water of the lake.

She wasn't alone, and the man she was speaking to—no, arguing with—didn't look familiar. Neither did the second man, standing slightly off, his expression concerned as he watched their growing fight unfold. I could hear them now, their voices rising, watched MC's right hand rise and fall, form a fist, strike her thigh loudly enough the sound reached us.

"Who," Crew growled, blue eyes locked on the fight, "is that?"

"Trouble," Chantal muttered back as MC finally spun away from the two men and marched toward us, her feet thudding on the wooden slats, shoulders tense, scowl dark enough to make me think twice about ever crossing her. Good thing she was on our side.

She swung up the ramp from the floats below to the main dock, joining us while the two men trailed behind her. I instantly disliked the smirk on the face of the one she'd been arguing with, despite his attractiveness. He had that dark-haired and blue-eyed look that was usually my type, but the clear arrogance that gave him a rolling swagger and the way he looked me up and down?

Yeah. Nope.

Besides, I was married to tall, dark and handsome. And if MC and her crew didn't like this asshat? I was team Tortuga all the way.

I gave the second guy a brief once over, not meaning to dismiss him but not really having much choice as MC joined us, jaw jumping before she inhaled to speak. At least Dude#2 looked innocuous enough, even a bit embarrassed to be there. So, our trouble was with Dude#1?

We'd just see about that.

"Crew." MC nodded to him. "Fee." I returned her head bob. "I'm afraid I have some... troubling news." She didn't turn around, didn't bother, as Captain BossyPants pushed his way into our little circle, facing off with my husband. Crew had at least six inches on the guy, but you'd think he was a giant the way he grinned at winked at the former sheriff.

Of course, my darling was never one to be intimidated. He glared right back while he addressed MC. "What seems to be the problem?"

"No problem." Mr. NoticeMe stuck out one hand in an aggressive show of the kind of masculine bravado that made me want to sigh and eye roll just to vent some of my anxiety. "You must be Turner." Crew's natural politeness kicked in and he shook the guy's hand, though I was more hesitant when he turned to me and offered the same courtesy. "And that makes you Fleming."

"And you are?" I glanced at MC and noted her

continuing unhappiness as the man, still grinning like he was having the time of his life, slipped one arm around her shoulders and squeezed in a clearly false show of comradery.

"Gregg Brown," he said. "Your new partner."

CHAPTER THREE

Um. *What?*

I wanted to protest. Fish lipped, I'm sure of it, my denial that this stranger—arrogant and instantly unlikeable or not—thought he could muscle his way into our treasure hunt without our permission making my stomach knot into a ball of intense need to shove him off the end of the dock.

I didn't. I behaved. Only because I was literally held in place by shock. If I'd been better prepared? Yeah, no promises he'd have survived the splash.

"Allow me to explain." He had to use that smarmy TV host tone of voice, that fake *let me take care of everything, honey, there's a good girl* kind of condescending attempt to get his own way, didn't he? Just when I was starting to despise him.

Snarl.

"Please," Crew said at his most dry, a sure sign he was about to implode or explode or something that would do damage to the still smiling man in front of us. "Do."

But it was MC who cut in, who growled a soft, guttural protest of a sound before taking the bull by the horns—or, more appropriately, my husband by his temper—and filled us in on what Chantal had called troubling news.

"Gregg's company owns the sonar equipment we rented." She bit out each syllable like they caused her pain, a deep toothache of acceptance. "He insists on joining our expedition." She flashed him a glare. "Apparently, taking part is in the small print of the contract."

"We didn't agree to anyone else joining us." I'd been John Fleming's daughter my whole life, that mountain of a former sheriff and master of intimidation without saying a single word well rubbed off on me. But it was clear this Gregg person wasn't aware of my lineage and nor did he give a crap about the dueling scowls worn by every single person in our little huddle.

Everyone, that was, but the man who hovered at his elbow, still looking contrite about the whole thing.

"Gregg." He spoke up, voice low and tense. "Maybe we should—"

Whatever Dude#2 was going to say, it was clear Gregg was the boss because a single dismissive motion with one hand while the smile vanished and the cold, calculating snake underneath made an appearance cemented the nature of their relationship pretty effectively.

"My equipment," Gregg snarled, "my rules." His smile flashed into view again, perfect and unnaturally white teeth too bright against his tanned face. "You don't like it? Find another set of sonar."

Sounded like he already knew that was going to be difficult. MC's scowl and head shake told me I was right.

"We booked a month ago," she said.

"So you did." Gregg laughed. "Gave me enough time to poke around into what you were looking for, MC." He tsked at her, glanced at the man behind him. "Right, Martin? Tortuga should have expected this, considering."

Huh? "Considering what?" Great. Had I missed something? Maybe my detective skills weren't anything to write home about after all.

Gregg's demeanor turned to transparent modesty. "Why, only that where she fails, I never do."

MC glared and if she could have killed him with that look? Oh, he'd have been dead so many times over he'd have run out of reincarnations in about ten seconds flat.

"You're a treasure hunter, I take it." Crew was at least keeping his head, even if I was still in a bit of a flabbergasted state. Or maybe I was just taking in this new information and processing it so I could make a logical and informed decision moving forward. Right,

Fleming. Lying to myself at that moment seemed like a good idea so I didn't lose my freaking mind. We were so close. Why did we have to run into problems now? I did my best not to blame MC while Gregg answered my husband's flat question that wasn't really a question.

"I am," he said, spreading his arms wide, bumping Anja who snarled her protest at his touch. "With a better record than Tortuga, I can assure you." He winked at me. "If anything, I assure you, my presence is an asset to this hunt. And I am only here to help."

Chantal snorted but didn't speak. No, that was MC's job.

"Just because you've scooped some of my finds—"

Gregg cut her off with an extravagant sigh. "That old complaint." He turned to the man behind him and laughed. "Tired of hearing it, aren't we, Martin?"

Martin just shrugged.

When Gregg returned his attention to us, I had a sudden connection of memory. And as was my brain's MO when it came to such instances, I blurted out what I remembered. "You were here, years ago." I jabbed a finger in his direction. "You were one of the hunters who debunked the treasure. Made Olivia a laughingstock." Not that I had all that much sympathy for the former mayor of Reading. Olivia Walker's attempts to lure tourists to what she'd dubbed the cutest town in America had succeeded, but I hadn't always agreed with her tactics. Still, here stood one of the very treasure hunters who'd made her life miserable and while she might not have been my favorite person—or me hers—she was local, damn it. Defending her was a matter of pride.

Gregg shrugged. "I did," he said, simple and frank.

"So, if you don't believe in the treasure," I said, vindication giving me a burst of justified argument that felt in the moment like the winning blow, "why do you even want to be part of our hunt?"

Gregg's smile returned, though this time tight, hungry, without any sort of filter to hide his clear greed and determination. "Because of this," he said.

And showed me the doubloon.

My doubloon.

Grandmother Iris's doubloon.

My. Head. Exploded. Good thing my darling, loving, caring husband was standing right next to me, because if I'd been alone with Gregg Brown in that moment?

I might have discovered twelve dead bodies over the last few years. But his would have been my first murder.

For one single instant, I caught the startled shock in his blue eyes, though it was gone in a flash, and I may only have imagined it. But his smirk disappeared, and he tossed the coin to MC as if divesting himself of my property would wash clean his filthy act. How dare he touch my treasure?

"Unless you want to wait for new equipment," he said, now brusque and sharp, amusement gone, "and trust me, there's nothing available," that made his good humor return if only for a moment, "you can either break the contract and I'll take my sonar and go. Or."

"Or," MC said, voice low and angry but filled with enough acceptance I knew we'd lost, "we let you join us." She met my eyes. "We need to talk."

Did we ever.

Gregg didn't try to follow us as I grasped MC's elbow and guided her away, down to the end of Crew's SUV where we huddled with Anja and Chantal, Martin speaking in a low, quiet voice to his boss while Gregg scowled and shook his head. I chose to ignore them, taking the gold coin from MC. She looked startled then a little hurt before rubbing both hands on her thighs in a quick, angry motion.

"The truth is, he has a stellar record," she said, quiet enough her voice wouldn't carry. MC looked like she was choking on that truth and even her team, as angry as they still visibly were, didn't argue so I had to take her statement at face value. "If he wasn't such a jackass about it, he'd actually be a good addition to the team."

"That's going a bit far, don't you think?" Chantal seemed to want to say more but held back while MC seemed to wait for the words that didn't come.

"You have history," I said, knowing I wasn't coming across as nice or polite or anything else that could be construed as positive work relationship building. Like I gave a crap at the moment. "Tell me it's not going to come back to bite us in the ass." I glanced behind me at the pair now whispering heatedly to each other. "And who's this other guy?"

"Martin Faller, Gregg's documentarian." Anja made a face like she was feeling ill. "Seriously, the man has an ego he needs an extra 7mm wetsuit and set of oxygen tanks just to carry it around with him."

Diver humor. I was still learning, though the context wasn't lost on me.

"He's been a pain in my ass for years," MC finally admitted, leaning against the back of the black truck, her face falling, anger draining away. It was in that moment I knew we'd lost and if we wanted to proceed today, we'd have to do so with Gregg's help. And hated it.

The dark sedan that pulled into the parking lot, coming to a halt next to the quiet, watchful driver in the matching one, disgorged the petite but always commanding form of Special Agent Elizabeth Michaud. She strode toward us after a quick nod to the watchful Darius, her happy expression switching instantly to flat G-woman on a mission as she took in our glum attitude. And the moment she looked up and caught sight of Gregg? Well. I'd never seen Liz's temper. Crew's former partner had always come across as level, collected and professional, even when she was happy.

At that moment she laid eyes on the unwelcome treasure hunter? Wow. I thought MC's glare had been deadly.

Liz came to a halt next to her friend, grasping MC's arm in one hand, her thin body quivering inside her perfectly pressed FBI standard-issue suit.

"What. The. Actual." She let MC go then, not missing a stride, covering the distance between us and the now watchful Gregg and Martin with her comfortable shoes barely touching the ground.

MC looked like she wanted to stop her, but it was Crew who went after his former partner, the Tortuga team leader finally following, while I grasped firmly onto my desire to fall into blame, fury and a hissy fit of gargantuan proportions before ordering Darius to toss Gregg into the center of the lake.

Big girl panties.

"Tell me I shouldn't be worried." I looked back and forth between Anja and Chantal while the two reacted in their own way. The tall brunette sighed heavily, looking out over the water like she didn't have the heart to answer while her counterpart seemed to pull herself together, faint smile returning, warmth to her eyes.

"MC is right about one thing," she said. "Gregg has an excellent track record. And while he's a risk-taker, he's known for getting the job done." Her returned calm actually made me feel better, even more when she reached out and touched my arm in that reassuring way of hers. "We all hate to admit it but having him as part of the team just increased our chances of finding what we're looking for."

"If it's out there to find," I said, hating my doubt but voicing it at last.

Chantal's good humor only increased and even Anja grinned. "That's the fun, Fee," she said. "Right,

Anja?"

"Exactly." The glitter of excitement in the young woman's gaze finished off the last of the tension and let me release my homicidal need to put an end to anything that might come between me and the hoard. Wow, was I really that possessive of a heap of maybe gold and possibly jewels that I'd kill for it?

Nope, not the treasure. The history, our town. And the fact I really, really didn't like Gregg Brown.

"So, he has a history of taking MC's jobs?" I let Crew and Liz deal with the mess, knowing it was kind of a coward's way out but happy to regain some semblance of myself.

Anja nodded, earnest expression sad all of a sudden. "Not just MC," she said, keeping her voice low, glancing over as if worried he might hear her. "He has a terrible reputation for scooping other teams."

Chantal seemed uncomfortable enough I felt for both of them.

"Why do people let him get away with it?" Seemed like someone might have contemplated a brief walk off a short pier for him along the way.

The girls shrugged in tandem. "He gets the job done," they said, also together. Like this was an old argument they'd shared enough times it had its own rote response.

Crew returned, Liz following with her firm grip on MC dragging the treasure hunter away from her conversation with Gregg. He was grinning again, so clearly the FBI agent had lost the battle she'd waged on her friend's behalf. It was obvious she knew exactly who Gregg was and, when the three rejoined us, her huffing fury emanated from her like the corona of the sun.

"You had to know this was coming," she snapped at MC who just looked tired.

"What do you want to do?" Crew's quiet, level tone seemed to cut through everything. I reached out and took my husband's hand while Liz tsked but relented, the Tortuga leader and her divers all exchanging glances as Crew went on. "We hired you," he said, "not Gregg Brown. If you think we should wait for new equipment, we wait. But if you trust him to help…"

MC's expression settled into her more familiar confident command. "A delay looking for replacement equipment could cripple us," she said. "Our rental costs are depleting our budget. Everything is in place now, today. And while my funders are patient, our resources aren't unlimited."

Crew nodded, squeezing my hand when I inhaled for one more protest. "How do we keep Mr. Brown over there from making off with our treasure if he finds it?"

So, my darling was on the same page as me? Good to know.

MC's face twisted into savage promise. "Oh, he won't try to cheat you," she said. "He just wants the credit and a small cut for his trouble. Trust me, Gregg Brown doesn't care about the treasure." She shook just a little, a tremor running under the crust of her forced collective calm. "All he wants is the fame."

"That's correct." Gregg chose that moment to interrupt, Martin hovering behind him. "And since I know how close you are to tapped out, MC,"—she what?—"I'm happy to share the find—and the fame—and even take on the rental bill for the sonar equipment. Just to make things equitable."

So, there were things she was hiding from us. I really wasn't that great of a detective, it turned out. As for MC, she looked like she wanted to throw up.

No way was I letting Gregg have the last word or take over this hunt. Before anyone else could speak up, I let my inner redhead out to play.

"Fine," I said. "But I'll tell you one thing, Mr. Brown. If you try to cheat us?" I jabbed a finger at the waiting water. "They'll never find your body."

CHAPTER FOUR

I had no idea anyone could throw up as much as Darius did that day. In fact, I was certain the giant bodyguard would eventually wither up and float away in a pile of dust. Surely, he didn't have a drop of moisture left in his hulking body, though, as he sank to the floor of the boat with a groan following one more go at letting his insides see the light of day, the greenish tint to his skin and the heavy, beaded sweat on his face was clear indication he wasn't going to stop any time soon.

"Are you sure you don't want to go back to the dock?" I'd been asking him the same question for the last three hours, three torturous and horrific hours while the black-suited and primly tied, polished shoed tower of typical stoic silence moaned a protest.

"I'm fine, Miss Fleming." It's all he'd uttered. And no, he wasn't insulting Crew. I'd kept Fleming, though I did wonder at the correct use of Miss vs. Mrs.

Fee. Darius was dying and I was thinking about social niceties.

"You should have told me you get seasick." I crouched next to him, the others firmly ignoring him as they had since he'd begun his little voyage into personal suffering not ten minutes after we'd set out across the crystal lake to the head of the Minute River, the feeding point at the base of Black and Ember Mountains. At least he'd distracted me from the nail-biting process of scanning the bottom of the lake for anything viable. I was almost grateful for the chance to focus on something other than the muttering and indecipherable shorthand even my beloved Crew participated in while the Tortuga team, Gregg and my husband tucked close, hunched over the small screen that delivered the sonar scans back to the surface one agonizing update at a time.

Exciting at first? You bet. Three hours later? Despite the canopy over the flat-decked boat, the heat was getting to me. Redheads and hot sun don't exactly mix. And the impatience that was my normal operating system wanted answers now.

Okay, so I was bored. Nursing Darius—about as stubborn as they come, considering he was on board a boat in a full suit in the middle of a July day when he knew he couldn't handle open water—at least gave me something to do.

I glanced up as we passed the two boats in the distance, my jaw tightening. We'd had a lovely—insert sarcasm here—encounter with Geoffrey Jenkins about an hour in, when we'd drawn near the Patterson dock. Two small boats had hurried toward us, the accountant at the head of one, his typical shark's smirk firmly in place.

"You don't have permission to search this part of the lake," he'd said. And while I wanted to argue, we all did, the presence of Sheriff Jill Wagner at his side, her unhappiness apparent, told me we weren't going to win if we decided to fight.

"Sorry, Fee," she'd called across to us. "They have the support of the council on this."

Whatever. So, we were cut off from a small portion of the lake. So what if Captain Reading's ship was under that particular stretch of water and the treasure long gone. So what?

Argh. Hard not to let it get me down.

Crew joined me, patting Darius's shoulder, the first real show of friendliness he'd offered the big man since Malcolm ordered his main bodyguard to look after me. Maybe seeing Darius was human warmed my crime-fighting husband's heart. Or maybe he just needed a distraction of his own.

"We're almost done," he said. "This new system covers a lot of ground." He grunted something under his breath I missed before going on. "I hate to admit it, but Gregg knows his stuff." He glanced over his shoulder at the monitor and its audience, just as the aforementioned treasure hunter laughed that annoyingly arrogant laugh of his, one arm sliding around MC's waist in a far too familiar gesture that told me they'd more than worked together. And knowing they'd been involved at one point? Added layers to potential complications.

Sigh. Could my day get any more frustrating?

"Are you finding anything?" From the lack of enthusiasm on Crew's face, I already had my answer.

"Nothing definitive," he said. "The problem is a wooden ship would have deteriorated a fair amount by now. Silt from the river, not to mention a few rockslides…" he sighed, rubbing at his face, eyes tired when he met mine again. "We're going to have to dive to be sure."

"We assumed that," I said, leaning in to kiss his cheek.

"Some of the areas we need to search are deeper than expected," he said, wincing a little. "Sorry, Fee, but you're going to be left out of most of the dives."

Well, that had been expected, too. "My fault for leaving my beginning diver course so long," I said. "I trust you, Crew. That's all that matters."

"That's it." You know, I'd thought Gregg's voice was jarring, but it just got worse with use. Seriously, could he be any more irritating? And taking over the whole project, muscling his way in. I scowled as he shut off the machine, while MC frowned like she was going to protest. "We've scanned your little lake. Nothing to see here, folks." He seemed almost pleased. A total counterbalance to the grim trio of Tortuga divers who sat back and exchanged looks.

Gregg, meanwhile, winked at MC with a smirk that rivaled Geoffrey's. "How about you and I have dinner, a bottle of wine, look over the results—"

"How about," Crew cut in, growl in his voice uncharacteristic since he rarely lost his temper, "you hand over our footage. Since we only needed your equipment. Not your analysis."

Gregg looked surprised a moment and I almost laughed as I realized Crew had the right of it. Outmaneuvered himself, the jerk.

"I'm the most familiar with the equipment," the treasure hunter blurted, staring right at MC. "And I'm the most likely to find what you're looking for."

She paused then nodded to Crew, to me. "I'm afraid he's right," she said. "Every sonar has its own peculiarities. And while we are definitely going to have a solid look ourselves, Gregg will have the best chance of spotting something we might miss."

Well, craptastic. Still, I'd be hugging my husband for trying.

"I guess that means we're diving tomorrow?" Chantal prodded MC who nodded.

"We'll prep our gear when we're done with the footage," she said. "You and Anja can divide up the dive locations once we have a list and assign teams."

The youngest of the Tortuga divers glanced at Gregg who grinned back. "We'll take care of it."

Clearly, they had a set way of doing things and our new arrival was gumming up the works. I waved to our captain and Wanda Beaman cheerfully waved back, turning us toward shore. She'd been happy to take the job despite the improvements in her fishing business and I was equally happy to have her, knowing the lake was her second home and had been her whole life. She hadn't expressed any opinions about the treasure one way or the other, however, merely piloting us with her steady patience. And kudos to her for not judging, at least visibly, as she raced toward the marina, leaving a v-shaped trail of white water behind us, sending Darius heaving over the side once more.

I noted Chantal and Anja moving away from the sonar equipment, huddling and whispering as they glared at Gregg. Martin had kept his head down, going almost unnoticed, fiddling with a camera he occasionally aimed at Gregg and, when Crew left me to Darius and returned to where Gregg and MC seemed intent on a conversation that left them looking more chummy than confrontational, I took a moment to lean in to Martin and smile though I'm sure my expression was less friendly and more snarl.

"I take it MC and Gregg were something more than just rivals."

The cameraman twitched, enough guilt on his face when he looked up at the pair and then down at his camera, I knew I was right. "Used to be," he muttered.

"I take it you disapprove." No questions. Just statements.

The small man shrugged, narrow shoulders rounding forward, the lines on his forehead creasing toward his receding hairline as his hazel eyes flickered to mine a moment. "It's none of my business," he said.

"Well," I shot back, "it's mine if it's going to interfere with this hunt."

Martin fiddled with his camera further. Was I making him nervous or was he hiding something? I have to admit, I wasn't trying to mask my animosity. I'd come too far, suffered too much, lost an immeasurable amount to allow anyone to come between me and the resolution of this mystery. Maybe I was being a bit overenthusiastic in my aggression but damn it, this was important. I owed it to Grandmother Iris to see it through and if he or Gregg or anyone got in my way?

Heaven help them.

Martin's refusal to answer only increased my already tweaked temper and, when we finally docked, I couldn't even bring myself to be kind to Wanda, despite the fact the older woman had only ever been kind to me.

She didn't seem to mind, though, and the flat look she shot at Gregg told me she must have understood my mood and was giving me leeway. Bless her.

I left Crew and the others to go over the footage, noting that Gregg left before me and good riddance. Though, what happened to him being the only one who could read the results? Grumble, mumble, whatever. I needed to get my head on straight and out of this funk I'd found myself in. And my day had started so bright, so full of hope.

Now? I just wanted to go home and crawl back into bed and start all over again.

Instead, I hopped in my car and, needing to spread the love that was my irritation and maybe get a bit of commiseration and support from caring and compassionate souls, I set my sights on the annex and, of course, Daisy and my amazing mother.

Because who else could smother me in adoration and chocolate chip cookies?

CHAPTER FIVE

I parked in my regular spot, the sweetly painted Petunia marker grinning at me as always. Hard not to let my gaze linger at the emptiness behind the cartoon version of my sweet little dog, at the carefully leveled green space that made my chest ache despite the fact I was absolutely and utterly over the loss of my B&B.

Right, Fee. Tell me another one.

Lingering over that not-so-distant pain did little to improve my mood. Rather than entering the annex from the front door and risk running into guests or staff who may or may not have been prepared for the redheaded cloud of doom and gloom who hunkered her way around the side of the house for the backyard, I chose to do my best not to make anyone else feel as rotten as I did and keep my crankiness to myself. At least, until I was able to get a solid hug or two in from my mother and bestie.

Today was supposed to be one of triumph and excitement. Instead, I felt like crying. How much did that suck?

As I passed the corner of the house, head down, jaw aching from clenching against throwing something violently enough to vent some of the stress shuddering through me, I missed the fact the back garden wasn't exactly empty. To make matters worse, the last person I wanted to see in that moment—his smirk still intact despite the crying woman who hissed in angry whispers at him—stood with his arms crossed over his puffed-out chest, shoulders back and feet planted in his ridiculous hiking boots like he was some kind of intrepid explorer ready to climb any mountain or dig up a lost city at any moment.

I hated his socks. Totally random, but the way the yellow stripes contrasted against the white, peeking up over the lip of his boots? Made me want to choke someone. Okay, him. Yes, they were just socks. Still. And those knee-length khaki shorts?

Seriously.

So, I'm positive it was obvious my dislike for Gregg Brown had grown to irrational proportions. But if the crying woman's reaction was a normal one? Maybe he had that effect on every female he encountered. I caught my forward motion and held still a heartbeat, trying to decide what to do. Not wanting to intrude on their conversation warred with knowing what they were fighting about even as I really, really didn't want to have to talk to him again today. Or any day. My inner busybody was actually willing to forgo finding out the details of their disagreement without a fight in exchange for never, ever having to see him ever again.

Irrationality was winning, apparently.

Thing was, as I was trying to decide the course of action that would let me escape without imploding or freaking out or anything else that I could and would blame on my temper, my options were erased as the big, white Tortuga Divers truck pulled into the parking lot and the three members of that team got out. And headed right for me.

The crying woman in Gregg's company looked up instantly, her attractive face a mess of mascara and red splotches from weeping, her short, dark bob in disarray, the crumpled handful of tissues in her grasp held tight to where the opening of her flowered button up revealed a gold heart locket. When she spotted MC? That seemed to be the last straw, her face twisting into a furious and pain-wracked expression that left me wanting to hug her and punch him.

Okay, wanted to punch him anyway. Any excuse.

She spun away from him while MC waved at me and approached, Chantal and Anja's conversation cut off when their boss slowed her steps as she took in the scene before me, the three watching as the weeping woman spun away from Gregg and ran toward the back door.

"Hannah!" He might have called after her, but he made no effort to chase her, eye-rolling when she slammed the kitchen door behind her. "Women," he said with a wink and a grin. "So emotional."

It took him a moment, I think, to figure out the four females standing in front of him not only didn't get the joke but that he was currently taking his life into his own hands just breathing in our presence. The sheer weight of our combined physical animosity actually made me feel better, though MC seemed to shake off whatever anger she felt toward him faster than the rest of us.

"Nothing's changed, Gregg," she snapped. "You have absolutely zero class." She continued on through the back door herself, Chantal and Anja following her, leaving me alone in the garden. With him.

Oh my god, please. Someone save me from myself.

"Fee!" The door opened one last time, my dear and darling Daisy sweeping out, her checkered pink and white dress so fifties fabulous it almost made me smile despite my mood. "There you are. Your mother needs you. If you'll excuse us, Mr. Brown?"

Gregg had zero problem up and downing my friend with that nasty gaze of his, smirking the whole time while I debated whether Daisy knew just how close I was to murder. He didn't seem to care, though, moving before I did, brushing past my bestie on the way by. He did *not* smell her hair as he passed.

Okay, I'd dealt with men I couldn't stand in the past. Lots of them. Still had a few I wished would vanish off the face of the planet. Looking at you, Robert and Geoffrey. But this guy? Maybe it was the fact it felt like he'd hijacked my treasure hunt—yes, damn it, mine—and maybe it was protectiveness toward MC. Then again, it could have been that my instincts were on point because really.

Just *gross*.

Daisy waited for Gregg to vanish into the dim interior of the annex, the sound of my mother speaking unclear in the words but sharp as a tack in the meaning—as in, get out of my kitchen—before meeting my eyes. Her gray ones rolled, lips tightening before she blew out a soft puff of air. It took a lot to make my Daisy mad, but it was clear Gregg had succeeded. Just like Mom, if her tone of voice just now was any indication. Good to know he managed to rub everyone the wrong way. Took the pressure off me feeling like I was overreacting.

Because I didn't have a penchant for overreacting or anything.

"Poor Hannah." Daisy's voice barely reached above a whisper as she leaned into me. Just feeling her hand take mine eased my stress as her gaze widened, beautiful face animated as she went on. "Gregg and MC were an item not so long ago and Hannah gave him one more chance. She's going to divorce him for sure, now."

"Day." I choked on a half-laugh. "When did they check in?"

"Hannah did about an hour ago." She shrugged and smiled, releasing my hand to smooth the front of her dress. Just like Daisy to have all the gossip. She should have been the detective, not me. One of her hands fluttered in front of her, smile beaming as she perked. "How was the sonar scan?"

Argh. "Long story," I said. "You know why Gregg is here?"

She nodded, confused clearly, biting her lower lip. "Hannah said he was invited, that he's doing a documentary." She exhaled then, one delicate sandal tapping in irritation on the decking. "He's not supposed to be here."

I filled her in quickly and quietly, the scene at the dock this morning still seared into my brain. Day led me inside, the darker interior enough of a contrast to the outside it took my eyes a moment to adjust, to spot my mother at the long, stainless-steel counter, prepping biscuits and watching us approach. The firm and rather abrupt motions of her hands told me she was in as bad a mood as I was. Not like Lucy Fleming to abuse dough in such a manner unless she was irritated. I finished telling them both what I knew while Mom rolled out a sheet of soft dough with enough force behind her rolling pin, I pictured her wielding it as a weapon.

So, I probably shouldn't have felt better just dumping everything on them like that, but somehow it always eased my stress, having those two amazing women to listen and nod and murmur their commiseration of utter and absolute agreement.

Made me sad, suddenly, as I leaned against the counter, realizing while I wrapped up and the pair exhaled at the same time, I'd miss this. The warm butt of my happy pug settled on my toes, Petunia making her presence known, contented sigh joining that of my mother and Daisy while I fought off the tingle of tears. Knowing I was going to have to eventually tell them this was my last season and, as soon as September rolled around, they'd be taking over the annex completely.

Sure, I could have rebuilt. But with tourism on the decline—no fault of Vivian's, she just didn't have Olivia's drive to keep the momentum of tourism going, focused as she was on other and more important issues—I'd be crazy to reinvest the insurance money in a business that likely wouldn't be needed in the next decade or so.

They'd be fine. The annex was paid off, and between the two of them they had more than enough side jobs to stay busy. And I had the chance, at last, to do what I always wanted.

Still. Hard not to regret the end of something truly special.

CHAPTER SIX

Liz passed me the platter of chicken, her own plate heaped with slices of the steaming roasted deliciousness, her fork stabbing violently into the pale meat as though the focus of her dissatisfaction was on the other end of the stainless-steel tines. Mind you, I would have been more than happy to jab Gregg Brown a few pokes with my own utensils, thank you very much, even more so after his blowhard entrance into the annex in which even Daisy rolled her gray eyes and had to fight to keep from sighing.

"Adequate," he said, voice booming loudly enough every guest in the place heard him (and I don't mean just at the annex, either—I bet they caught his gust of hot air all the way up the mountain at the White Valley Lodge and if he didn't like it, he could just go get a freaking room there already). He seemed to enjoy the attention his appearance created, the other visitors staring as he moved through my (our, sophistry) lobby like he owned the place. Meanwhile, Martin lugged two giant suitcases behind his boss, face tight with something that could have been anger but seemed far too ineffectual to me to end in anything that might right the wrongs clearly circling around inside the cameraman's head.

Hannah, to my surprise, waited at the foot of the stairs for her prize of a husband, head down, arms around herself, tears dried up but the ravages of her unhappiness still visible. He'd taken his time following her up to their room, Martin grunting in their wake, and I let the documentarian do the dirty work since he was obviously so willing to walk that path, he didn't need me to help him embarrass himself.

Yeah, I still wasn't over the whole takeover of my treasure hunt. Sue me.

Liz had returned shortly thereafter, Gregg and company exiting the annex for dinner in town, leaving the rest of us—MC, Chantal and Anja included—to take over the dining room for what felt like a last supper.

I missed seeing Dad, knowing he was out of town on a case, one that had blown up on him and dragged him away from this most important weekend. He'd been torn, almost abandoned the clients in favor of staying behind, but Mom talked him out of it.

"Johnathan Albert Campbell Fleming." I loved it when she used all of his names like that. "This treasure has waited for just ages. Your client takes precedence."

Dad had hummed and Dad had hawed, but, in the end, he'd left, grumbling and shoulders hunched under a thundercloud, the rumbling rattle of his pickup exiting town more like the toll of doom.

I should have known him leaving was a sign that things weren't going to go according to plan. I grimaced at Crew who didn't seem to notice, eyes locked on his own heaping plate, digging into the chicken dinner Mom had so carefully prepared for us. It wasn't lost on me our mayor was also missing from the table, though Vivian French's absence had been agreed on ages ago.

"I have to appear to remain loyal to the Patterson family," she'd said when I broached the topic of our going public. "But keep me posted, Fee."

Our relationship might not have been perfect or as close as me and Daisy, but the rekindling of our friendship since she'd taken over as mayor—and revealed to me the truth of why she was in bed with the Pattersons—had taken the last of the edge off our mutual animosity. As had the realization we had a mutual enemy in the (murder) drowning of her brother, Victor.

These days, just seeing Robert's 70s 'stache and beer gut made me want to throw up for more than one reason.

It didn't help that Liz kept shooting angry looks at MC or that her diver friend wouldn't meet her eyes. The room was uncomfortable enough as it was, and despite the fact Mom's delicious cooking was even more incredible than ever, every bite tasted flat and empty in my mouth.

It wasn't until we were silently staring at our dessert bowls of fresh biscuits slathered in crushed strawberries and vanilla ice cream that the mood in the room changed. And not for the better. Because despite the fact the doors to the dining room were closed and the "Private Function" sign had been set out, at least one of the two men who pushed their way through didn't seem to care he wasn't invited.

Gregg grinned all around before helping himself to the only empty seat at the table. Oh. My. God. He sat in Dad's chair. Okay, so not officially or anything, but that was always where my father sat when we used the dining room for family purposes and the sight of Mr. Asshat with his butt in my dad's seat almost set me off.

I didn't get the chance to react, not when he happily helped himself to a serving of Mom's strawberry shortcake, sitting back and taking a big bite while Martin remained standing, as though trying to hide behind Gregg's chair, distinctly uncomfortable. I wanted to say something, do something, in response to his blatant arrogance. But I was honestly so floored by his clear show of don't give a crap I couldn't think of a thing to say.

Gregg polished off his serving in a few hearty

bites before setting the bowl aside and nodding to Mom. "Delicious," he said and rose to his feet, in his mind a welcome guest satisfied with himself, winking at Liz. "See you all in the morning." And then, just like that, he strolled out as though nothing untoward had happened and this was all just tickity-boo.

Was it possible to despise someone so much you couldn't breathe?

Apparently, that's a yes.

"God damn it, MC." Liz's fist slammed down on the table, making everyone jump, Daisy letting out a little meep of nerves before covering her mouth with both hands. The FBI agent instantly looked contrite, inhaling sharply with that same fisted hand now reaching out toward my bestie. "I'm sorry, everyone." She visibly pulled herself together, though she was clearly still angry when she again focused on the Tortuga team leader. "You had to know he was going to pull a stunt like this."

MC shrugged, tossed her dark ponytail over her shoulder, the freckles on her tanned nose meeting as she scowled at her friend. "Gregg Brown is always a possibility," she said, voice low and angry. "And not my fault, Liz." She finally did meet another gaze, but it was first mine, then my silent husband's. "Fee, Crew, I'm sorry about this. But I made you a promise. We all did." Chantal and Anja might not have looked happy either, but they both nodded their agreement as MC went on. "If there is a treasure to be found, we'll find it." She stood abruptly, tossing her napkin to the table, nodding to Mom. "Dinner was amazing, Lucy. Daisy, thanks for getting us set up. And now, if you'll all excuse me, I'm going to turn in early." She strode out without another word, her dive team hesitating before also rising to their feet.

"We'll keep an eye on her," Chantal said right to Liz who grunted and shrugged sharply.

"This isn't her fault," Anja spoke up before Chantal shot her an angry look. "It's no one's fault," she hurried on as if placation was necessary. "He's a predator and we either have to work with him or stay ahead of him."

"Or we could shoot him," Liz growled. "That's what I'd do with a predator. Put it down before it could do any more harm."

Crew sighed softly, face no longer blank and quiet, a faint smile pulling at his lips. "Careful, Agent Michaud," he said. "You do know this town has a reputation for murder, right?"

"Makes her the prime suspect," I said, silently thanking Crew for lightening the mood. Even Mom giggled a little, Daisy's faint smile but giant eyes showing her nervousness.

"I guess he'd better not end up dead, then," Liz snarled. And relented with her own headshake and tight grin, eyes narrowed. "Then again, no body, no crime."

Not exactly accurate, but we all laughed. Yup, going to hell, the lot of us.

Chantal and Anja said their good nights, leaving my little posse in quiet contemplation. Funny that

Mom didn't even try to rise, clear the table, bustle off like she always did. Instead, she sat, quiet and with her napkin clutched in her lap, on the other side of Crew, between him and Daisy, while Liz's fingertips tapped over and over on the bell of her water glass.

"Clearly you know more about him than we do," Crew said, leaning forward, one big hand taking mine absently. Comforting, knowing his default was touching me in some way.

Liz tossed her own napkin before crossing her arms over her chest, white button-up straining across her shoulders, black dress jacket draped over the back of her chair. She didn't let her hair down often—proverbially speaking—but seemed comfortable enough with us to shed the shell of her persona and show us the real Liz under the suit.

"I've known MC forever," she said. "We dove together when we were kids, got our diving certifications together. She's always wanted to hunt treasure, I told you that." Liz's scowl didn't change but her tone of voice flattened out. "She met Gregg about a dozen years ago, in Roatan, I think."

Crew grunted softly. "Honduras?"

She nodded. "They were doing their DMT together."

My husband squeezed my hand. "Divemaster training," he said.

I didn't comment as Liz went on. "Gregg convinced her to go on a treasure dive with him and MC was hooked." She made a face, lips twisting, eyebrow arching. "In more ways than one. He had her convinced he was in love with her, and they were the perfect team. Yada. Yada." Liz tsked softly under her breath before going on. "They didn't last, but that didn't stop MC from going back to him over and over again when he called. Every time he screwed her over, every time. But she just couldn't seem to shake him."

"And Hannah?" I felt for the woman, though honestly, she had to have known what she was marrying. Grunt.

Liz eye-rolled. "Fell for his charm," she said, "what little he has." Snort. "Their marriage supposedly put an end to MC and Gregg. Or so she told me." She slapped both of her thighs with aggressive attention. "I should have known better."

Daisy surprised me by speaking up. "Hannah blames MC for her marriage issues." She seemed equally shocked she'd spoken but Liz nodded to her in support.

"Because women are idiots about men," the agent growled.

Hmmm. Really made me wonder about Liz's relationship history.

Fee. Mind your own business already.

"I'm not going to lie," Liz said, leaning ahead, hands clasped in front of her, forearms straddling the bowl of melting ice cream dessert. "I'm nervous about them diving together." She stared down into the mess and shrugged. "But I have to admit, she's right about one thing. If there's a treasure to be found, Gregg will find it."

We broke up our little party a short time later, without much more to say about the matter. Not like we had much choice, right? Or did we? I let Crew leave without me, pausing to help Daisy lock up the annex, Mom heading for the kitchen and cleanup. Day went one way—upstairs—and I went the other—down the back hall—while my head spun, and I thought about calling the whole thing off.

I hated not being in control of what was going on. Hated it. And, as I exited the back hall with a bag of garbage for the dumpster, my anxiety about the whole plan ramped up at the sight of two people arguing in the dark in heated whispers.

Because it wasn't MC and Gregg, or even Hannah and Gregg who huddled just outside the back deck light, hands gesturing in angry waves at each other. Nope. It was Gregg, sure. But the woman having the fight with him?

Surprise, surprise. It was Chantal.

CHAPTER SEVEN

Then again, maybe not so surprising, but their intense conflict reached the point, as I watched, that she actually looked like she was going to hit him. But not before she looked up and caught me watching, likely with my mouth hanging open.

The two went their separate ways, Gregg brushing past me with his now characteristic wink while Chantal disappeared through the serving door to the dining room. Avoiding me? Hardly took a massive pass of deductive reasoning to reach that assumption.

Part of me prodded at my curiosity to go after her and find out what was going on while the rest of me—the tired and flustered and suddenly overwhelmed part that preferred the arms of my loving husband to pursuit of whatever private issue Chantal might have had with Captain Annoying—shrugged and went about her business.

You know what? Regardless of what happened with this treasure hunt, the actual hunting part wasn't the point. So, who cared, if it came down to it, which of the people we'd hired and accidentally allowed into our investigation via a loaded contract uncovered the actual Reading hoard?

That was me. Mrs. Brightside.

Still, it was impossible to completely shake the uncomfortable feeling lingering in the back of my mind as I finished up my chores and headed for home. Maybe that part of me that loved a good mystery refused to let go on sheer principle or perhaps it was the lurking worry that nothing positive could come from something so screwed up in the first place that had me slump my way into Crew's house, shoulders down, a frown on my face surely deep enough to hide a treasure in.

My darling husband took one look at me, glancing up from the sofa where he re-reviewed the video feed on his laptop, and shut the lid with a click, rising to come to my side while I abjectly kicked off my shoes at the door and, lower lip jutting at an appropriately unhappy distance, held out my arms to him.

Of course, he obliged me with a sweet and loving hug. Didn't comment on my settle into sulk, or the fact he was in the same conundrum of aggravation as me. Because he was a good husband, wasn't he?

Crew knew to give me a minute to poor me before kissing the top of my head, then my cheek, then my lips.

The perfect distraction.

I came up for air a few minutes later, hands wound into his dark, thick hair, breathing into him while I exhaled the tension I'd carried with me since our arrival at the dock that morning. "Hissy fit officially over," I said.

"Damn," he whispered, nose brushing mine, voice husky. "Did I miss the hissy part? I love the hissy part."

Smartass husband. I snorted a laugh, loved his chuckle over my mouth, kissed him again before patting his stubbled cheek.

"It's going to be okay, isn't it?" Like he knew any better than I did. But if Crew told me it was? I'd believe him, no question, 100%.

"It is," he said, telling me exactly what I wanted to hear, bless him. "I promise, Fee. One way or another, we're going to prove if the treasure is here once and for all. And no one can stop us."

I hesitated in that moment, not wanting to shake the firm conviction in his voice, exhaling finally with enough concern his lips tightened and he nodded.

"Go ahead," he said. "You won't feel better until you tell me everything. Even if I don't want to know."

How did he know me this well? I filled him in on Chantal's fight with Gregg while he fetched us both a beer, cracking mine open before handing it to me and popping the seal on his own.

"Well, according to Liz none of them get along," he said, taking a long drink, blue eyes locked on me.

I nodded, sitting at the counter, hating being a doubter. "It just seemed pretty personal, that's all," I said. "Maybe he had an affair with her, too." Would be like him, I guess. Yup, judging Gregg Brown was my new favorite game.

Crew leaned across the tile, setting his bottle next to mine, free hand covering my drumming fingers and silencing their rapid beat. "Let's see how tomorrow goes," he said. "There are a few spots that look promising." He circled the counter then, gesturing at the computer. "Want to see?"

I sort of did, but shook my head finally, reaching down to lift my watching pug into my arms. She'd been slow and plodding on our walk home, probably tired, the dear.

"I trust you," I said, wishing I didn't feel so disillusioned all of a sudden. This was supposed to be fun, right? Had been only this morning. Why then was there a giant, black cloud threatening rain with a chance of disaster looming over me? Because, I realized, the training I'd just taken hadn't lost its repeated impact just yet. And, when I finally understood what was really making me panic—yup, that was the underlying feeling, good to know—the word I'd just uttered at him resonated like no other. I reached out for his hand, clutching Petunia to my chest with her butt in my lap, head against me like a toddler, as I blurted what I was thinking. Classic

Fleming. "You're supposed to be able to trust each other out there," I said, barely above a whisper while I gave voice to what was weighing so heavily on me. "And I don't trust him."

Crew's blue eyes flashed, and, in that moment, I knew he was as worried as me. More so, maybe, given his training. He'd been diving since he was a kid, took the sort of education underwater reserved for those who, as far as I was concerned, came closer to being astronauts (was that oceanauts? Aquanauts?) than divers.

But, before I could really fall into the pit of despair waiting to engulf me, Crew shook his head, kissing me again, this time with tenderness. His steady hands grasped my shoulders, shook me just a little, faint smile lifting his lips, lighting his blue eyes.

"You know I would never put you at risk," he said, never mind himself, right? "These people are pros, Fee, with years of experience. Not one of them will let their grievances get in the way of safety."

So he said. But I did feel better. He seemed sure, so what choice did I have?

"Do you want to stay out of the water?" Crew hesitated before going on while I fought for the usual irritation that typically flagged as a precursor to him trying to protect me, shocked when it didn't rise to the surface immediately. "You don't have to dive tomorrow."

It was sheer force of will that spoke for me then, and old habit, rather than conviction. "I'm diving," I said, rising with Petunia in my arms. "And that's final."

Crew just nodded, let me go. Thing was, as I climbed into bed and tucked the covers under my chin, my pug snuggled against my hip, it wasn't my husband who prodded me to think it over.

Nope. Traitor brain. It was me.

CHAPTER EIGHT

You know when you have something big weighing on your mind and you toss and turn all night in between flashes of nightmares and uncomfortable half-dreams that leave you unsettled, unrested and, in general, at odds with the world?

Not saying that was my night, but. Yeah. Sigh.

That's how I ended up out of bed and in the office at Fleming Investigations, Petunia on her dog bed next to my desk, tackling paperwork at 6AM while my husband still slept at home. An early text and the looming thunderstorm that had rolled over Reading the night before delayed our first dive of the day for at least a few hours. No way could I stay in one place without a distraction—non-Crew related, get your mind out of the gutter—which meant an early morning trip into the wilds of my hometown where I even had to make my own coffee since Sammy's didn't open until seven.

I wondered, as I glanced at the end of the long, narrow room that was the headquarters of my new profession, when Darius slept or if he even did. He sat, quiet and watchful, my protective shadow, at the door to the office, ramrod straight and android focused. Not the first time I wondered if, in fact, somehow Malcolm had not hired but created the hulking bodyguard like some Irish mobster Dr. Murraystein. The fact the lurking giant of humanity drank tea instead of coffee and preferred opera to regular music—a fact I'd discovered when he drove me home once when my car wouldn't start—leaned me in the direction of invention instead of birth, but I digress.

Whether man or machine, Darius wasn't going anywhere and certainly wasn't contributing to an upswing in my present mood.

Made all the better (sarcasm, my old friend, how nice of you to make an appearance) when the door swung open, and a gust of wind blew trouble into my life.

How, exactly, did I know the woman marching toward me, her normally perfect dark bob tossed by the lingering gale outside, her dark eyes locked on me, practical pumps thudding on the runner carpet leading all the way to my desk, meant discomfort to my existence? Because I knew that look on Olivia Walker's face, had seen it so many times in the last number of years it barely phased me anymore.

The former Reading town mayor came to an abrupt halt, nodding to me in a sharp and decisive manner, one fist tapping on the surface of my desk as if she needed me to pay attention and didn't already have my undivided. Well, almost undivided, as I caught and tracked Darius's silent and blank-faced approach behind her. What was he seeing in her I wasn't? He had, after all, been trained to spot danger when others might miss the signs. Was I overlooking something? Or, as usual, was he simply being overprotective as Darius seemed to adore doing just to irk me and, more notably, my former law-enforcement husband?

"Fiona." Olivia drew a deep breath, clearly unaware she was being tracked by a watchful hunter ready to pounce on her if she made the slightest wrong move in my direction. I actually had a faint heart palpitation in worry for her and almost waved Darius off, surging to my feet instead and circling the desk to join her, knowing putting myself between her and him might be the only way to preserve her from disappearing suddenly and never being heard from again.

I really needed Malcolm to retrieve his trained gorilla already. My nerves weren't up to my own safety and that of my family, let alone random others who might wander into a perceived field of threat only Darius seemed aware of.

"Olivia." I hadn't seen much of her since she'd been ousted in the November election, Vivian taking the seat in a landslide vote of support. I wondered if Reading residents—especially business owners—were feeling the implications of the loss of the tourism-centric former leader? I gestured for her to take a seat, but she shook her head, the shining bob she preferred falling into silken place from its previously ruffled condition. How did she have even her hair trained to behave and obey like that? She'd always run a tight ship, our Olivia Walker. Guess her entire person reflected the precision she'd always used to keep Reading on the map.

"I can't stay," she said, rushing through her words before stopping in a lurch, swallowing hard. She glanced behind her then, blanched, two bright points on the tips of her cheekbones showing as her eyes widened at the sight of the looming bodyguard. I waved Darius off this time, shooting him a glare that made him start slightly before taking one—count 'em, *one*—step back, hands folded in front of him, flat gaze still focused on my visitor.

His retreat seemed to do the trick, though, as she pulled herself quickly together, smoothing the front of her pale yellow suit jacket, the press pleat line of the front of her trousers so sharp they could cut paper. I never liked her in that color, thought it made her olive complexion sallow, but she'd failed to ask me for fashion advice, so I kept my opinions to myself.

Considering my favorite outfit the last few years had been faded t-shirts and jeans with sneakers and a messy bun/hanging ponytail of unbrushed red curls?

Yeah. I wouldn't have trusted my judgment either.

"Well, nice to see you." This was awkward. She stared at me with her pupils slowly growing huge, throat working like she wanted to speak, hands clenching at her sides as though she fought some epic internal battle that meant the be-all and end-all of Olivia Walker. I was a heartbeat from reaching out and asking her if she was okay when she finally blurted out why she'd come.

"You have to stop the treasure hunt," she gasped. "Before it's too late."

Hang on. She said what?

I gaped, knowing I was doing it, not sure what this was about. Did she know about Gregg Brown and his interference? Had she learned something about the Tortuga dive team I didn't know about? My own panic and sudden reticence about the project, so fresh and fed by my night of bad dreams resurfaced as a wave of anxiety that gave me goosebumps while Olivia reached out and grasped my hand, almost painfully tight.

"Trust me," she hissed in my ear while I hastily shook my head at Darius who—oh my god, he did not reach under his jacket for something that couldn't be a gun—closed the distance so fast I almost hit him when I raised my other hand to warn him off. "It's not worth it, Fee." She backed off then, sweat visibly beading on her upper lip, her forehead, the fingers that released mine shaking when she wiped at the moisture. "They won't let you succeed. I should know." Olivia's own panic fed mine. They?

My mind blanked while she went on, voice almost a moan of fear. "Even suggesting we use Captain Reading as a tourist draw brought me more trouble than I could ever have imagined."

Wait. Of course, I knew who she was talking about. And, unlike the intrusion of Gregg Brown, the doubt and discomfort his invasion had caused, her fear of the family I now understood she was warning me about? Couldn't have firmed up my resolve more.

Whether she knew it or not, Olivia had just sealed the deal on the treasure dive as far as things went, Gregg Brown or no Gregg Brown. Because no matter what else went on in this town, as far as I was concerned the freaking Patterson family could suck it.

But before I could tell her as much—surely, she saw my utter and consuming rejection of her warning on my face as my realization woke and flamed in the all-devouring Fleming fire of *hell no*—Olivia's lips were at my ear again. And she uttered one word, only one, before retreating.

"Blackstone."

She spun then, hustling past Darius who let her go, who followed her all the way to the door and closed it firmly behind her when she left. I stood there a long moment, waiting for the entry to thud softly shut, sinking slowly to the edge of my desk, hugging myself tight.

The mysterious corporation that had been a thorn in my side—okay, I always had a thing for taking stuff personally—since the fake extinct woodpecker sighting had almost cost my friend Jared and his partners their zipline park. Even if that corporation hadn't employed my former cheater boyfriend, Ryan Richards (said a lot about their low brow taste and choice in employees), the fact they were impossible to track, had their fingers in so many weird and seemingly unrelated pies while hiding the true nature of what they were up to while poking their collective corporate noses into the inner workings of my town?

Yeah. Blackstone. They could suck it, too.

Thing was, though, they had their own little private army, didn't they? And were somehow linked to the Patterson family. I'd found that out firsthand when I'd tried to sneak into Alicia and Jared's wedding last fall, break and entering into the Marie Patterson Olympic Equestrian Center and Super Secret Criminal Mastermind Lair™ (okay, I was making up that last part, but partially believed it, don't tell me I'm the only one). Only Crew making me a deputy and Liz joining me in the ensuing murder investigation I'd stumbled on (like anything else was new) kept me from being either a) arrested b) ejected or, most likely, c) waterboarded and then taken out back and shot or something equally nefarious by the black-outfitted super soldiers with their giant guns and sunglasses that made me want to stir rebellion in the lower classes for no real reason except *rebellion*, yo. Down with the man and all that.

I guess I was glaring because when I looked up, Darius had joined me, his own normally empty expression creased in a frown.

"Want me to take care of her?" He didn't ask like it was a big deal. To the contrary. He might as well have been inquiring if it was time to take the garbage out.

Okay, so I didn't intend to lose my crap that morning, not on Crew, not on anyone. Certainly not on the giant mountain of manhood in the dark suit with the very large and very deadly gun under his double-breasted jacket. In fact, if it had been an ordinary morning and I'd had a solid night sleep and breakfast even, or maybe a coffee someone else had made instead of the crappy cheap one I'd thrown together from Dad's jar of instant that had been all I had access to, I might not have lost my epic Fleming temper.

Hmmm. Yeah. Or maybe not.

I don't think Darius expected it, likely one of the only reasons I remained alive and breathing as I lurched toward him and hit him in his very broad and very solid chest with one shaking index finger, the flames of my fury washing over me and consuming every scrap of self-preservation I'd ever had the good sense to cultivate.

"Don't you ever," I hit him again, noting that my finger hurt, and he felt distinctly like a rock wall under that dress shirt, "ever," okay I was going to need a splint for my poor, injured digit, "poke your nose in my business again." Shaking? Check. Pissed off? Check. A little worried in a tiny but growing seed of oh my god what did I just do kind of way that the behemoth of manflesh with the gun might not like the tiny redhead poking him ineffectually or telling him what to do.

Oh, checky-checko-checkeroo.

It could have gone badly. Should have. Darius worked for Malcolm, after all, not me, not really. Though he did have orders to keep me safe, he wasn't mine to push around and if shove came to guns blazing, I wasn't betting on the bulky beast of Mob burden to put up with the likes of little old *moi*.

Except, apparently, not only were the Irish organized crime gods smiling on me, one look at the amused expression on Darius's face told me he found me adorable and, at the very most, my demands in line with the antics of my pug.

Yeah. That went over well.

This time when I jabbed him it was with my fist since my finger wasn't up to the task. He grunted in shock, eyes widening, and he actually backed up half a step in response. Okay, swayed back and shuffled one foot. But I'm not above giving myself kudos in the pay attention and take me seriously department.

"I. Mean. It." Three hits, not hard, but solid enough even that chest of solid stone had to feel it. "You've been on my butt and lurking in my shadow far too close for my comfort. And I'm done."

Rebellion in those normally flat, empty eyes.

Oh no, he did *not*. "Darius," I said, voice dropping in volume and temperature, "I will call Malcolm and have him assign me one of the other boys. Don't think I won't."

Okay, that got through to him. Definitely panic

and unhappiness at war with—wait, was that sorrow?

He nodded, backed down for real this time, taking a long stride in retreat before staring at the floor.

"Sorry, Miss Fleming," he said in that always surprising tenor voice of his. "I'll behave."

Huh. Well, okay then. Though his insistence on Miss instead of Ms. still rankled. I wasn't exactly sure what to do with the rest of my bubbling confidence in my ability to bully a bully and so, rather than let him know that—heaven forbid—I seized my purse in a firm grip and stomped for the exit, the clock telling me it was coffee time at well past 8AM and that the distraction of paperwork had done its job. Feeling at least as though I'd conquered something if not quite knowing what, exactly, I headed for Sammy's with my anxious pug on her lead, my head high and my temper singing.

Boo-yah.

CHAPTER NINE

It didn't take long for the gusty wind to make me regret my decision, though the rain had stopped, and the sun was trying to come out through the clouds overhead. It wasn't often we dealt with storms of this nature in July, but they did happen. Mountains made for odd and unpredictable weather sometimes. Petunia was clearly smarter than I, the darling, had stayed clear of Olivia's visit and the subsequent conflict I'd created—taking responsibility for it, sure was—I'd stirred with Darius. Not like her to mind her own business so the continual nervous looks she shot me were obvious indicators she'd sensed trouble and was worried about me.

Her level of anxiety should have cooled me down. I hated causing her stress, after everything she'd been through. But even Petunia's discomfort did little to cut through my layered animosity toward anything and anyone that might tweak my last nerve.

As I stomped my way to Sammy's, though, I had to admit part of my irritation was tied into the delay in the first dive this morning. How sad I'd reached the point I just wanted to get it over with. The childlike delight and excitement of the hunt for the treasure to this point had carried me through some truly horrible events and tied me closer to the people I cared most about. Losing the bright shiny of that made me almost hope we didn't find anything at this point.

Disappointment seemed a fitting end, somehow.

Now, don't get me wrong. If we found the treasure, great. And. The bitter taste in my mouth was going to be hard to wash away. Olivia's warning about Blackstone wasn't helping any, and I couldn't help but wonder at the worry nagging me suddenly, a worry I gave full examination to as I approached the glass doors to the coffee shop.

They'd interfered before, covertly, like assassins in the night. A sick feeling invaded my temper, stomach now in the kind of knots that took weeks to unravel. Because it wasn't entirely inconceivable Gregg Brown was working for Blackstone, was it? His out-of-the-blue arrival smacked of their tactics, didn't it? And if he was, indeed, tied to that most secret of corporations, could I bear to allow them a hand in discovering the Reading hoard? I had no proof, of course, though you could bet the moment I got the chance I'd be doing my best to find out. It had always proven difficult in the past, however, to find out anything substantive about Blackstone, so it was very possible even if they were funding Gregg Brown and his treasure hunting exploits, I'd never know the truth of it.

Wasn't that a vile and bitter bit of gristle to chew on. Growl.

I kept my head down, not wanting to have the rehashed conversation I seemed to have to go through every time I stuck my head out the door these days, hurrying past a pair of older women who watched me go by. I could feel their curiosity burning a hole in my back, though when I glanced out of the corner of my eye I noted, at least, Darius was doing as asked and was keeping almost a block between us.

There was that silver lining to hang onto. If I was in the mood for such things. Instead, I lingered over my predicament about Gregg Brown while avoiding questions about Petunia's, sympathies mixed with questions about when I was breaking ground, not to mention endless inquiries into the treasure.

I was over today, and it was only 8AM.

The only distracting moment came when I looked up at the last moment before passing through the entry, attention caught by a young man in a suit climbing into the back seat of a dark sedan. Not that black cars and people in such attire were entirely foreign—case in point following me around everywhere like a double-breasted shadow—but his youth and something familiar about his face and the way he carried himself caught me and held me, door half-open, wash of coffee-scented air wafting over me, while the lean, dark-haired kid looked up and met my eyes.

And waved before disappearing into the car and closing the door.

I watched the sedan go by, a weird tightness in my chest making breath difficult. I couldn't place him, but it was clear he knew me, wasn't it? And though I had no reason to feel uneasy, something about him and his attitude gave me pause and only added to my layers of anxiety.

So, now you know the state of mind I was in as I finally stepped through the front door of Sammy's coffee, my pug tugging on her lead in the knowledge she was about to get a sugar-laden snack from the girls behind the counter and came face-to-face with Rose Norton. Not my favorite person to begin with and, from the snide look of judgment and disdain creasing the folds of her near-gaunt face, the feeling was as mutual as possible.

We didn't talk much these days, both of us usually satisfied with matched sets of glares since I'd decided screaming incoherently in public at someone who clearly didn't deserve my focus or attention wasn't worth the negative press it gained me every time I lost my crap on her.

Thing was, today? It had become impossible to stay silent. Not because of anything in particular she'd done, but due to the glaring and obvious affront the nasty little piece of work wore in her hair.

Now, I had no proof that the butterfly pin holding back her bangs over her left eyebrow belonged to my Grandmother Iris at one point. In fact, I was sure the collection of identical pins I had tucked into the music box that had been one of her gifts to me were likely purchased from some department store in Montpelier either by my grandfather or her lover, Daniel Munroe. However, as my eyes locked on that familiar shape, worn so brazenly like a fully-intended attack on me and mine—made worse by the loss of Petunia's and my mood and just everything, I admit it—it took everything in my power not to reach out and jerk the butterfly from her hair before punching her right in that upturned nose of judgment and vitriol.

"You thief," I snarled before I could stop myself, pointing at the pin, hand shaking, a rush of fury uncoiling from where it had been bubbling since yesterday, happy to have a target. "That's Grandmother Iris's pin. Where did you get it?"

Rose's shock at my snarling attack was so genuine it helped cool some of the heat of my rage, but only some. She recovered quickly, hand rising to her hair as if to protect the butterfly. I only then noted some of the jewels were missing from one of the wings. What had she done to my grandmother's hairpin, the wretch?

"I have no idea what you're talking about," she snapped back. "This was a gift from Robert." She huffed past me, tossing her dark hair. While my hateful cousin had been growing a beer belly over the last few years, Rose seemed to be donating herself to his expansion at expense of her own physique. If she lost any more weight, she'd be a skeleton. And while I refused to feel an ounce of compassion she might not be well, I instead decided that's what happened to horrible people like the two of them—eventually, one just consumed the other in an evolutionary cycle of nature determined to eliminate evil.

I almost reached out to stop her as she exited the coffee shop, gritting my teeth to restrain my hand that ached to grasp her and spin her around to face me. But I knew better. No way I was putting myself in a position to be charged—specious or not—with assault on her precious little person. But I'd be getting my pin back (mine, damn it), you better believe it.

And if Robert stole that from my grandmother what else did he have he wasn't supposed to? Never mind the slice of the treasure map I knew he had in his possession. The possibilities of what he'd taken? Endless.

After all, it had taken me a bit to get home after my grandmother died, leaving the B&B empty of guests but open to someone who, clearly, had no problem taking a five-finger approach to helping himself to the precious possessions of others.

I guess I'd been standing in the doorway, fuming, with my mind running, for longer than was considered normal or necessary because when I finally came back to myself and shook off the tension of the encounter, I realized everyone in Sammy's was staring at me. And, in that same moment, when they discovered themselves staring, went back to instant conversation and pointedly ignored me. Why did I suddenly feel like I was in a badly directed TV sitcom?

My life. I really had to get over myself.

Except, I had this magnetic personality, it seemed, that attracted the sort of people who gave my blood pressure reason to skyrocket. A short moment of visual connection with one of my least favorite people, Barry Clement, ended in mutual scowls as Dr. Aberstock's assistant and traitorous lackey of the Patterson family looked away, held nothing against my next, more physical, encounter. As evidenced in the subsequent appearance of the shark-like also Patterson pain in my backside, Geoffrey Jenkins.

"Fee." I turned to find him entering the shop, pausing at my side, that cold and calculating smile not reaching his eyes. Far too close for my comfort, though when I tried to increase the distance between us, one of his arms slid around my waist and, to my shock, tucked me firmly against his hip. "How nice to see you."

So, he'd hit on me a few times before (gross, just gross), sometimes covertly, once or twice more openly. But this was the most overt, the aggressive way he held me firmly in his grasp, his face hovering over mine, tongue snaking out to moisten his lips as he stared at my mouth with intent the first time I'd ever actually felt like I might need to take self-defense action to protect myself.

Dear. God. Was he thinking about kissing me? I was going to throw up.

This day couldn't get worse, I was sure of that. Except, this was Reading, right? And I was Fiona Fleming. Worse was not only expected, it was the kind of constant companion one wished would take a flying leap already.

It wasn't Darius who came through the door in a rush. At first, I assumed it would be the looming bodyguard who took Geoffrey out. I had a flash of the mountain of a man whipping out that giant gun of his and flinched at the expectation of a gunshot even as my mind processed the tall, broad-shouldered and furious former sheriff I'd married who grasped Geoffrey by the shoulder, spun him toward him and, in an uncharacteristic show of lost temper, punched the accountant full in the face.

CHAPTER TEN

It all happened so fast I could only stand there and gape, though the whole world seemed to slide into a wobbly kind of agonizing slow motion I could do nothing about. Instead, as though encased in the thick and gooey passage of time, trapped and forced to observe in horror rather than have any ability to intervene in the unfolding drama, I watched Crew's follow through, Geoffrey falling back from the blow, a stream of blood flying in tiny droplets through the air, shining bright red in a ray of emerging sunlight streaming through the coffee shop door. The Patterson accountant hit the floor and seemed to bounce, eyes huge, mouth gaping open, while Crew drew back, shoulders wide, fists at his sides, looking for a moment like some kind of avenging superhero.

Only then did Darius intervene, appearing like the shadow he was, restraining hand on my husband's shoulder as time sped up to normal and the hubbub of patrons and staff flooded my ears in a cacophony that gave me an instant headache.

Too late, Darius. The damage was done. And as I met my darling's eyes, and noted the deep shame there, the regret and his own self-judgment for losing his temper like that, I knew I wasn't the only one carrying the burden of all the crap we'd been through, and not just the treasure hunt, either.

Geoffrey made it to his feet with the help of a pair of customers, though he snapped a snarl at them and pushed them off once he was upright, dabbing at the blood flowing from his nose with the back of his hand.

"You've done it now, Turner," he said. "You'll be hearing from my lawyer."

Crew let him go without speaking, without meeting his eyes, before pulling me aside, Darius standing guard beside us while the excitement died down and, as was typical of my town, everything went back to normal.

Not so normal, though, the contrite expression on Crew's face, how he wiped at his mouth with one hand, wincing as I took it and examined it for injury. He'd have bruises on his knuckles, but I didn't think he'd broken anything, at least.

"Fee," he said, low and intense, "I'm so sorry. I don't know what got into me." He cleared his throat, glanced around, clearly embarrassed. "I can't believe

I lost it like that."

I hugged him, near to tears. "We've been through a lot," I whispered. "It's okay. We'll handle it."

But Crew shook his head, pulling back, jaw jumping, that tic under his eye leaping into life. I hadn't seen it in ages, used to be the cause. Knew I wasn't this time. Not that it made it any better. "I know better than to be jealous," he said. "I trust you. It's just…"

I'd always wondered if Crew noticed Geoffrey's attention, but I'd never asked. Clearly, that had been a mistake. "I'm sorry," I said. "You know I'd never—"

He kissed me then, took his turn embracing me. "I know. I do. I just can't stand to see him touch you."

"Well, I don't really enjoy the experience myself." I tried for lighthearted and barely reached bitter. "It's my fault. I asked Darius to back off. If I hadn't, Geoffrey wouldn't have gotten anywhere near me."

"No," the big bodyguard grumbled, interrupting. "It's my fault. I should have shot him ages ago."

Crew and I both stared, and I know my husband had the same thought. Should we laugh? Darius wasn't known for his sense of humor. And the big man's threat, considering his line of work, was real.

Until a slow smile spread across his face. "I was kidding. You can relax."

I returned my attention to my husband, still not sure if I could trust Darius and not able to bring myself to care if Geoffrey did turn up the worse for wear. "My hero," I said. "Now, stop it. Okay?"

Crew swallowed and nodded, but not in agreement. "I'm just so sick of them, Fee," he said, barely above a whisper. "The Pattersons, Rosebert, Geoffrey, this town. All of it."

"I get it." I squeezed his hand. "Of anyone, I get it, Crew." He nodded again, body uncoiling. "Do you want to walk away from this? From all of it? Because, you say the word, and we're out." I was shocked to discover I meant it. Not just the hunt, but Reading. If it meant my husband was happy, I would leave this all behind and to hell with the hoard, with the cutest town in America, and the lingering mysteries that still ate at me.

Crew inhaled, smiled, kissed me once more, himself again. "I love you, Fiona Fleming," he said. "Let's go find the gold and shove it in their faces."

There was that. Vengeance it was.

CHAPTER ELEVEN

It wasn't until I was sitting in the passenger's seat of Crew's SUV, my pug deposited safe and sound at the annex, the vehicle carrying us toward the yacht club and our first dive that I remembered to tell him about the hair clip.

Crew listened without comment before sighing. "I'm sorry, Fee," he said. "I wish there was something I could do."

I reached over and squeezed his hand, trapping it in mine. "It's just a hair clip," I said, feeling my shoulders sag. "And it didn't even have all the jewels. She can keep it."

We both knew it was less about the clip and more about the principle of the thing. I hated sucking my sweet husband into the downward spiral of my mood, but considering he'd had his own disheartening experience this morning, it wasn't all my fault, I suppose.

Picture us, then, as we pulled in and parked, our overjoyed enthusiasm as we exited the cab of the truck, our bubbling excitement while we schlumped our way to the dive shack, the abundance of our positive optimism when MC opened the door to us, a frown on her own face, Anja and Chantal looking about as perky where they worked with the dive equipment that was going to keep us all safe underwater.

Yup. We were a sorry bunch, weren't we? And frankly, professionals or not, the heavy state of unbridled why are we here again wasn't endearing me to the idea of diving in these conditions.

Made worse as I peeked over the edge of the dock into the water at the murkiness that sloshed back. Which meant the typically clear water would be less than ideal when it came to visibility, making what we were about to attempt all the harder.

Naturally.

Okay, Fiona Fleming, shake off the miasma of dejected loserdom or go the hell home already.

Whitecaps in the distance reminded me of Darius's seasickness even as the hulking bruiser paused behind me, bending to tap me on the shoulder. I turned to look up at him, knowing by the unhappy expression on his face I wasn't going to like what he was about to say.

"I don't want you to dive today." He sounded

like just letting the words out hurt him. And winced when he was done. I had a flash of realization when he did and almost laughed, despite myself.

Was he scared of how I'd react? Did I really make that big of an impact on him back at the Fleming Investigations office? Or was the bodyguard actually worried about what I thought of him?

Honestly, that second question was so odd to me it had to be the first despite the fact there was no way someone like him was afraid of someone like me. Then again, we'd been kind of co-conspirators about Malcolm for years now, his lurking presence a constant when it came to my Irish mob godfather. Did Darius like me?

No, not like me, like me. But think of me as a friend as much as a job? Did he really want me to like him back?

I reached out on impulse while Crew joined the dive team, squeezing his hand as I had my husband's, managing a smile. "I'll be okay," I said.

Darius swallowed, glanced at the water, looked queasy a moment, then swallowed again. "I can't go with you." There was almost a wail in the back of his voice. Had this morning's altercation between Crew and Geoffrey added to Darius's concerns? He'd said it was his fault. Was he blaming himself?

I could have just asked him. Instead, I squeezed one more time and let him go. "I'm with professionals," I said, regurgitating Crew's answer. "I'm trained for what I need to do. I'll stay in shallow water. Trust me, Darius. And trust Crew. He'd never put me in harm's way, and you know it."

The bodyguard nodded slowly, though he still looked wretchedly doubtful. "I'm supposed to protect you at all costs." So soft, that tenor voice. "Miss Fleming?" I waited with arched eyebrows in response to that hesitant use of my name as a question until he sighed and shook his head, tension leaving him. "You are the worst assignment I've ever had." And then, he laughed, a big, loud guffaw of releasing stress that triggered my own funny bone.

"I know," I said around a giggle. "I'm sorry, Darius. I really suck at behaving and not putting myself in danger and listening and all that important stuff."

His laughter died but not his good humor and, when he softly patted my shoulder, there was enough affection on his face I knew I'd made the right assumption. He really did like me. Imagine that.

"Just come back in one piece," he said. "Mr. Murray will never forgive me." And Malcolm Murry would likely follow through on "never forgive me" with "never find the body" so fair enough. Though Darius seemed less concerned about his own safety if something happened to me than the actual risk I might come to harm.

How sweet was that?

I left him to his ineffectual observation, unhappiness showing in flickers of glances over the choppy water of the lake, as I entered the dive shack to suit up.

"Not that one," Chantal snapped at Anja. "The

other one."

"Then get it yourself," the tall brunette bit back. "I'm not your servant."

"Temper, ladies." Gregg's grin and amusement weren't helping as he zipped himself into a full wetsuit, Martin already dressed and ready, checking out his camera equipment and keeping clear of the growing tension.

"Mind your own business," Chantal shot back before throwing a wetsuit at MC. "That's the 3mm."

The icy waters of the lake would require much thicker suits. I wasn't going past thirty feet and was totally wimping out wearing 7mm. MC's face darkened as she threw the suit back.

"Wear both," she said, turning away while both Chantal and Anja made rude faces at her. "And hurry up. We're already behind and I want to get two dives in today."

The rest of our prep went about the same, the surly team butting heads while Gregg just seemed to derive amusement from the clash of personalities and his cameraman practically hid behind his boss. I couldn't help but glare at the treasure hunter, Blackstone's giant gold B logo in my mind's eye. It might as well have been tattooed on his forehead at this point. I was more and more certain—proof? Who needs proof?—that we had a bigger snake in our midst than we'd first thought.

I was about to say something to Crew when he jerked MC aside, stopping me from interrupting.

"Get the team under control," he said, low and

commanding, "or I'm pulling the plug."

Her sullen expression leveled out, but she didn't apologize. "It's nerves," she said. "It'll pass. Let's get to the boat."

I quickly got out of Chantal's way as she heaved on the handles of the wheelbarrow, loaded with tanks, pushing past me without a glance, trundling toward the boat, I stood back and let Gregg go next refusing to be baited by that smirk of his and mostly succeeding. At least, I didn't smack him as he passed me, so that was a win, right?

Crew and MC were already gone, and I headed after them, only to realize I'd forgotten my regulator. Because diving without the means to breathe was brilliant, Fee. I sighed at myself, wondering if this boded badly or well, and turned back to the shack and my missing equipment.

The door was partially ajar, enough I caught sight of the fight before I heard it, and paused, heart in my throat, while Anja, entire body shaking with clear rage, hissed something in Martin's face. He looked distinctly distraught as if she'd broken his heart, before she turned and stomped out of the shed, ignoring me, bangs hanging over the thunderclouds in her eyes.

The documentarian didn't say anything to me either, keeping his head down and hurrying by, camera clutched to his narrow chest. I took a moment to sink to the bench and rest my face in my hands, heart pounding painfully, worried all over again.

This was a terrible idea.

That's why I canceled the dive, right? Why I marched up to MC and Gregg and told them in no uncertain terms we weren't going underwater today or any day, not together, not like this.

Exactly.

Snort.

My retrieved regulator in my hands and my sense of self-preservation badly askew, I headed for the boat and our first dive of the day.

Please, let it not be my last.

Thing was, it turned out MC was right, at least to a point. The moment the boat was loaded, Wanda at the helm taking us to the first location, the team had settled into a quiet stillness, looking outward across the water, the rough ride forcing all of us to hang on. Their chatter turned from snarky jibes to the low-level hum of experienced divers ready for the job ahead. Even Gregg's smirk disappeared as he double-checked the gauge on his tanks. I ran through my own list of things to do I'd been practicing in my head since I finished my first open dive, feeling the repetition of the process calm and collect me.

By the time we reached the first dive site about five minutes later, I was actually bordering on optimistic no one was going to die today.

CHAPTER TWELVE

Freezing lake water was still freezing, no matter how thick the dive suit. I caught myself shivering as I peered through the gloom surrounding me, spotting Anja a few feet away where she gracefully explored the area we'd been assigned, looking more like she belonged underwater than anyone should.

Me? Yeah, no mermaid-like elegance here. I'm sure I was much more floundering fish-out-of-water. I still struggled a bit to control my fins and the work it took to turn, not to mention the silt thickening the water's view to the point I was squinting despite myself. It wasn't helping me see or anything, just a reaction to the reduced visibility caused by the storm. All-in-all, not the best dive I'd ever had.

Right. Because I had a huge list to compare to.

Anja turned to me, shot me an OK symbol with her thumb and index finger and I had to fight the urge to give her a thumbs up in return. I'd learned quickly that meant I needed to go to the surface, but I was still trying to imprint all the hand signals in my brain. It took me a stuttering moment for my chilled mind to return the message and when I did, she nodded and continued on.

The cold seeped into my bones, swimming helping a little but my mind—that ever-vigilant and obsessive controller of all things Fiona Fleming— whispered about hypothermia while I argued with it we were fine, thank you very much and shut up already. This was supposed to be fun, not a lesson in oh my god I'm going to die, why didn't I listen to Darius, this is the stupidest thing I've ever done, and if I make it back to land, I'll never dive again.

Okay, a bit over-the-top and I wasn't that close to panic, but the novelty was wearing off and I was over it.

At least we were in shallow water. I couldn't imagine the added difficulties of diving to the depths the others had taken on. Though, Crew assured me it was likely the water was clearer deeper beneath the surface, where the storm would have been unable to stir up the lakebed. I'd watched the boat carry off the other two teams as Anja and I went under, Chantal and MC heading for an area near Black Mountain and the mouth of the Minute River while Crew and Gregg—Martin and his camera along for the ride— had a spot closer to the center of the lake to look into.

Ten minutes later, according to my dive watch, and Anja signaled for us to surface. I exhaled my relief as we slowly rose, forcing myself to relax and breathe normally while my body ejected the excess nitrogen that had built up in my blood, the slow ascent carrying us up the line to the buoy left for us as our target. As we surfaced next to it, the boat was just returning, Wanda piloting it carefully to a stop a few feet clear of us and helped us board.

"Nothing?" She shrugged her broad shoulders and didn't seem surprised. "Maybe the others had better luck."

I heaved off my equipment with Anja's help, envying the ease in which she divested herself of her own gear and helped her stow the now empty tanks while Wanda guided the boat onward to the next location.

"Well done, Fee," Anja said, clearly back to her bright and sunny self, smiling at me with her green eyes sparkling. She brushed at her bangs clinging to her forehead. "Refreshing, wasn't it?"

She could say that. I shivered inside my wetsuit, tucking a heavy towel around me as I huddled onto the bench seat.

"Is the ocean this cold?" My nose twitched, tickle warning a sneeze or four was coming. Great. I'd better not be getting sick.

FEE. STOP IT RIGHT NOW.

Anja shrugged as she toweled off, crouching next to me, the boat's rocking doing nothing to budge her amazing balance. "Go deep enough," she said, "and every body of water is."

I guess.

"Disappointed?" Anja's clear gaze locked on mine.

Was that why I was grumpy? "A little," I said. "I guess I wanted to be the one to find the treasure." I laughed, then. "Silly, right?"

She laughed too, patted my knee before joining me on the bench with a deep, contented sigh, eyes locked on the water, smile on her face. "It's what we live for, Fee," she said. "And the dive. So, it's a Catch-22. We want to find what we're looking for, but we never want to leave the water."

If she said so. "Do you think we'll find it?" I hope I didn't sound too plaintive.

If I did, Anja wasn't judging me for it, at least not openly. I had a feeling she wasn't the type to anyway. "Whether we do or we don't," she said, "at least we're trying." Her sunny smile made me feel better.

That was until we pulled up to the second buoy and the pair that waited for us boarded. I blinked in confusion at the sight of my husband, his face creased in anger, as he returned to the boat, turning on Chantal with what was clearly an ongoing argument bubbling inside him.

Before he opened his mouth, my own mind made the connection to his unhappiness. And I got to speak what he clearly was about to say, if in the form of a question instead of an outburst of dissatisfaction.

"Where's MC?"

Crew frowned at me while Chantal took Anja's silent assistance in removing her gear, not meeting my eyes, her own face expressionless but in that flat and empty way that said she was wearing a mask of discontent.

"Where do you think?" Crew tossed his gloves with enough force they thudded against the hull of the boat.

Chantal didn't comment, Anja's unhappiness returned. I realized I could have prodded my husband for more information, but it was pretty clear what happened while we headed out to the middle of the lake for the final buoy.

Gregg had wanted to dive with MC, and, despite the fact things weren't supposed to go his way, he got what he wanted. Story of his life? Seemed that way. Wondered what it would take to shake up that belief system.

I was willing to give it ago.

Crew sat, staring at his hands, frowning deeply enough I let him be. He didn't look up as we stopped at the final buoy, didn't say a word to anyone while MC and Martin climbed on board, a jubilant Gregg the last one to return to the safety of the vessel.

"We're on the right track!" Only when he spoke did I realize Martin still had the camera running, had been filming all along, the awkward way he'd entered the boat due to his careful framing of his boss who held up something shining in his gloved fingers.

It was bittersweet, seeing that round, gold coin in

the hands of Gregg Brown. I knew what it was immediately, had been studying the one Grandmother Iris left me for years now, knew it was a doubloon even before Gregg lowered his hand and laid it in his palm, turning slowly toward Martin and the camera.

On the one hand, this was proof. More proof. Maybe the ultimate. And, on the other... he had to be the one to find it, right? Crew's dark expression wasn't hard to read, though I admit, it was me making the assumption my husband was furious the treasure hunter had scooped Crew's chance to find the coin.

I should have known better. The former sheriff instead confronted Gregg, angry face tight, tall, broad body shaking when he faced off with the treasure hunter.

"Stupid and dangerous and if you pull something like that again, Gregg, I swear to God, contract or no contract, I will beach you permanently." So, it wasn't the find that my husband was angry about?

Gregg's expression flattened out, empty hand on my husband's chest as he firmly pushed Crew away. "My call," he snapped.

"Not yours," Crew bit back. "MC was in command of the teams. She made the pairings. Our dive plans were designed around those pairings." My normally calm husband was losing it for the second time today and there wasn't much I could do about it. "Your last-minute decision to run the show put everyone at risk."

"Dial it back, cowboy," Gregg snarled.

"I won't," Crew said, now cold, quiet and far more dangerous in my estimation. Yelling Crew was scary to me. Intensely still and collected Crew?

Yeah. Look out.

"Crew's right," MC said, sounding tired, rubbing at her face with both hands. "It was stupid, Gregg. Selfish. Next time, dive where I assign you or don't dive."

He shrugged, smirk back. "And yet," he said, "amidst all your complaining, who was it that found what we were looking for?" He didn't even seem to realize he'd missed the point, turning toward the camera once again, brandishing the coin like the prize it was. "Success!" Gregg's mood shifted instantly to self-satisfied smugness as he spun on my husband. "You're welcome."

I had to hold Crew back. Literally had to grab him and use every ounce of my strength to contain the fury I knew welled in the gorgeous man I loved. I'd never seen this side of him, not really. Sure, I'd seen him angry, pissed off at me, irritated, scared. But never flat-out furious. Dare I say murderous? And twice in one day?

Maybe we really did need to leave Reading.

Crew resisted me only a moment before turning his back on Gregg, resuming his seat on the bench, his stare at his hands, silent and fuming. I joined him, one hand on his lower back, just sitting with him while the others talked over the find.

By the time we reached shore, Crew had pulled

himself together enough that he held me back, the two of us the last to leave the boat as the dive team lugged the empty tanks and other equipment to the shed for refills.

"That idiot," he said, voice low, for me alone. He was shaking, and not from the cold. "We got to the second dive site, and he refused to dive. Practically pushed me in. I had to finish gearing up underwater, Fee." No wonder he was so angry. "I'll tell you one thing, he might be good at finding treasure, but he's a menace to himself and everyone else he dives with."

"So, we pull the plug?" I have to admit, I almost didn't say it. Sure, I wished otherwise, too. But Gregg found a doubloon. The truth of that was finally sinking in.

My husband shook his head, dark hair drying in the breeze, forming curls around his ears and the nape of his neck. I wanted to run my fingers through it, to kiss him and make it better, but that wasn't going to happen.

"No," he said. "We follow through. But I'm keeping my eye on him. And I'll be damned if I'll let either of us dive with him, Fee. Ever."

Since I had no desire to go in the water with Gregg, that suited me down to the ground.

By the time we joined the others, their excitement had won out over the disagreement on the boat and, while Crew might still have been furious, apparently, his decision to keep both of us out of harm's way by any means possible—out of Gregg's way, that was— seemed to have released the truly frightening tension in him.

I sat at the picnic table next to Chantal, Crew on my other side, Anja joining us from a short trip to the dive shed. Chantal left me then, Anja taking her place, her own trip to the storage building meaning she missed the arrival of the next best part of the day as lunch arrived.

Mom took a moment to kiss my cheek and hug Crew before depositing hampers of soup, fresh biscuits and a deliciously hot lasagna on the table she first draped with a cloth. I almost laughed at her attempt to keep it smooth in the remaining breeze, but this was my mother we were talking about. Like wind was going to win out over the indomitable Lucy Fleming.

I was already warming thinking about her amazing cooking, knowing everything in those hampers would hit the spot. Her delight over the doubloon brightened things further, the gold coin rolling over and over in her hands while we served ourselves like starving street urchins who'd never seen food before—diving was hard work!—and dug in.

"How beautiful," she said.

"Thank you," Gregg answered with a wink around a mouthful of biscuit.

Mom's empty, rather chill expression in return, while she handed off the prize to my husband, told me she wasn't a fan herself, for whatever reason. My mother didn't suffer fools lightly and had years as a high school principal to back her confidence when dealing with those she deemed worthy of her more pointed attention. Case in point. With slow deliberation, she looked down at Crew and kissed him softly on the cheek. "Well done, dear," she said.

I honestly thought Gregg was going to split in half and combust on the spot. Meanwhile, the Woman of the Year, my shero and all-around Amazing Lucy Fleming beamed a smile at the rest of the team.

"Good job, all of you," she said. "Have a wonderful dive this afternoon and keep us posted."

No one said a word as Mom left, while I hid a giant grin behind one hand and Chantal choked on a bite of pasta, her lips twitching.

Gregg ate in sullen silence from then on, the rest of the team chattering in happy supposition. Even Crew let out a chuckle or two, the coin in front of him gleaming a promise of more to come.

Were we really going to find the Reading hoard? It hit me suddenly, breathlessly, in a wave of massive surprise so overwhelming I clutched at my husband's bicep and leaned into him.

"Crew," I whispered, knowing I was being an idiot for finally getting it. Finally letting it in.

He looked down at me, grinned. "I know," he said. And kissed the tip of my nose.

Real. Oh my god.

"Okay," Anja said, brushing crumbs from her lap, leaning toward Martin. "Let's see it."

He hastily swallowed the bite he was chewing before retrieving his ever-present camera, setting it on the table. The small viewer was still big enough for all of us to crowd around and watch as, through a haze of murk thinner than what I'd dealt with but still present, Gregg spotted and then retrieved the doubloon.

We watched it twice, first Chantal, then MC, asking for another viewing and Martin didn't argue. It was while we were starting our fourth review of the footage that the sound of a car door slamming interrupted, Hannah Brown joining us. She pointedly ignored MC, leaning in to kiss her husband's cheek, an act he seemed disgusted by.

"Any luck today?" His wife was obviously trying. MC said something incoherent and left the picnic table, heading for the dive shed while Chantal answered.

"Some," she said. Um, finding the doubloon was some luck?

"What are you doing here?" Gregg didn't even look at her, asking the question a moment before he grinned and jabbed Martin in the rib for the fourth time—the same point every viewing as his hand on the screen closed over the coin and brought it up from the lakebed. "There's the money shot!" Again, for the fourth time. Seriously.

Hannah hesitated, clearly sensing she wasn't welcome, and my heart went out to her. I should have done something, said something, but everyone ignored her from that moment on, even my husband, chatter returning to the video and the discovery, and, with a downcast expression, she finally left, though I noted she stopped off in the dive shed before exiting a few minutes later, climbing in her car and leaving.

Weird. She had no reason to be in there.

Lunch devoured, I headed for the yacht club proper and the washroom, returning from the still 70sesque and in bad need of a renovation interior to the delightful show of the sun on the exterior. It finally won against the clouds, the blue sky overhead making me dread less getting in the water once again. Surely this was an excellent sign?

I headed for the others, noting Martin entering the dive shed alone. I followed him on impulse, wanting to congratulate him. After all, he'd taken some amazing footage in really difficult circumstances and despite my dislike for Gregg, the treasure hunter was right. From what I'd seen, the discovery of the doubloon was the money shot, all right, and Martin had captured it in breathtaking fashion.

As I entered the shed, the dimness making me blink now that the sun had returned in full force, I almost missed the small man hunched over a set of tanks. I froze, realizing they weren't his and as he registered I was there, caught the tell-tale flash of guilt on his face while he lurched away from the set clearly marked with MC's name across the front.

CHAPTER THIRTEEN

I was about to call him on it when he blurted out his excuse.

"I thought it was Gregg's." He glanced down at the clearly marked tanks and blushed. "I always check his gear before his dive."

From the gauges, someone had already refilled all the tanks. "Nice of you," I said.

A shadow fell over us, MC entering the shed, and, in that same moment, Martin hurried to the door. He glanced at me in a hasty and nervous way before exiting, the dive leader not even noticing, head down, focused on the afternoon ahead, likely.

"MC." I had to say something, didn't I? Even if I was just being paranoid. She glanced at me, arched an eyebrow in question while she reached for her regulator and began to examine it, her pre-check on her mind. "I don't know if it's relevant." I stopped, didn't know if I should go on. Maybe I was blowing this out of proportion. Surely Martin didn't wish her harm. She stopped what she was doing, waited for me to speak, patient and watchful. "I caught Martin doing something to your tanks. I thought you should know." The right thing to do. So why then did I feel like a tattletale?

MC inhaled sharply, spun and crouched, examining the gauge, the connections. "Did you see what he was doing?"

"No," I said, miserable now. "I'm sorry, it was probably nothing."

She stood slowly, met my eyes. "Thanks, Fee," she said. "For having my back. I'll check everything over."

Okay, so it *was* the right thing to do. I nodded in return and stumbled out of the shack into the sunlight, fighting the urge to apologize to someone. No one in particular as I rejoined the others at the table, Martin not looking at me at all, his color still high. Wait a second, why was I feeling bad about warning MC he might have been up to shenanigans? The last thing I wanted was another dead body on my hands and, innocent or not, I refused to beat myself up for looking out for the people around me.

It took pulling myself back from the brink of guilt to realize my husband was gone. I looked around, noticed the SUV was missing from the parking lot, while Anja leaned in.

"Crew got a call," she said. "He'll be back in twenty minutes."

Huh. Must have been some call to make him leave. Had to have been Liz, since Dad was still out of town. Or Jill? Whatever the reason for his departure, it would have had to be pressing to drag him away from the club.

My questioning text received an instant answer. *Be right back. Don't sail without me.*

One thing was assured. Gregg Brown's attitude or not, we were not leaving the dock without my husband on board.

True to his guestimate, fifteen minutes later, as the annoying treasure hunter huffed over the delay (that was really barely a delay, putting us off by hardly any time at all), Crew's SUV returned and, silent and with that blank expression that told me his unhappiness had returned, he joined us.

"Well, finally," Gregg snapped, pushing past my husband. "Who's ready to find a treasure?"

The others followed, Crew holding back but when I tried to ask him what was up, he shook his head.

"Leave it, Fee," he said, blue eyes dark and snapping with anger. "We'll talk about it later, okay?"

No, it wasn't okay, but, well.

Okay.

The ride out wasn't quite so rough, the afternoon warm, breeze dying out at last. Though I knew the water would still be low visibility, the thought of going under again wasn't quite so daunting this time.

I admitted quietly to myself part of my issue this morning had been nerves, the whininess just a symptom of hating this feeling of being way behind everyone else in experience. At least we'd all be diving close together this time. The area where Gregg found the doubloon was a deep pocket surrounded by shallower water.

"Chantal, you're diving with Fee." I glanced her way as MC made the assignment, worried she might be disappointed not to be going deep, but her grin and okay gesture told me otherwise.

"Easier to spot gold closer to the surface," she said.

Grateful, I grinned back.

Wanda anchored the boat near the morning's discovery, where she'd left the last buoy in the water as a marker. "Have a great dive, kids," she said. "Find that treasure, won't you?"

"That's the plan." Gregg stood, Martin assisting with his tanks. "MC, you're with me." Not a question and definitely not up to him. But Crew didn't argue, and the dive leader didn't either.

Instead, my husband fist-bumped Anja who enthusiastically returned the gesture. And then I realized, from here on in, it was a competition. Which team would find the next piece of the puzzle or, even better, the hull of the *Darkling Dragon* and Reading's hoard?

Okay, even I was getting excited, spine-tingling, heartbeat elevating as the tension and anxiety of the last twenty-four hours was devoured by the return of that drive I'd felt from the moment I'd discovered the treasure might be real. I waited my turn to leave the boat, Crew and Anja going first, sinking beneath the surface before Gregg and MC, Martin with his camera rolling, sat on the edge.

"Historic day!" Gregg was clearly working the footage as he clapped MC on the shoulder. "Beat you to the gold, Tortuga!" He settled his mask and regulator then tipped backward, almost smacking her with his fins on his way by. MC muttered something around her own mouthpiece before rolling back, disappearing after him.

I joined Chantal in the water when Martin vanished after them, forcing myself to calm despite my renewed excitement. That sense of adventure died pretty quickly as I sank beneath and realized, unlike this morning, the murkiness wasn't just cutting visibility, it was almost eliminating it.

I floundered a bit, already out of sight of Chantal, disorientation taking over. Panic rose despite the fact I knew I was close to the surface, safe, with plenty of air and the means to rise simply by inflating my buoyancy device. And yet, it still took me a solid minute of heavy breathing to pull myself together, a tiny meep of fear escaping when something touched my shoulder.

Chantal was there, so close I could see the color of her eyes, OK signal a question. I nodded, OK'd back, even though I wasn't. But no way was I missing this. I looked down, hoped that the deeper we got the clearer the water would be and followed her as she descended.

I tried to keep up, but she was a stronger swimmer and it wasn't long before the black flip of her fins disappeared from view. I refused to lose it, continuing on what I hoped was my proper trajectory, knowing I'd encounter her sooner or later. Funny, it seemed like I was swimming for a lot longer than usual, and, when I finally thought to check my dive computer strapped firmly to my wrist, I swore softly to myself.

Fifty feet. I was too deep, ten feet further than I was trained for. Time to panic yet, Fleming? No way. Stubbornness settled in and I stopped descending, straightened up, tried to get my bearings. And spotted, rising beneath me from the dark water, another diver.

Thank goodness. I was saved. Except, the moment that thought crossed my mind I realized two things. Whoever it was? They were rising far too fast than was good for them. And, from the limp way they hung in the water? Something was terribly wrong.

All about a half a heartbeat before the surging body hit me and forced me up toward the surface.

CHAPTER FOURTEEN

I managed to slow our rapid rise, though whether it was actually anything I did or the sheer weight of my additional equipment and the fact I was literally carrying weights in my BCD that kept us from rocketing all the way to the top. I knew we were still rising too fast, panting into my mouthpiece, going lightheaded when my oxygen intake bottomed out from rising panic. It took every ounce of internal fortitude I still possessed to force my breathing down to a more normal intake, to make my shaking hands work at the other diver's lines and BCD hooked into mine. I'd gone through some emergency procedures when I'd taken my diving course, but I doubt anything could have prepared me for this eventuality.

I tracked our surface speed, knowing I was in

trouble but, at least, hopeful I wouldn't black out from the elevated nitrogen in my system. I'd suffer, but I would be okay. At least that's what I told myself, unable to spare much worry for the limp figure, still trapped against me, a stream of bubbles from their BCD fighting against my weight.

It wasn't until we were almost on the surface, I managed to identify the person now tethered to me, the pressure of our ascent and the close proximity of his body making it impossible for me to separate us. Maybe if I'd had a bit more experience, or if he'd been conscious, I could have found a way to part myself from Gregg Brown. But, as things stood, I was helpless, unable even to unhook my tanks and shed them, to separate us.

I broached the surface, immediately struggling to turn, to locate the boat, slowly spinning with Gregg beneath me, pushing me partly out of the water, and finally spotted the hull of our vessel not so far away Wanda could miss me waving frantically for help.

My chest twinged, though I knew I had at least an hour before the full effects of decompression sickness would set in. Sympathetic reaction wasn't helping any, though, nor the gnawing worry we'd risen too far too fast and my typically overreactive brain wailing in the background I was going to die.

The surge of the boat's engine at least felt urgent enough I knew rescue was at hand. Enough I could finally focus on the state of the man, clearly unconscious, still attached to me. Though it was likely the wrong thing to do under the circumstances,

I forced my hand between us and our tangled gear and, through sheer will, unclipped myself from my tanks, sinking out of my BCD and spitting out my mouthpiece, pawing at the mask on my face, panting into the July afternoon while the boat rushed toward me.

Gregg bobbed sideways, the weight of my tanks taking him off balance and I realized with the dull understanding of someone who'd been through this far too many times I'd known all along he wasn't just unconscious.

Considering his eyes stared, empty and cold, back from behind his mask as he tipped over on his side, his mouthpiece floating free of his gaping mouth, I knew I wasn't the one who had to worry about death.

I inhaled deeply from the oxygen Dr. Aberstock offered me, the warm blanket around my shoulders doing little to kill the chill that had settled over me. Despite the heat of the sun now beaming down as if unaware of the present circumstances, I couldn't get warm.

I'd never be warm again.

As usual, the doc had made it to us way ahead of the EMTs, though I knew an ambulance would be along any moment and wouldn't fight them when they loaded me in the back and took me to the hospital.

"We're lucky Curtis County General has a hyperbaric chamber," Dr. Aberstock said, inserting an IV line into my wrist. He looked rather odd in his dive suit, that familiar Santa Claus roundness stuffed into shiny black rubber. "And that I'm a diver." He winked at me, then nodded to Crew who hovered, his worry obvious, though he stayed out of the way since the doc arrived as if knowing he wasn't helping otherwise. I reached out and took my husband's hand, tugging him down to sit next to me at the picnic table while Dr. Aberstock elevated the bag of fluids now pumping into my system. "We'll get you sorted, Fee. Right as rain in no time. Treated early, you'll barely know you were sick."

I wasn't so sure he was being totally honest, but I'd take it. "Any idea what happened to Gregg?" I'd lowered the oxygen mask to ask that question, only to have both men move my hand out of the way, Crew replacing it for me.

The doc patted my shoulder. "I don't know yet," he said, "but I have some suspicions. I'll have to examine him more thoroughly." He'd only given the dead treasure hunter the briefest of inspections in between shoving an oxygen mask on my face and going to his car for the bag of whatever it was he was feeding into my bloodstream. "I don't want you to think about that right now. We've been through this enough times before you know I'll get to the bottom of it." That wink. Yes, I knew it well.

Far too well.

Dr. Aberstock checked my dive computer again,

frowning slightly. "It's been over a half-hour," he said. It had taken a bit to alert the other divers, to gather them and return to shore. I'd insisted, Darius immediately calling the doc, it turned out, when he saw us returning early. I guess he knew me better than I thought, assumed there was trouble, and I was the cause. Fair enough we'd practically flown to the dock, so his worry was warranted. "Are you feeling any dizziness, nausea, shortness of breath? Joint pain?" He examined my eyes while the faint wail of the approaching ambulance finally reached us.

"No." My voice sounded odd, muffled under the oxygen mask. "I'm okay." At least for now. I knew symptoms could show up at any time, my muscles only aching from holding myself tense in anticipation of the agony I knew was coming but never manifested.

"We're not taking any chances," he said. "Your dive computer says you need recompression treatment and I'm not risking your health." The ambulance pulled into the parking lot, and he waved them over. Crew's arm around me felt firmer than usual, and the tightness around his eyes, the super controlled way he held himself, was all I needed to know just how afraid he was for me.

And was likely blaming himself. Because Crew.

I rose when Dr. Aberstock's soft touch encouraged me to, and, for the first time, I took note of the rest of the team. They huddled together, heads down, despair clear on their faces, even Martin and his endless filming silenced as his camera dangled uselessly from his shaking hands. Shell-shocked, like a band of warriors who'd seen too much and simply couldn't process yet.

I wished I could join them, whisper my condolences, hug them and commiserate. Despite my feelings previously, no matter how I'd railed against Gregg Brown's presence, I'd seen too much death to truly mean all the previous wishful thinking something bad would happen to him. Even my hot temper couldn't survive the death of a human being, even if he really was despicable.

Oh, Fee. Enough already.

I waved off the offer of the gurney, despite Dr. Aberstock's tsk of disapproval, perfectly capable of climbing into the ambulance, thanks. As I did, a car squealed its way into the parking lot, Hannah Brown barely at a halt before leaping out of the driver's side and running toward us, already sobbing. She knew, how? Didn't matter, though it was obvious she wasn't here to mourn, not when she didn't stop, didn't pause an instant, before throwing herself at MC.

"You killed him!" Hannah's words were barely coherent, but her intent was clear enough. Lucky for MC Darius loomed nearby and caught the grieving widow around the waist, practically picking her up off the ground to keep her from assaulting the Tortuga dive leader. The fact MC didn't fight her, misery on her face, broke my heart. She'd be blaming herself, too, wouldn't she? Gregg might have played at being the boss, but I knew from talking to MC initially, she took her responsibility as leader very seriously.

She did respond, though, shaking her head, slow and heavy. "We don't know what happened yet," she said.

"I'll sue you for negligence!" Did Hannah understand Gregg had been the intruder in this dive? That his own actions just this morning had, according to Crew, put MC herself at risk? Doubtful, and nor did it matter to the clearly distraught woman who struggled against Darius's mountain of immobility while sobbing with tears washing her mascara down her cheeks. "I'll ruin you and you'll never dive again!"

"That's enough of that, Mrs. Brown." Jill had appeared about thirty seconds after Dr. Aberstock, Robert lazily following behind her in his own car. But she'd disappeared after a brief chat with me, leaving me to the doc to start her investigation elsewhere. She'd returned from the boat with Wanda, Robert emerging from the dive shack, hiking his pants up under his round belly, inhaling an impressive amount of air through his nose—enough to make his nostrils vibrate, even from a distance—before expelling the resulting cache to the pavement.

Delightful as ever.

Hannah sagged in Darius's arms just as Jill gestured for the big man to let her go. He did as he was told without a word, backing off to join me. The EMTs didn't seem eager to leave, clearly as fascinated with the show as I was, and since they weren't hustling me toward the ambulance I found my natural sense of curiosity—that usually got me in trouble, I know, I know—cut through my mind's fearful chatter I was going to implode or something.

"Who was diving with Mr. Brown?" Jill turned to Anja when she raised one hand in a tentative admission of association, though she looked like she wished she'd stayed out of it.

"I was closest to him when we first went in," she said. "I saw him leave Martin behind and go deeper, but that was early on. I'm not sure what happened after that."

Martin swallowed hard, his own tears making it clear he was taking Gregg's loss personally. "I tried to keep up," he said. "But something caught his attention, and he was off like a shot." He looked down at his camera. "I was having trouble with the equipment and before I could sort it out, he was gone."

MC nodded, again in that slow and weighted motion, like her head rocked independently of her spine, a bobble doll, not a human being. "He signaled to me he'd seen something about five minutes in," she said. "Went deep, fast." She glanced at her dive computer, pressed the surface. "I made it to 160 feet. He had to have been even deeper than that."

Jill turned to my husband who shrugged before she could ask the obvious. "I was on the other side of Anja," he said. "The water was so murky I didn't see a thing." He sounded frustrated by that, still hugging me close like I was the only thing anchoring him to the world at the moment. I was happy to be that connection if he needed me. Heaven knew he'd do the same for me. And had.

"And I was with Fee initially," Chantal said, face a twisted mess of regret. "When I realized the water was dirty deeper than I expected, I turned back to tether to her, but I'd already lost her." Chantal's green eyes met mine and she choked on a soft intake of breath. "I'm sorry, Fee. This is my fault. You should never have been out there alone like that. I take full responsibility."

I shook my head at her, tried a weak smile and made it. "Trust me, Chantal," I said, "this is par for my particular course."

Didn't seem to help, but I tried.

"For all we know, he had a heart attack or an aneurysm or something." Anja seemed suddenly angry, lurching to her feet, arms crossed over her narrow chest. "He wasn't the safest diver, we all know it." She jerked her head to the side, defensive but clearly unable or unwilling to stop talking. "He was an arrogant ass who took stupid chances and got himself killed finally."

"Shut up!" Hannah lunged for the tall diver this time, but Jill managed to get in between them, holding the furious woman back from clawing at Anja with savagely swinging arms. "You shut up about my Gregg!"

Anja just shrugged and looked away, face dark, body tense, though she did sink back to the bench again, falling silent.

"I'd like to talk to each of you individually," Jill said, crisp and professional, handing Hannah off to my cousin despite his expression of disgust at having to support the weeping woman. "Fee," she turned to me, sympathy present but all cop, "I'll come see you in the hospital when you're feeling better."

Since I was feeling okay at the moment, she needn't have bothered. But if I didn't get treatment soon, her words would be prophetic, so I nodded.

I watched Jill loading tanks and gear into the sheriff's pickup as I settled into the back of the ambulance, the doors closing on us while Crew took his place next to me, holding my hand.

CHAPTER FIFTEEN

I did my best to relax inside what had looked, essentially, like a giant duffle bag, the dark blue canvas surface more like the home of someone's stinky hockey gear than a life-saving hyperbaric chamber.

"We use it for cancer treatments," Dr. Aberstock told me, holding my hand as he encouraged me to step into what I tried not to think of as the means to dispose easily of my body if this didn't work, my silly brain imagining being tossed into the trunk of a car and taken somewhere to be disposed of forever. His sweet, cherub smile wasn't helping. If anything, it only made my nerves worse, and my claustrophobia wasn't helping. "Might not be perfect, but it will do the job."

I'd closed my eyes and forced myself to relax when the zipper slid shut, the pressure instant in my ears as the interior of the chamber inflated with oxygen. I plugged my nose and pushed outward like I did when I flew, feeling my ears pop softly, the white interior at least bright enough I didn't feel like I'd been sealed inside a flimsy coffin.

An hour to lie there and think about what happened wasn't the best idea in my condition, but I had little choice, though I'd been offered headphones and the option of music to distract me. Instead, I went the typical Fiona Fleming route and drove myself crazy by replaying the events of our last dive over and over.

Gregg rising toward me so fast, too fast for my inexperience to avoid him. Yes, that much I would accept. But our gear getting tangled, my inability to slow us down enough to pressurize properly, my panic? Sure, I might have been a new diver, but I should have been able to disengage, to offer him assistance. If I'd been on the ball, would I have been able to save him? That question ate at me the long sixty minutes of the oxygenation treatment and persisted as the pressure inside the chamber released and began to dissipate completely as the hour came to an end. Could I, with more experience and less freakout, have saved Gregg's life?

I was sweating when Dr. Aberstock unzipped the bag and Crew helped me out. I hugged my husband, not caring the hospital robe likely gaped in the back, or that I was about to break down all over again.

The doc's hand fell on my shoulder, and I pulled away from my husband, even as Dr. Aberstock smiled faintly at me in sympathy.

"I know what you're thinking, young lady," he said. "And I can assure you, if Mr. Brown was already unconscious by the time he reached you, had already expelled his mouthpiece, there was nothing you could have done for him." He paused, nodded once. "Nothing. You did the best you could."

I did cry then, wiping at the tears, before hugging Dr. Aberstock, too. He softly rubbed my back before handing me gently off to my husband who helped me into the wheelchair the doc had insisted on and returned me to my room.

I settled into my bed, Mom there, anxiously tucking me in, patting at my hands, my hair, before bursting into her own tears. Dr. Aberstock found himself hugging yet another weeping Fleming, though he didn't seem to mind and, instead of passing Mom off to my husband, held my mother for a bit, letting her pull herself together and make her own decision to let him go.

"Now that I know for certain Fee is going to be okay," he said, beaming that smile of his at all of us, "if you'll excuse me, I have an autopsy to perform." With that, he left us in that brisk stride of utter confidence that always made me feel better.

I didn't get time to settle long, Mom and Crew barely turning to focus on me, when Jill appeared at my door. I waved her inside when she hesitated, joining us with an unhappy expression and not looking at Crew in a way that triggered new anxiety.

"You're not here about Gregg," I said.

"I am," she said. "And." She finally glanced at my husband who, grim, nodded back. "I have to ask you both questions about the incident this morning." Incident? What was she talking about? "I've already spoken to your... friend outside." Crew had made Darius remain at the door, on guard, not that the big man argued. I think he preferred that position.

But why would Jill want to talk to—and then, it hit me. "Geoffrey." The ass. "Did he actually press charges?"

Crew answered before the sheriff could. "That's where I went at lunch," he said, voice low and soft, filled with embarrassment. "He filed a restraining order. I went to talk to him about it, but I couldn't find him." He glanced at Jill, his shame so clear I hurt for him. "I know, I was breaking the law doing so. But I wanted to apologize."

Jill seemed sympathetic enough. "Just tell me what happened."

Mom stood to one side, her anger clear in her flaring nostrils and flashing green eyes as Crew and I told her everything that unfolded that morning at Sammy's. Funny, with the discovery of the doubloon and Gregg's subsequent death I'd completely forgotten about Geoffrey and his bloody nose. Seemed inconsequential in light of what happened, and yet, if he was really going to press charges, this could mean a headache for Crew that we didn't need.

If he decided to sue? Yikes. Well, we'd deal. We

always did.

When we were done, Jill inhaled, exhaled, shrugged. "You should know Geoffrey has made an official complaint and has gathered witnesses." Sammy's was full. Not hard to find people who saw what happened. Still, thanks a lot, Reading residents, for taking his side. "He wants you charged with assault."

Mom tsked brusquely. "And what about his assault on my daughter? What about that, Jill?" I'd seen my mother's reaction to being manhandled and, it turned out, she was just as protective of me being mauled as having her own person touched against her will.

Jill seemed like she would have liked a giant black pit to open up and swallow her rather than have to answer my mother. "That will all have to come out in court," she said. "I'm sorry. There's nothing I can do."

"We'll just see about that." Mom turned toward me, her shoulder to Jill. "If you're done, Sheriff Wagner, my daughter has been through a terrible trauma and needs her rest. Not some ridiculous and petty questioning based on the petulant reactions of a truly distasteful human being."

Jill flinched. I knew she adored my mother. Everyone did. But I had no idea Mom's approval meant so much to her. It was pretty clear, though, as my friend turned to me, face tight with regret but knowing she had no choice. "I hope you're feeling better," she said. Hesitated. Then left with her head down and her footsteps quick but quiet.

"Honestly," Mom said before falling still herself.

"It's my fault, Lucy," Crew said. Sighed. "I'm an idiot. But I'll handle it. For now, Fee needs to sleep."

I was tired, and oddly hungry, though I wasn't going to tell them that. Not when my next visitor appeared and distracted me. MC looked ten years older, face pale, shoulders rounded, hands in the pockets of her jeans, boot soles squeaking on the floor as she shuffled just past the threshold and waited for us to invite her further before coming to my bedside.

"I'm so sorry," I said. "You must be devastated." Yes, still feeling guilty over not being able to help Gregg, though Dr. Aberstock said otherwise.

"I'm sorry, too," she said. "Thanks to this disaster, the hunt will have to stop. My funders are tapped out and when they found out someone died, they decided to stop sponsoring me altogether." She shrugged faintly, like someone who'd lost everything in one tragedy. Which, I guess she had. "I'm done."

I couldn't help but wonder what bothered her more, though. Gregg's death or the loss of her business? Mind you, I knew my own mind would have led me to feel sorry for myself, so I wasn't about to judge her. Or shouldn't have been calling kettles black, since I'd been a pot a few times myself.

Still. For the first time, it crossed my mind Gregg's death might not have been an accident. Now that I knew I was going to be okay? I could focus on what actually happened. Or what didn't.

MC didn't linger long, especially when a massive yawn took me over a moment later, my mother instantly shooing the Tortuga dive leader out of the room, pausing herself only long enough to softly kiss my forehead before taking her leave.

I sent Crew home, too, though I could see the argument brewing. "You need sleep. I need sleep." Like I was going to get much in the hospital, but whatever. "We have a lot to deal with tomorrow. Get some rest, please."

He left then, a long kiss for me before he exited, the soft sound of his voice outside my room and Darius's answering tenor telling me while my beloved might be going home (or so I told myself despite knowing he was as bad as I when it came to leaving things alone already), my bodyguard would watch over me.

Which actually gave me the security I needed to sleep enough over the next twelve hours by the time Crew came to pick me up in the morning, I was feeling much more myself than I probably had the right to.

Dr. Aberstock cheerfully discharged me, though when I tried to quiz him about Gregg's murder, he wouldn't tell me much. "Still investigating," he told both of us. "Now go home and lie down before I change my mind and readmit you."

He might as well have told me to stop breathing. Crew dropped me off at home, Petunia snuggled next to me and hovered for about ten minutes before I huffed a sigh and glared at him.

"If you're going to be Captain Protectivepants for the next few days," I said, knowing I wasn't being fair but needing him to back off already, "you can just forget it, Crew Turner. Go to the office. Have a run. Something. Anything. Just beat it."

Crew's frown couldn't win against my determination, and, after a short standoff, he shrugged before kissing me and leaving.

I waited until I heard his truck pull away before getting out of bed, getting dressed and harnessing my pug. No way was I sitting still like some good little girl, tucked away from all the action. I couldn't just convalesce when I felt totally fine, knowing that a) my husband was about to be charged with assault and b) someone else might find the treasure thanks to the mess of yesterday and c) a man was dead, and I had no idea if he'd been murdered or killed himself out of his own idiocy.

I couldn't help thinking, as Petunia hopped down off the bottom step and headed out in her rolling waddle toward the sidewalk, about Martin fiddling with MC's tanks. The guilt on his face had been epic. He claimed he thought they were Gregg's, though, and my natural suspicions rose to the surface like air bubbles from a regulator. What if he really had mistaken MC's tanks for Gregg's and was planning to do something to his boss's equipment? But why? He'd seemed genuinely broken up by the treasure hunter's death. I had no frame of reference for conflict between them, so research was in order.

As for the others, they'd all had access to the

equipment in the shed and, if I recalled correctly, even Hannah had been alone with our gear yesterday, hadn't she? I'd seen her go into the shack before driving off while we were finishing lunch.

That was assuming murder, of course. My default. Frankly, the pool of suspects, if I was going to be honest, was as wide as the lake. From what I could tell, everyone involved had a reason to hate Gregg, me included. Crew included. And, if my leap of accusation about him was accurate, if Gregg was working for Blackstone as I'd suspected, maybe that entity had something against him.

Not to mention the Patterson family. Hadn't Olivia just warned me to stay away from anything to do with the treasure? If Gregg's death wasn't an accident, could this have been something that founding family organized as the means to keep me from finding the truth?

Too many questions, not enough answers. I followed Petunia as she meandered her way down the street, doing nothing to encourage her to walk faster as I usually did, content to wander and think while she led the way. I was surprised when she turned at the end of the street and headed downtown, considering she usually wanted to go to the annex—or, if I was being honest, the empty lot where the B&B named for her, and her predecessors once stood. Happy she didn't seem so obsessed with the loss of her familiar home, I continued to follow her while she plodded at a steady if slow pace toward the center of town.

Two blocks in, my head spinning, I finally shook off the seemingly endless spiral of thoughts I could do nothing to satisfy in my present circumstance. Worrying over questions that had no answers only made me tense and uptight and, frankly, more than a little cranky. It was in that state of mind I looked up, came back to awareness, and spotted the young editor/reporter who was now the voice of the *Reading Reader Gazette* entering that paper's office.

I'd only met Christopher Jenkins once and did my best not to hold the fact he was Geoffrey's son against him. While he might not have been as hard-hitting in his reporting as Pamela used to be (as soft as she'd become in the final months of her control of the paper), he didn't seem to be the pro-Patterson mouthpiece I'd expected when I heard he'd taken over the *Gazette*. Or, had it handed to him, more than likely. He'd been polite enough but in a hurry that day, handsome where his father was shark-like, earnest but guarded, dark hair and eyes reminding me of my dear friend who'd been kept from me by Christopher's family. But my assumption he was anything like Jared Wilkins was a guesstimate, nothing more.

No time like the present to find out if the apple fell far from the rotten tree. And if he had a worm at his core or was just what the doctor ordered.

CHAPTER SIXTEEN

Christopher looked up as I entered, his curious expression turning sullen and unwelcoming, telling me everything I needed to know before I could even open my mouth.

"I know why you're here, Ms. Fleming," he said, looking down instantly, bitterness in his voice. "I have zero influence over my father, so asking me to do anything about the assault charge is a waste of time." He met my eyes again, then, chest puffing out under his golf shirt, lips a tight line of disapproval. "Not to mention the fact your husband should have controlled his temper. Now, if you don't mind, I have work to do and zero patience with the Fleming family, unlike the rest of this sad little town."

Wow. Okay then. He turned his back on me, sat

down at a computer and put on headphones, proceeding to ignore me completely.

I suppose I shouldn't have been surprised, and honestly getting offended by the temperamental little snot did me no good. But the temptation to march up to him, tear off those headphones and give him a piece of my mind was so strong I willfully spun myself to the exit and marched out.

The last thing we needed in our family was two assault charges and that's the way I was heading if I decided to follow through on impulse. Look at me, adulting and everything. Crew would be proud.

It wasn't until I hit the street again, I realized my shadow was missing. No dark sedan followed me, no sign of Darius whatsoever. Had Malcolm done something horrible to him after finding out about Gregg's death? A shiver ran down my spine, fear for the big bodyguard replacing my annoyance with the brat I'd just left behind me, and good riddance.

I returned home, texting Malcolm as I went, but didn't receive an answer. Instead of retreating inside, I bundled my pug into my car and took a drive to The Orange, to check in in person. But the small collection of dark-suited men matching my own Darius—okay, so I had claimed him after all, it seemed—didn't know where their boss was and seemed surprised my protector had gone missing.

I did drive to the house then, settled on the couch with my pug for an hour of TV, restlessly paced and refused to call Crew, pretended to be interested in the episode I was watching and then, knowing it would make me mental if I stayed any longer, stuffed Petunia full of strawberries and left her snoozing on her pillow while I went out again.

My tolerance for doing nothing had never been lower, though pacing the streets of Reading wasn't really helping all that much. I could have gone to the annex and checked in with Daisy and Mom, but I was positive those two would be horrified (Day) and motheringly furious (guess who) in equal measure before sending me home or turning me in or insisting on babysitting me when all I really wanted was some answers or something to do.

I briefly considered bugging Dr. Aberstock but knew he'd be in touch the second he had something. And honestly, going to the annex meant I might run into the dive team, and I really didn't feel like encountering any of them at the moment.

Instead, frustrated and feeling a bit frazzled, I headed for town hall and the one person I never thought I'd have on my friend list but who I now considered one of the most trustworthy people in my life.

Olivia's old space hadn't changed much since Vivian's takeover, even Hugh Farcourt the familiar face of the mayor's office. Though, when I peeked in to see if she was around, her assistant was absent. Which meant neither of them was in the office at the moment.

Grunt. I hesitated at the top of the steps, thinking about Geoffrey and feeling anger grow from the lingering seed he'd planted yesterday. No, not yesterday. Long ago, as in the first time he'd hit on me, standing on the steps of the sheriff's office, offering me protection and support if I'd back him. I'd been horrified and grossed out then. And even more so over the span of time he'd decided to increase his apparent bid for my affection. Never mind he'd been married to his wife, Gail, for at least twenty-five years, if not more. Or that he knew, beyond a shadow of a doubt, I loved Crew more than life itself.

Angry? You bet I was angry. Because that piece of work wasn't going to get away with taking his jealousy and disgusting plans to make me feel uncomfortable at every turn out on my darling husband.

Wasn't.

Time to give Geoffrey Jenkins a piece of my mind and an ultimatum. Either he stepped off Crew or I'd make him regret it.

I spun and marched down the hall, past Vivian's office door and to the end of the corridor. I'd worked up quite a head of steam by the time I paused at the wood and glass entry to Geoffrey's office, hating the sight of his name etched there. Now, it was possible I'd wasted that buildup to action, considering he had an accounting office a street over. The likelihood he was even here was slim to none. But I wasn't really considering I might have to march myself out of town hall to confront him.

And, when I noted the door was ajar, I almost stopped and turned around. Not because I knew it meant he was likely here, but because I wasn't sure this was a good idea after all. I had to catch myself, catch my breath, a soft wave of dizziness taking me over, forcing me to lean against the dark wood paneling of the wall, hands on my knees, doing my best not to pass out as the rush of darkness closed in around the edges.

It took about a minute, I think, for the spell to pass and I knew despite my treatment I still had lingering effects I really should report to Dr. Aberstock. I dabbed at the cold sweat standing out on my upper lip, my forehead, and promised I would. But the reminder of what I'd been through had a positive shift in my mood. I was so lucky to be safe, alive and well yet again, despite everything that happened. Geoffrey Jenkins wasn't going to take that away from me.

My temper broken but my determination no less powerful, I pushed open his door. The curtains were drawn, the lights dim, his chair turned toward the windows. But it was clear he was there, one hand visible on the armrest. I approached while taking slow, calming breaths, planning what I wanted to say before planting myself in front of his desk.

"We need to talk." I kept my tone low and clear, rational. I would *not* lose it, not in front of him. Not when Crew's safety and reputation were at stake. "We both know you provoked my husband this morning. I want you to drop the charges, Geoffrey. If you do, we'll just let this go."

I knew my argument was weak, but I had some

ammunition at least. If he decided to push back, I'd suggest he might want to reconsider since I was thinking about my own assault charges, with "sexual" tagged on for good measure.

He didn't respond right away, so I marched on, taking his silence as a sign he was, at least, willing to listen.

"Crew is genuinely sorry," I said. "And willing to publically apologize." Okay, I was speaking out of turn, but I knew my husband would agree if need be. "We don't want this to get ugly, Geoffrey. Let's be reasonable, shall we?"

Still no response. Seriously, the guy was a total jerk. Why was I even trying? Temper rising once again despite my decision to the contrary, I circled his desk, ready to hand him my ultimatum, only to stop in my tracks.

Inhale.

Exhale.

And shake my head with a terrible fear growing in my chest.

Because he hadn't stayed silent out of some kind of attempt to piss me off. Not if his staring, empty gaze—my second in less than twenty-four hours—was any indicator.

No, he'd stayed silent because Geoffrey Jenkins had touched me inappropriately for the last time.

CHAPTER SEVENTEEN

Was it just me, or did Jill's lack of surprise as I quietly filled her in on finding Geoffrey's body tied to a long-suffering soft sigh of acceptance and, dare I say, expectation? She didn't comment as much, but it wasn't hard to see that Sheriff Wagner's attitude toward my discovery had little to do with sympathy and much more with overwhelm.

Okay, fair enough. She now had two deaths to investigate, both of whom could very easily have been murdered. In fact, I wasn't about to think we'd be so lucky to discover they'd both died of natural causes. This was Reading, after all, and since when did my stumbling over dead people ever end well?

I guess it wasn't helping that Rosebert prowled Geoffrey's office, looking for clues (i.e. making idiots of themselves), glancing our way over and over again. Rose's uniform shirt made her look like a little girl who'd raided Daddy's closet and the color did nothing for her sallow complexion. As for my hateful cousin, he'd been packing on the beer belly sufficiently, while failing to consult a tailor, it seemed because the outside of him was trying very hard to show itself through the closure of his khaki button-up.

If I had to catch one more flash of his pale fish belly or the line of dark, curly hair that peeked out the gap between buttons, I was going to throw up all over this crime scene.

It felt like I'd been answering questions for ages, though likely it had only been fifteen minutes or so. Just long enough for the entirety of the Reading town council to make individual pains in the asses of themselves by either poking their noses in (both Terri Jacobs and Sophia Bell at least held back from invading the space utterly) or actually walking past Jill's scowl of anger at the intrusion (looking at you, Oliver Watters) to take their own turn investigating where they had no reason to be.

Since I really didn't have a reason, either—aside from what I'd already told Jill—the fact it had taken this long to get through my interrogation wasn't boding well. Maybe she was just being thorough since this was, after all, my second dead guy of questionable morals and popularity in a single day. Or perhaps it was simply the oversight of the council and the revolting presence of her two deputies that prompted my sheriff friend to grill me like we'd never met, and I was under suspicion of murder.

Or if I was going to be totally honest, it was probably just my guilt at being at the center of attention once again that made it feel like Jill had it out for me.

When Vivian finally made an appearance, the last of the council to do so, I felt my tension ease just a little. Sure, we weren't besties, but the events of December and her subsequent reveal to me her plan to uncover the truth about the Pattersons had endeared her to me. And, since our typical sniping had ended and trust built between us, I actually really liked her, respected her and sought out her advice and opinions.

Still felt weird, but I'd take all the help I could get.

She nodded to me as she entered, her pale cream suit perfectly tailored, a Grace Fiore, naturally. Like she'd wear anything but her (and my) favorite designer. And, to my surprise, she wasn't alone. Crew followed her in, scowl aimed at Jill before he hurried to me and hugged me, tucking my head under his chin, big body rocking me a little.

"Are you okay?" He sighed in my ear. "Stupid question. You're always okay. Fee, what happened?"

"I'd like to know, too." Vivian joined us, Rosebert lingering. Only when she spun on them and pointed at the door, imperious and cold, did they leave as a unit, though I noted Rose pausing by the exit on the other side of the threshold as the mayor returned her attention to me. "Are you okay, Fee?"

I nodded, pulling free of my husband, hands sliding deep in my jeans pockets as if I could anchor myself by stopping their shaking. "Sorry about this, guys," I said. "Kind of a Fee Fleming record I wasn't planning on breaking." My joke didn't win any support, so I rushed on. "I was actually here to see you, Viv." I leaned into Crew who instantly supported me again. "When I realized you weren't in your office, I decided to talk to Geoffrey about the assault charge." I looked up into those gorgeous blue eyes I loved. "I should have stayed away, too, I guess. But I couldn't let him ruin everything, Crew. Not after what we've been through."

He kissed my forehead. "You didn't do anything wrong," he said.

Jill sighed, her phone on record still held out between us. "As long as you didn't kill him," she said, voice dull. "Or that diver yesterday."

Even Vivian looked shocked at the suggestion while the sheriff winced and shook her head, her blonde ponytail bouncing against her back.

"Sorry," she said. "Rough day."

Tell me about it. "No, Jill," I said, then tried again, "Sheriff Wagner, I did not kill Geoffrey Jenkins or Gregg Brown. And, until we have proof either of them was murdered, maybe there are other questions to be asked."

Jill chewed her bottom lip, only then meeting Crew's eyes. "I'm sorry," she said, "but I'm going to need a timeline of your activities since last night."

He nodded while outrage hit me hard in the gut. "It's all right, Jill," he said, deep voice tired. "I understand." Crew met my gaze again. "She has to eliminate me as a suspect, Fee. I'd do the same thing."

Dr. Aberstock arrived, saving Jill from a very angry tirade in which I was about to tell her just how far she could shove her questions for my innocent husband. He left me to join the sheriff in a corner, voices low, while the doc headed around the desk and immediately went to work on Geoffrey's still body.

"Apologies for my late arrival," he said in his familiar joviality. "Busy day in the morgue." His eyes met mine, a slow wink descending. "Keeping me on my toes, are you, Fee?"

I shot him a wry smile with no humor in it. "Tell me he spontaneously expired from being a horrible person, would you?" And Gregg Brown, too, for that matter.

But the faint frown on Dr. Aberstock's face told me he already suspected murder. "I'll have to conduct an autopsy to be sure," he said, "but I'm afraid this death doesn't look natural." He sighed and straightened. "Sorry, Fee." He fiddled with what looked like a turkey thermometer, pointed end disappearing out of my view, thankfully, because I knew where he was sticking it and my stomach was already upset. "I have a general time of death, Jillian, if you'd like?"

She seemed to hold her breath, but nodded once,

sharply, in response.

"Liver temp is no help," he said while I did my best not to let the panic in my chest win. "But he is in full rigor." The doc stood back a moment. "From the corneal clouding, I'd say sometime between 10AM and 1PM yesterday."

Yesterday. Encompassing lunchtime. When Crew was supposed to be at the yacht club with us but had gone to town to talk to Geoffrey by his own admission.

I guess I should have felt vindicated no one reported Geoffrey missing, not even his wife. Did that mean he was also out of favor with the Pattersons he always seemed so keen on protecting?

I met my husband's eyes, saw his grim understanding, caught his faint headshake before he and Jill spoke again, whispering now. Crew had both hands on his hips, jaw tight, a sure sign of agitation. No way did my husband kill Geoffrey. I knew him better than that. But did he have a solid alibi?

Not from his wife.

Apparently, Jill didn't like what he had to tell her because a moment later she and Crew headed for the door. He paused long enough to kiss me one more time, quick and soft on the lips, before leaving with her.

"I'll be home later," he said in passing on his way out, as though there was nothing to worry about. I let him go without comment, surprised when Vivian's hand caught mine and squeezed it. She still startled me sometimes. I'd never been at the receiving end of her empathy, didn't even know it lived inside her. I'd first seen the fact she could care about another human being when Grace had been accused of murder. With Vivian's compassion aimed in my direction, I appreciated fully the strong and silent presence of the powerhouse woman I'd come to admire and, even, adore just a little bit.

Just a little.

"Olivia warned me," I whispered while Vivian glanced my way.

"About?" She kept her own voice down, the sound of Rose and Robert talking loudly outside the door telling me they were delighted to help Jill escort my husband to the sheriff's office for a conversation. I hesitated. Maybe I should go with him. Only to feel my phone vibrate. I looked down at the incoming text message while Vivian waited for me to answer, and relief washed over me.

John and I are in the lobby. Liz's text read like she spoke, terse and professional. *Escorting Crew personally. Let us handle this.* And then, a moment later. *Hope you're okay.*

I sighed over the last line and shrugged. Looked up at Vivian. Who waited, patient and silent. Right, she'd asked me about my cryptic Olivia comment.

Was it any wonder I had the beginning of a splitting headache?

I told her about the former mayor's visit while the two familiar EMTs—I needed to learn their names if I was going to be in their presence as often as this, just to play nice—arrived with their gurney to take the body to the morgue. Dr. Aberstock joined us, snapping off his rubber gloves and watching as the pair took care of Geoffrey's corpse.

"Does this mean you're thinking the Pattersons are targeting you and Crew?" Vivian waited until the EMTs had left before speaking, still in a whisper.

"It's possible," Dr. Aberstock answered for me. "And I certainly wouldn't put anything past them."

"But why Geoffrey?" As far as I knew, he was a line-toeing member of the clan. Their heavy, the shark face in charge of bullying everyone into submission. Why kill him if he was loyal? I shook my head, angry again all of a sudden. "Gregg Brown, fine. I can see that. The man was far from loved. But Geoffrey?" It didn't make any sense.

"Unless he'd recently done something to betray the family." Vivian seemed tense all of a sudden. "There has been some unrest." She crossed her arms over her chest, tapping her French manicured fingers on her forearm. "One thing is for certain, however. Neither you nor Crew had anything to do with it."

Nice of her to be so sure. Dr. Aberstock nodded. Okay, so I had these two on my side. Our side. If only I could be sure of Jill.

"Liz and Dad are going with Crew to the sheriff's office," I said. "They'll keep an eye on things." As much as I wanted to be there for him, those two were much better equipped to handle legal matters. Besides, my presence would cause more harm than good at this point. And anyway, my strength lay in uncovering truths people normally didn't talk about

out loud. I had to accept my husband knew how to handle himself.

"I do have some information for you about Mr. Brown." The doc took a half step closer while Vivian and I leaned in to take in every whispered word. "First, I'm positive he was murdered." Great. "And while I'm pretty sure I know how I'm waiting on final lab results." Sometimes I thought the doc loved holding off information just to make me nuts. But he was right to keep it to himself until he knew for sure. Still. "The other item, however, is much more exciting." Leave it to Dr. Aberstock to find something thrilling in murder. "It's less about what I found in the body and more about what I found on it."

"I'm not in the mood for a riddle," I said, not meaning to grumble, but come on.

"I'd rather show you if you don't mind?" He leaned away. "Meet me at the morgue and I'm happy to share my findings." With that, he left.

And, like a sucker for a mystery, I followed him, but not before pausing to hug Vivian in thanks.

"It's going to be all right," she said. Was she choked up? When I pulled away, she cleared her throat, blinking a moment before her poise returned. "Take care of yourself, Fee."

It was a tense and pensive drive to the hospital, though when I passed through the doors to Dr. Aberstock's domain, he pounced on me so quickly my tension turned to startled shock at the sight of his beaming smile.

He dragged me without a word to the far end of the room, to a small, locked drawer under one of the larger doors where he stored his guests. He quickly opened the narrow lock with a small, silver key, sliding it out so quickly three round, gold objects impacted the front of it, ringing softly from the contact.

While I gaped down at the shining doubloons, Dr. Aberstock's jocular mood was justified.

"I found these in his waist pouch," the doc said. "Fee, I think Gregg Brown found the treasure just before he died."

Which meant regardless of what I'd thought of the man, he'd done what the others said he would.

Dead or alive, the treasure hunter had uncovered the Reading hoard.

CHAPTER EIGHTEEN

A small jolt of panic set in. "Tell me he didn't die before he could tell us where." That would be just awesome.

But Dr. Aberstock winked and held up a familiar-looking dive computer. "I have the coordinates and the depth at which he made his find," he said. "Which means, now, so do you and the team."

I hugged him quickly, on impulse, though it was honestly hard to maintain any level of excitement with the headache I was dealing with and the events of the last twenty-four hours weighing on me.

Dr. Aberstock paused, good humor fading into concern. "Fee," he said, looking in my eyes, his own narrowing. "Are you experiencing any further symptoms?"

No way I was going back in the duffel bag of death. "I'm fine," I said. "Just a headache. Can you blame me?" He stared at me, didn't speak for so long I sighed at last, and eye-rolled. "Fine, and a little dizziness. Also understandable since I didn't sleep well last night." He continued his long, silent stare. "I'm okay. I promise."

"If you experience any further dizzy spells…" he hesitated. "I should make you go take another treatment right now."

"I don't have time for that," I said. "Thanks for this, Doc." I took a step away, distance like a shield between us. "You can't give me any hints as to how Gregg died?"

The doctor shrugged. "To put it in the simplest terms," he said, "Mr. Brown drowned after ejecting his mouthpiece at 180 feet." He spread both hands wide, the chubby digits steady and level, unlike the faint shaking still plaguing mine. "As to why he did so… there are causes such as epileptic seizure, heart failure. But," he gestured for me to follow him to a desk near the door where a monitor showed what looked like a slice of tissue with bubbles in it. "The most likely is some kind of issue with his oxygen mix. I can't be certain, however, without the lab report. So, until it comes in, I want you to go home and get some rest." He reached out, touched my shoulder, kind smile almost making me cry. I really had to pull myself together. "Promise me, Fee."

I nodded and retreated, heading for home. Two painkillers and a snuggle on the couch with my pug did wonders, though I texted my dad and Liz every two minutes, demanding updates. Which, after answering me once or twice, they both ignored.

I was about ready to head out to the sheriff's office myself when Liz sent one final text.

Don't you dare come down here, she sent. *I mean it. We've got it. You'll just make a mess.*

What did that mean? Growl. Fine. But now restless and unable to pretend otherwise, I paced a moment before my eyes settled on the music box, the frame tucked behind the sofa, and my mind went to the three gold doubloons in the metal drawer.

If I couldn't help my husband, maybe I could finally solve the mystery of the missing Reading hoard once and for all. I'd take a win, thanks. Earned it.

I retrieved the map from inside the frame, rolling it up and carrying it with me, heading out in pursuit of assistance, my pug left at home this time, napping with a full belly. By the time I reached the annex, I was a bit out of breath, oddly, but refused to worry about it. I was tired like I told the doc. And the headache had retreated, no further bouts of dizzy taking me over. So, I was a little weak. Fair enough.

When I poked around the annex, however, I quickly discovered Mom, Daisy and even the dive team were nowhere to be found. And the few staff I hunted down were no help, which drove me back out onto the street. Knowing the last thing I needed right now was caffeine, I headed for Sammy's anyway, not sure where else to go and not wanting to return home just yet. Didn't hurt the coffee shop was within a block of the sheriff's office, though, right? Just in case I could be of assistance at some point.

I guess I shouldn't have been surprised to find MC, Chantal and Anja sitting at a table by the window, sipping coffee in silence. I joined them, knowing their terrible mood might not be lightened by what the doc found but needing extra eyes anyway.

As I sank into the open seat, I spotted Daisy at the counter and waved her over while MC nodded to me.

"I have news." I told them what Dr. Aberstock found on Gregg, Day pulling up a chair in time to hear about the doubloons. MC looked interested, Chantal, too. Only Anja, however, showed any surge of enthusiasm, reaching for the map and unfolding it in front of us. Maybe we shouldn't have had it out in the open like this, but honestly, I didn't care at the moment who saw what we'd found. The gap where the piece Rosebert possessed remained missing had been filled in by my guesswork, but I couldn't help but think I'd only had a glance at what was there and maybe I'd failed to spot some important detail.

And yet, if Gregg had found the treasure, did it matter anymore?

"Here." Anja pointed at the odd red line running off in a random direction. "Isn't this where we were diving yesterday?"

MC finally caught the bug, leaning in with her brow furrowed. "Along that trajectory, yes."

"I hate to be the only naysayer," Chantal said, sitting back and glaring down at her coffee lid, "but three coins doesn't make a treasure." She shook her head, looked out the window. "I know, they could be proof. They could still be a long way from the main hoard. And we're out of funds to look any further."

"Leaving the find open to some other team to scoop." MC snarled at her teammate before thudding one hand down flat on the center of the map. "I know, I get it. But with the coin discovery, maybe we can convince our funders to step up and front us more cash."

Chantal didn't answer and didn't look hopeful, either. I considered suggesting I step in to fund the search but didn't want to do so without talking to Crew first. We had time and if the treasure really was down there and Gregg found the trail to it, I knew my husband would be on board.

We'd sort it out, I had no doubt. Which lightened my attitude while the others seemed to sink back into their depression over the whole thing.

"It doesn't matter right now," Anja said, sounding like she'd given up after all, map clue or not.

MC seemed to agree, though she sounded on the interested and cautiously optimistic side. "Fee, when will the doctor release the coins so we can have a look?"

I hated to throw a troublesome wrench into her renewed enthusiasm, but I didn't have much choice. "Considering they are evidence—since the doc gave

me the impression he thinks Gregg was murdered—
it could be a while."

All three women stared at me while I winced.
Whoops. I hadn't meant to deliver that particular
piece of information in quite so callus a way. But
there it was.

Chantal spoke up first. "Your sheriff told us not
to leave town," she said, sounding sullen and more
than a little like she'd been doing her best to keep her
temper in check, was failing at last. "I thought it was
because she had more questions about the dive. But
if Gregg was killed... I guess we all need lawyers."

Grim, the next few moments. I left them, heading
for the washroom, my head pounding all over again.
A quick splash of water on my face helped a little. I
stared at myself in the mirror, shocked at how
horrible I looked, skin pale despite my faint tan,
freckles standing out, dark circles under my eyes.
Yup, I'd been through the ringer just about enough
for one day, thank you.

As I grasped the door handle to leave the
washroom, I paused at the sound of hissing voices
on the other side. The back hallway where the
bathrooms were located carried sound pretty well, so
as I eased the door open a crack it was pretty simple
to catch the two arguing Reading residents in the act
without them spotting me right away.

Olivia was in Barry Clement's face, her fury
written all over her. "And I'm telling you," she
snarled, "if this comes back on me, I'll make sure you
never see the light of day again."

"I'm taking care of it," he said, sounding faintly panicked. "They won't find anything that ties either of us to it."

"You just be sure of that." She poked Dr. Aberstock's assistant firmly in his narrow chest, hand shaking from the violence of the jab. "I won't be drawn into something that has nothing to do with me, and if they find out Geoffrey was part of things—"

The sound of someone approaching drove the two of them apart and, before I could go after them, they both left in a rush, disappearing as a pair of teenage girls headed my way.

I thought about going after them both and asking some pointed questions. After all, mention of Geoffrey Jenkins so soon after his death? Suspicious, as far as I was concerned. Barry wasn't exactly my biggest fan and vice versa. He'd been team Patterson pretty much from the start, though. So why would he want Geoffrey dead? As for Olivia, I couldn't bring myself to believe the former mayor might actually kill someone.

Then again, I'd seen how driven she could be. What if Geoffrey found out something about her, something he was using against her? Would she ever get to the desperation point where she'd act to protect herself no matter what?

If I'd learned anything, it was that people were capable of things they wouldn't normally do under the oddest circumstances. And that no one was completely innocent.

My mind turning, I thought about calling Jill to fill her in about the overheard conversation. Instead, I texted Liz, shared with Dad, and got an almost instant response.

Thanks for this. Will have agents look into it.

Crew's okay, Dad sent then. *Good work, Fee.*

I really couldn't take credit for what I'd overheard, but if fate had taught me lessons I could count on, I was a magnet for other people's troubles being dumped on me. Listening and paying attention paid off in the past. I'd just have to keep up the trend and hope what I'd stumbled over could help my husband.

Darius's hulking form flashed in my mind, and I firmly pushed that thought aside with the kind of loyal faith he'd vanished for reasons that had nothing to do with murder. Because I wouldn't be hanging him out to dry, thanks.

Still, his disappearance coincided with Geoffrey's death, didn't it?

I returned to the table to find everyone still quiet and withdrawn, even my normally sparkly Daisy. She looked distraught and caught my hand as I sat down.

I might not have been able to solve Geoffrey's murder right then, nor Gregg's, for all that. But I wasn't going to just sit here and mope. I sighed and shrugged, trying to shed the mood along with my headache. "There's nothing we can do about what happened to Gregg," I said. "But if we have a chance to find the treasure, shouldn't we do everything we can to take it?" Selfish, who, me?

But the women were collectively nodding even as my bestie stared hard at the map. And, as if on impulse, touched the folded corner where Anja's fingers rested. Just above the red line.

Before any of us could do a thing to stop her, she quickly slid the map out from under our hands and folded it, first one end on an old line that looked like it had been creased by accident, a faint crust of rubbed-in dirt showing where it had been abused in the past, and then the other, down below the compass pointing at the wrong angle if its purpose was to point north.

And then, in one last fold, brought the edges together. Where the now halved compass and red mark formed a clean junction as if the two were made for each other.

Creating a line that started at the yacht club and ended its journey, not on the lake at all, but on the mountain that was part of the Patterson family property.

CHAPTER NINETEEN

Fresh excitement did wonders for our mood, though my worry about Crew certainly made things uncomfortable for me, if not the three divers huddled over the map now relocated to the annex, spread out on Mom's stainless-steel counter. She'd quickly moved aside her bread-making in favor of the Tortuga team's rekindled treasure talk and, with Daisy beside her, hovered and listened as the three experts debated the details.

I, for one, had no doubts whatsoever the line ending at the Patterson land was our true goal. Questions lingered, like the three small, odd marks more like mistakes than clues bracketing the Patterson end, making no sense and likely just dots of dirt left behind by age. The debate raging about what the line itself meant and how to infiltrate said property lost my interest as the swinging door opened and Liz walked through.

Rather than interrupt her friend and the other two divers now nose to the map, the FBI agent came right to my side. I found I was less interested in what the Pattersons might be hiding on their mountainside property and far more what was going on at the sheriff's office.

Liz kept her voice down, hand on my arm, face that familiar blank professional stare that I found so hard to read. "He's okay," she said first, thankfully, clearly understanding I had to have info about Crew and if she didn't get to it quickly, I'd be irate in three, two, one...

I exhaled and hugged her, knowing such a demonstration might not be her choice at the moment, but grateful for the embrace she dished right back. When I let her go, she even cracked a smile.

"Just be patient," she said. "John is handling it. That's not why I'm here." She glanced over her shoulder at the team then back to me. "Have you had much of a chance to research Gregg Brown?"

I shook my head, wondering what she'd come up with, the FBI database at her beck and call. "I take it you've found some interesting details I need to know about."

"Not so much about him," she said, lips barely moving, and volume turned down so far I had to lean close. "Did you know that the only other person in common with MC every time Gregg scooped her finds is in this room?" Liz's words were light but full of meaning. "Suspicious, if you ask me. Despite working with him in the past and personal tensions aside, how well they hunt together, I know MC would never hand over her own jobs to him. Not without admitting it."

Which meant the link between was a suspected culprit in betraying Tortuga's owner. I bit my lower lip. "Which one?" I did my best not to stare at the two divers, though I now had my suspicions. I'd seen them arguing, hadn't I? Were they more closely connected than I'd given them credit for, distracted by the MC tie-in to drama?

Liz's soft exhale was followed by a single name. "Chantal."

It kind of hurt. Not that I wanted it to be Anja. I liked them both, a lot. Part of me was hoping it had been Martin. And I wanted to reject the truth, though Liz's steady surety wasn't up for debate.

"Let's see what she has to say about it, shall we?" Liz's interrogation style wasn't the same as my husband's. He preferred long, careful and drawn-out question periods that left the suspect rather flustered and more likely to hand over information they might not under normal circumstances.

Liz, on the other hand, had a more direct approach. She spun before I could stop her and headed for the counter, laying one hand on Chantal's shoulder. The diver looked up, startled, while the FBI agent smiled her enigmatic good nature at the other woman before hitting her with both barrels.

"How long have you been giving Gregg Brown information into Tortuga dives, Chantal?"

She paled instantly, unable to speak for a long moment while MC's head whipped back and forth, first to Liz, then to her diver, while Anja took a surreptitious half-step back, arms crossing over her chest, head down.

"I have no idea what you're talking about." Chantal spun and marched past me, out the back door, while MC stared after her, eyes wide, mouth gaping open.

"I'm sorry," Liz said, sounding like she really meant it. "You had no idea?"

The Tortuga leader shook her head, sinking to a stool Mom rapidly supplied. "None." She swallowed hard. Then laughed, guttural and without joy. "All this time." She glanced at Anja who wouldn't meet her eyes, then at Liz, suspicions clear. "You're certain?"

I didn't get to witness Liz's assurances or hear her evidence, not when my phone rang, Dr. Aberstock on the other end of the line. I ducked into the dining room, closing the door behind me, as the cheerful voice of the coroner greeted me.

"That information you were asking about," he said. "My suspicions were confirmed just now." I heard paper rattle, so he must have printed off the lab report. That was the doc. Not satisfied with the digital version, so old school. "How familiar are you with oxygen mixtures for diving, Fee?"

I'd had the basics, obviously. "I know the deeper you go, the less oxygen you're supposed to have in your tanks."

He grunted his agreement. Cool, I got something right. Yay me.

"When I conducted my autopsy, I noted a mass of air bubbles in his heart, and petechiae in both the heart and lungs. There was enough micro-tearing in the soft tissue I had a feeling I knew what I was dealing with. But the cerebral edema and microscopic perivascular hemorrhage in his brain?" He sounded satisfied while I struggled with the medical terminology and waited for him to get to the point already. "All consistent with a grand mal convulsion brought on by oxygen toxicity."

"Dr. Aberstock," I said, slow and low. "In English."

He chuckled, the creaking on the other end of the line from the unoiled base of his office chair, familiar enough I didn't have to guess to know he was at his desk. "Mr. Brown had a seizure due to elevated oxygen in his blood, far too high for the depth he was diving." He paused a moment, then resumed. "According to his dive computer—state of the art, these new dive watches—shows that his heartbeat became erratic shortly after he reached 180 feet. And while the seizure itself didn't kill him, it did cause him to spit out his mouthpiece, and prevent him from replacing it thanks to the convulsions, causing him to drown."

Okay, but not proof of murder, was it? "Could he

have made a mistake in his air mix?" My mind flashed to Martin, to MC's tanks, while the doctor answered.

"Someone of his experience? Impossible." He actually sounded a bit offended. "Besides which, his dive computer shows a completely different air mix to the one in the tank."

"Which means someone purposely sabotaged his equipment." Got it.

"Correct." I guess he had forgiven me for questioning his results. "You have a murder on your hands, Fee. And several experienced divers who were perfectly capable of making sure Mr. Brown didn't come back up from that depth alive."

CHAPTER TWENTY

I hung up from Dr. Aberstock, lost in thought a moment as I stared out the windows into the backyard at the annex, considering what to do next. Thing was the doc was absolutely right. Between MC, Chantal, Anja, Martin, even Crew, there were more than enough people on the list of experts—Liz included—who had the know-how to tamper with Gregg's equipment.

And, if I recalled correctly, everyone had the time and access to the dive shed, didn't they? I'd even witnessed his widow take a side trip into the shack before leaving, right around lunchtime.

Which left me with more questions and people to prod for answers than ever. I knew right where to start, spotting my first as she paced past the glass in the sunshine.

I slipped out the back door, hearing Liz talking in the kitchen and leaving her to the others, joining Chantal as she huffed a furious line back and forth between the rose bushes. Her shoes crunched on the gravel, kicking fine bits of it across the heavier flagstones where benches offered a normally peaceful oasis for visitors to enjoy the quiet of the sunny space.

She spotted me as she made her turn, but didn't stop, face scrunched in anger, hands jammed into her pockets, shoulders hunched in that particular protective fashion that told me she had things to hide, guilt to keep compressed as deep as possible.

Could it be I'd found Gregg's murderer without much of a treasure hunt of my own?

"Is Liz right?" I was careful to keep accusation out of my voice, opting for level and merely curious. Maybe I should have been angry. After all, if Chantal did tell Gregg about the treasure and the evidence we had to prove it existed despite his initial attempt to debunk the find, that meant his dead body was on her. Though, that thought made me shudder because she hadn't borne the brunt of said body, had she?

Nope. That had been on me. And I was so over it.

Okay, maybe a bit of heat rose inside me, even as Chantal shot me a furious look but didn't deny anything. She didn't even try.

"I just spoke with Dr. Aberstock," I said, same tone, though fighting to maintain it now. "According to him, Gregg's tanks were tampered with. Too high an oxygen content. And his dive computer, too." She stopped, turned to face me in the reverse of her stalking pacing, eyes wide. "Which means, only someone with the kind of knowledge, say, you have, could have arranged for his death."

Chantal spluttered, shook her head, and despite myself, I believed her wordless denial. I might not have been a great judge of character at the best of times, but I knew true shock when I saw it.

She sank to one of the benches, hands on her thighs, staring off into the distance now. "Murdered," she whispered before clearing her throat. I joined her, watched her sag back against the wood slats of the bench. "I didn't kill him."

"But you did scoop MC's finds," I said. "For Gregg."

Chantal squirmed a little, her light brown hair tracing across one pale cheek as the breeze picked up and took control. Her hand brushed the errant lock away from the corner of her mouth, fingers trembling. "I've known Gregg a lot longer than MC," she said. "He asked me not to tell her when they first met. I thought he was just being careful. Treasure hunters." She snorted. "We're all suspicious of each other."

"So, you betrayed MC out of loyalty to Gregg?" She started at my use of the "B" word. "Don't tell me you had a relationship with him, too?"

She shook her head then, lips a thin line. "No. His brother, Walter." She looked away again as if she couldn't bear to meet my eyes. "We didn't last, but Gregg and I stayed friends."

"Did you go to work for MC just to spy on her?" I'd liked her. Really liked her. Was she so despicable? And was I proving to myself, yet again, I couldn't read people at all and maybe I was in the wrong job, despite finding dead bodies on a regular basis?

"It wasn't like that." Chantal lurched to her feet, started pacing again. "MC and I met a few years later. Became friends. I didn't even think about Gregg, to be honest, until he approached me when we were heading out on a job. He just wanted to know what we were looking for." She stopped and finally met my eyes, hers full of regret. "I thought he was my friend, just asking. I should have known better." She stilled, sighed. "When he showed up, took over, I knew he'd used me. But when I confronted him, he threatened me." She seemed more broken up about that than his death. "Said if I didn't continue to share information with him, he'd tell MC about hiding our history and that I'd sold her out." Chantal wiped at a tear that escaped, panic taking her over while she settled next to me, grasping for my hands. "Fee, if anyone finds out, I'll be blackballed. Even Gregg said if word got out, he'd never hire me." She choked out a bitter laugh. "He said I wasn't trustworthy."

"That's what you were fighting about the night before the dive." I was trying very hard not to judge her, but I wasn't going to win for long. Family and friends, loyalty and trust? Yeah, if I only had those things in the end, I had enough.

She nodded, misery clear on her face, as though she knew despite her attempts to the contrary her career was over. "I told him I was done. He threatened me." She tensed, eyes narrowing. "And now you do think I killed him."

"So do I." I hadn't heard MC join us and neither, apparently, had Chantal, because she bounded to her feet again, backed away as if expecting the Tortuga leader to attack her physically. Instead, MC just stared, Anja coming to stand beside her boss, Liz joining us. "Did you, Chantal? Did you kill Gregg?"

Chantal didn't respond, so I did. "She had the necessary skills," I said and filled them all in on how he'd died. As I did, the utter disgust and revulsion on the women's faces shocked me, but not for long.

"How could you?" Anja pushed past MC whose dark expression spoke volumes the younger diver gave voice to. "Using what we love against him like that? You're a *diver*." She seemed most distressed by that fact. "To send him to his death underwater… Chantal, how *could* you?"

Liz met my eyes, hers flat and furious. "Honor code broken," she said.

Okay then. Divers. Sheesh.

"The thing is," I said, interrupting and sending Anja back to retreat behind MC, tears trickling down her cheeks, "Chantal wasn't the only person with a grudge against Gregg." I looked pointedly at MC, even the weeping younger diver. "You three all had access to the equipment. So did Martin. And Hannah." I had to track down Gregg's widow. But first, a bit of research was pending.

Chantal grasped onto my reasoning and held tight. "She's right," she said, words tumbling over one another. "It could have been anyone." She jabbed a shaking finger at MC. "I saw you in the shed."

"I saw *you* in the shed," the Tortuga leader bit back.

"Well, I didn't do it," Anja said, tears now dried up, while I wondered about her conversation with Martin. Happened right before he was in the shack poking around MC's tanks. Maybe it hadn't been hers he'd been fiddling with. Maybe he'd actually been checking Gregg's. Or sabotaging them.

Too many whys and too many furious expressions going around to get any clear insights.

"Why don't we have a chat, Chantal?" Liz gestured for her to join the FBI agent inside. She hesitated a moment, glanced at me, of all people.

I nodded instantly. "Just tell her what you know," I said, feeling zero guilt about acting like her supportive friend if it meant finding out who murdered my first dead body of the weekend.

Chantal pushed through MC and Anja on her way to the house, the other two watching her go with sullen expressions. Liz paused at the top step, Chantal preceding her inside. "I expect both of you to make yourselves available for questioning."

MC spluttered but Liz waved that off.

"I'll be with you presently," the cucumber cool agent said before disappearing inside.

Leaving me out in the garden's supposed peace with two very angry and now suspicious divers. Thankfully, a text message set me free and had me moving a moment later. You know what? Even if one of them had tried to stop me and confess they were the one who killed Gregg Brown? I would have left the collar to Liz.

My husband was home, and nothing was going to keep me from him.

CHAPTER TWENTY-ONE

"I would never," Crew started the second I walked through the front door, silenced almost immediately thereafter when I threw myself at him, locked my arms around his neck and my mouth on his and shut him up already.

Because, duh, Turner. Just *duh*.

When I leaned back, catching my breath, he grinned like it was funny or something. Almost earned himself a smack for that attitude. Until he held out one hand, tight in a fist, with a bit of a flourish. I offered my own. Crew upended his over my empty palm, a small, warm bit of metal coming to rest there. I stared in shock and then delight down at the small butterfly clip, three gems missing from one wing, now in my possession.

I looked up at him, caught his slow wink, and shook my head. "Crew Turner," I said. "Where did you get this?"

"Someone made the mistake of leaving it on her desk," he said. "I figured I'd make sure it got back where it belonged."

I tsked. "Theft, my love? Really? Is that what your retirement from law enforcement has brought you to? A life of crime?"

He reached for the clip. "I'll just give it back if you're going to be like that about it."

My hand closed reflexively over the clip, tucking it against my heart while my husband laughed at my possessive response.

"Over my dead body," I said.

He sighed at my choice of words. "Too soon, Fee."

Whoops. "Sorry, sweetie."

Crew hugged me before heading for the kitchen and the beer he'd been enjoying before I walked in the door, Petunia sitting firmly on his feet as though expecting him to leave again. "Rough day?"

Like he was one to talk. "You first."

Crew took a long drink of his beer, blue eyes tight. "I'd rather not," he said. "Did you hear from the doc?"

I filled him in on everything while he finished his drink and fetched another for himself, with one for me, too. I joined him behind the counter, helping him prep dinner like he wasn't under investigation for the murder of Geoffrey Jenkins, and I hadn't found two dead bodies in two days. Right, because this was Reading, and we didn't exactly have a regular relationship.

Frankly? As I sat down to my plate of spaghetti, the love of my life beside me, Grandmother Iris's last butterfly clip safe in the music box (missing gems or not, it was nice to have the set) I wouldn't have had things any other way. We'd faced adversity and death and murder investigations and worse before. We had each other and that was more than enough.

The dishes rattled in the sink, my usual grumbling about the fact Crew didn't have a dishwasher vanishing as my phone buzzed. My husband peeked over my shoulder when he heard me squeal in surprise, but he needn't have bothered. I instantly turned the screen toward him, showed him the message, relief washing over me, more powerful than I expected.

Meet me at the annex, Pamela Shard's crisp text said. *I have a lot to tell you.*

It didn't take much convincing to leave the dishes undone, to harness Petunia for the walk, the pair of us hurrying as much as the pug's meandering pace would allow. Crew finally hefted the weighty canine into his arms, rewarded with a loud fart of delightful vintage and the eager tongue swipes of the grateful girl.

Hard not to laugh, to feel a bit lighter-hearted. It had been ages since I'd heard from Pamela and though I knew she was alive and well, not vanished in the same manner as Fiona Doyle (I'd half expected to find the newspaperwoman's body floating in the lake some morning), I still worried about her. Knowing she was back in town, that she'd likely only returned with information of note and use, definitely improved my mood.

We found her talking with Mom and Daisy in the annex sitting room, the sun long set past the mountains though the sky remained blue. To my surprise, she wasn't alone, the tall and willowy Fleur King rising from the sofa to smile at me, shake my hand before I could cross to hug Pamela about as tight as I could without choking her.

She patted my back, a bit awkward but genuine enough. "I missed you too, Fee," she whispered in my ear, cleared her throat, voice thick. When Pamela pushed me back, her eyes glistened with a rim of moisture and I wasn't too proud to admit I had to wipe at a pair of tears, knowing I was beaming at her.

"I'm just glad you're okay," I said, glancing over my shoulder at Fleur. The investigative journalist hadn't shown her face in Reading since my first encounter with mention of Blackstone. She'd worked with Pamela years ago at the *Boston Globe*, had assisted with the investigation of the death of Lewis Brown, while being a suspect herself, if briefly. I had always thought the two might have some kind of personal past that was unrelated to the job but had no proof of a relationship that wasn't simple friendship. Not that it mattered. Pamela had married the love of her life in Aundrea Wilkins, finally free to do so after years apart. Surely the appearance of Fleur meant nothing.

Then again, I was quick to note the gold band Pamela had accepted from her wife in this very annex during their wedding ceremony was missing from her left hand. And her absence from Reading, abandoning Aundrea—at least, I could only imagine she was forced to do so—to the Patterson family she was part of, could have meant a few things I wasn't ready to face.

Not yet anyway. Not when my friend was tugging on my hand, pulling me down next to her on the couch, while Crew took the armchair and Mom and Daisy the loveseat. Fleur hovered instead of sitting, as though feeling out of place in our inner circle.

Another sign of something I didn't want to poke a stick at?

"Let's save the catching up for later," Pamela said, all business as she leaned forward and pulled a thick file out of her attaché case, a thumb drive dropping on top with a soft thunk. "We've uncovered information on Blackstone we need to share." She looked up at Daisy. "But we need Vivian here to make sense of it."

"I called her," Mom said, hands folded in her lap but tense enough I could see it in the set of her shoulders. She still wore her apron, dusting of flour on her knuckles. She'd been interrupted mid-bake. "She didn't answer but I left a cryptic enough message she should know it's important." The door to the sitting room swung open, Dad poking his head in. Another big gush of relief hit me, and I waved him inside. He sat on the arm of the love seat next to Mom, one big hand settling on her back and she instantly relaxed, smiling up at him, her fingers cupping his knee. So adorable, my parents, and hard not to hope Crew and I had that kind of love to look forward to when we were their age.

"In the meantime," Pamela said, forging on, a second folder emerging from the well-worn black leather, "you might want to have a look at this." Gregg Brown's name was written in bold block letters in thick black marker across the top. "Take a guess as to the identity of his main financial backer."

A few names popped into my head while I flipped the cover open. Names like Marie Patterson, Greggory Jenkins. But I think I already knew, had suspected and now had confirmation, that it was not a who, but a what, that sent him to Reading.

Blackstone Corporation owned Gregg Brown.

I shared the file but said it out loud so everyone would know the truth. "Is Blackstone after the treasure, then?" Dad whistled low under his breath, Crew scowling all over again. Pamela spoke as the folder made the rounds to Daisy, Mom and then the boys in turn. "Over my dead body."

Crew hissed at me. "Don't say that."

Yikes. Right. Ouch.

"Whatever their reason for interfering, yet again, in our town," Pamela said, sounding like she was ready for that interference to be over with once and for all, "it's clear they have motives we're still at a loss to uncover. Until now."

Fleur barked a laugh, fast and brittle before falling quiet. But she and Pamela were smiling at Daisy who seemed stunned by the attention.

"Why are you looking at me like that?" She met my eyes, her gray ones huge. "Fee?"

Pamela reached around me and patted Daisy's knee. "Your father passed away, leaving you in possession of stock in a company, is that correct?"

My bestie shrugged, sad in response, while I struggled to figure out what Pamela was after stirring up Daisy's hurt all over again. Hard not to feel protective of the sweet woman I'd always adored whose heartless dad left her nothing in the will aside from those useless shares.

"He did," Daisy said. "They aren't worth anything, Pamela. I looked into the company. It's just a shell. Emile helped," she smiled at me, "but even he couldn't find any real purpose for it." She shrugged then, dainty, almost helpless. "I'm sorry, I don't understand why they are important."

Pamela's evil smile made my stomach clench, in a deliciously devilish way. She was up to no good and I was all in all the time.

"There's a second shareholder, did you know that?" Pamela glanced up at the tall, pale woman she'd brought with her. "We only know thanks to Fleur."

She jerked her own shrug, almost like a puppet whose strings had been cut, suddenly awkward as if Pamela's praise made her uncomfortable. "I went digging into Blackstone after the woodpecker incident," she said like it was no big deal. "When Pamela came poking around, asking the same questions I did, it made sense to pool our resources." That far-too-familiar smile told me that even if Pamela wasn't in love with Fleur? The younger journalist had feelings unrequited.

Well, damn.

Not my problem right now. "You wanted Vivian here," I said, mind rushing to put two-and-two together.

Pamela nodded while Dad looked up from the file about Gregg, his second pass after retrieving it from Crew. "She's the other shareholder?" He frowned down at the photo of the treasure hunter. "Ranier French and Donald Bruce were old friends, yes. But they were never in business together."

"We're still trying to figure things out," Fleur said, shooting Pamela a look, a silencing look. "But from what we've uncovered, whatever they were up to? They left the results to their daughters."

CHAPTER TWENTY-TWO

Daisy's shock didn't dissipate in the least. If anything, it only grew. I reached across Pamela to grasp my bestie's hand while she shook her head, that surprise turning to sorrowful rejection.

"My father didn't care what happened to me or my mother," she said, without a trace of the bitterness she was entitled to as far as I was concerned. Daisy's fingers grasped mine tightly while she held on.

"I don't think that's true." Pamela didn't move, holding still. To prevent separating me from Daisy? If so, that kind of empathy was, to be honest, new for her. "If anything, I'm more inclined to believe that Donald was doing his best to protect you and your mother from his business dealings."

PIRATE GOLD AND MURDER

Daisy couldn't have looked more lost, more vulnerable, and I wished Emile was there to hug her because I wasn't sure one of mine was up for the job. Still, I finally rose, pulling her up beside me, and embraced her anyway. She clung to me a moment while Pamela stood as well, patting my bestie on the back just as awkwardly as she had me.

"Whatever the case may be," Fleur said, interrupting the moment, though I was grateful for it since Daisy was hanging on tight enough it was starting to cut off my oxygen, "we need to finish digging. And we need Vivian French's permission—along with yours, Daisy—to do it."

Of course, Day nodded, gulped, wiping at tears on her cheeks. "Anything," she said. "I just want to help. To understand." She met my eyes, her gray ones bright and shining with fresh tears. "Did I misjudge him all these years?"

If she had, she wasn't the only one.

My phone rang, how opportune. I left the group to talk, Liz huddling over Crew's shoulder, the two of them fighting Dad for the Blackstone folder and answered Olivia Walker's call after a short bout of hesitation. She'd done her best to warn me, hadn't she? She had earned a conversation even if I wondered about her talk with Barry and the murder of Geoffrey Jenkins.

"Fee." She practically gasped my name as I thumbed the green button and answered. "Please, I need your help. He's arrested me."

"Who?" Like I didn't know who. I was already

heading for the door, waving at my husband. But it was Liz I wanted and, when I motioned for her to come with me, she was on the move instantly.

"Robert." Olivia sounded desperate, voice a bit high-pitched and breathless. Not like her at all. "I'm at the sheriff's office. Please, you're my phone call. I need you."

She should have called a lawyer, but my lack of reticence to go running? Maybe her instincts were right. Considering I hadn't been allowed to interfere in any way with Crew's interrogation, I'd been itching to get my hands on details of Geoffrey's death. Busybody or not, this was my opportunity to find out what happened.

"On my way." I hung up, whispered what was happening to Liz on the way through the lobby so the few guests mingling didn't have to have their vacations disturbed. She drove, her rented SUV covering the few blocks quickly, while part of me—a guilty and regretful part—felt terribly I was relieved Olivia was under arrest.

That meant Crew wasn't a suspect anymore.

Oh, Fee.

Thing was, that truth cleared my head. No longer fogged by worry for my husband's safety, I'd be able to focus, right? I could help Olivia better knowing Crew was no longer in the line of fire.

Whatever it took to sleep at night.

Jill looked pretty harried when we walked into the office, toe-to-toe with Robert while Rose stood off to one side, snide expression the kind you'd love to wipe off her face by rubbing it against pavement at fifty miles per hour. I ignored her sour expression in favor of catching Olivia's eye where she sat, head in her hands, behind the bars of one of the holding cells. She looked up when I entered, hurried to rise, to grasp the metal in her shaking fingers, to wait for me with her brown eyes huge.

I didn't bother asking permission, pushing my way through the swinging half door into the bullpen. Jill nodded welcome while Robert spun on me, gut stuck out as if the prow of a well-rounded ship had crested the buckle on his belt and threatened to beach itself.

"You're not welcome here," he started.

"I am a private investigator hired by Ms. Walker to look into her case," I shot back. "Try and stop me." I looked him up and down, making sure he took note of the disdain I carefully released at the sight of his slovenly appearance. Seriously, had he washed that shirt in the last week? And how many drips of whatever it was he'd eaten did his belly have to catch before he noticed he was a pig? "Deputy."

I might have been going to hell for enjoying it, but that felt really, really good.

"She has the right to be here," Jill said in her long-suffering tone. "Step aside, Robert. Now."

He didn't do so immediately, the scent of his body spray wafting over me in a wave of noxious fumes I was positive had to be radioactive. That vile upper lip covering had thickened as if taking on sentient life, crawling as though alive as his mouth twisted into a sneer.

"Good luck proving her innocence, Fanny." He hiked his pants, the belt buckle barely held in place by the oversized hole in the leather that clearly wasn't intended to carry the kind of load he'd forced it to support. "We have video footage of her entering Geoffrey's office minutes before the doc says he died. And she was the only one to come or go in that window." He seemed very pleased with himself and while I usually didn't take anything Robert said as gospel, it did sound rather damning, didn't it?

"The doc's TOD wasn't precise enough for that kind of accusation, Robert." Unless he'd come up with a pinpoint he hadn't told me yet.

"I'd like a look at that footage." Liz's calm drawl always triggered my need to grin, for some reason. Like she was bored or underwhelmed and fully in control of every situation and if the bumpkin in front of her would just step aside she'd save the day.

Apparently, she intimidated him. I had no idea. But the clear flicker of nervousness wasn't hard to miss, the way his tongue snaked out and licked his lower lip—that disgusting mustache rippling from the motion, now oiled with his spit and making me gag from the view—was impossible to miss.

A moment later, he caught himself, clearing his throat, macho attempt at throwing his shoulders back making his belly bounce. "This way, Agent Michaud." Oh my god. The way he said her name. Was he attracted to Liz?

The poor thing. I just. I just *couldn't*.

She didn't seem to care, brushing past him, while Rose's own flicker of emotion told me she was acutely aware her Robertkins had a thing for Crew's ex-partner. And immediately my evil mind went to work on ways to use that to our advantage while secretly apologizing to Liz for even thinking such a horrific and revolting thing.

Still. Hmmm.

I waited for Rose to follow Robert, trailing Liz to his desk, and watched a moment as she sat with firm authority. Hard to miss his hand attempting to settle on her shoulder, Rose batting it away, Liz ignoring both of them while Jill, her jaw set, joined me.

"Fee." She swallowed, hands on her gun belt, looked down, then up again. "Just shoot me. Please. I'm begging you."

Poor Jill. I wanted to hug her but knew any sign of weakness wouldn't be welcome. "I'm sorry I'm in the middle of all this again."

She shrugged, gestured for me to go to Olivia as she followed. "Not your fault," she sighed. "But I'm wondering how Crew lasted as long as he did." She stiffened as we stopped on the other side of the bars and she focused on Olivia who stared at me, not giving Jill a moment's notice. "No thanks to you, either, Ms. Walker," she said. "Fee, you married a saint."

"I did everything I could for Crew Turner." Olivia shook, her voice vibrating with it, only her grasp on the bars seeming to keep her from flying apart. She pulled herself together visibly, wiping quickly at sweat on her upper lip before her grip on the metal in front of her resumed. This was the second time I'd seen her worked up this way in a very short period of time and I wondered if life outside the mayor's office was taking its toll worse than life in it.

Not my problem.

"I didn't kill Geoffrey." She said it like she needed to defend herself. Thing was, I knew she didn't. It would take a lot to convince me otherwise. Video footage could be tampered with, the doc's TOD was too wide for anyone to use against her, and I wasn't putting anything past Marie Patterson or Blackstone.

"You admit to being in his office." Not a question. Jill waited but again, Olivia didn't give her an instant of attention, hyper-focus on me and me alone.

"I knew about them, Fee," she hissed, leaning in until her forehead pressed against the bars. "I admit it. I knew the Pattersons were up to something. And I looked the other way. On purpose." She drew a trembling breath. "I had to play their game. To put this town on the map. I was sure I could stay out of whatever it was they were doing. Even when they asked me to…" She glanced sideways at Liz, Robert, Rose, then back to me, as if oblivious of the fact the town sheriff stood next to me. Oblivious or didn't care because Jill couldn't do anything to hurt her but maybe Rosebert was another story? "They asked me to interfere with certain parts of our town's governance and I did it. To protect Reading. I'm sorry about Crew." She shook her head. "He was a casualty of all this. He suffered like no one suffered. Fee, they tried for years to get me to fire him. I protected him as best I could. I even tried to convince him to just quit to keep him safe. But he's stubborn." She laughed then, with humor, with respect. "He surprised me. And despite everything, I couldn't betray him in the end."

"Which is why Vivian is mayor, and you're not." I nodded, though resentment welled. I'd known she'd had a hand in the torture my husband went through. I still didn't have all the details, partly because he would never tell me. But I'd sussed enough and heard bits and pieces I'd pieced together—yes, even from him—about how he'd been professionally maligned and compared endlessly to my father. To me, for some reason. All the Patterson's bid to get rid of him.

But why? "Why did they want Crew out?"

Olivia glanced over at the occupied desk again, face shuttering dark. She didn't speak, looked back. And in that moment, didn't have to.

Jill did it for her, whistling low. "The FBI." She whispered it, glanced at me. "They didn't want the FBI poking their noses in."

"How many times did I deny Crew's requests for help from state troopers?" Olivia sagged against the bars. "On the Patterson's orders. Fee, they own this town. And they had Geoffrey killed."

"And Blackstone?" I prodded her, hoping for

more, but the mention of that corporation shuttered her completely.

Olivia backed away, head shaking slowly from side to side, her dark bob swinging its own denial. "I'm not sorry," she said, voice deep and shaking with emotion. "I'm not. I'd do it again. I saved this town. But I lost, lost the game. And all the pieces are tumbling down."

She stumbled into the bench at the back of the cell and sat abruptly, shoulders rolling forward. When I prodded her to speak further, she refused, falling silent, hugging herself in her pale yellow suit until I turned away, frustrated and without the answers I'd come for.

"Jill," I said, "can you spare a few minutes for a walk to town hall with me?"

She looked a little startled but nodded. I waved at Liz who waved back, knowing she understood I needed her to keep Rosebert occupied when Robert looked up and, before he could follow, the FBI agent reached out and touched his hand.

Got his attention. And Rose's. Bless Liz for taking a giant one for the team.

We hurried down the street, passing through the main doors of town hall and up the steps. I stopped outside Geoffrey's office, looked around. Spotted the camera at the end of the hall.

"That's the source of the footage," Jill agreed.

I entered, the hinges humming softly as I did, the room quiet and still smelling faintly of death. Okay, I was probably imagining that, but hard not to when the last occupant had died in that very leather chair across the desk.

I hoped whoever got this office next knew so. Could office chairs be haunted? Didn't matter. Just the thought of placing my butt where his expired one had rested made my skin crawl.

"Jill." I turned toward the far right, where a door stood ajar. She didn't seem surprised, waited for me to check it out. The private bathroom on the other side wasn't offering the exit I'd been expecting.

"There's no other way out," she said. "The windows were sealed, screens on for summer." She followed me into the bathroom, waiting for me to take a good look around before we exited into the main office again. I tugged at the heavy, green curtains, velvet of all things, exposing the full bank of windows.

And heard Jill let out a very bad word as I took note the four main glass panels were, in fact, windows. But the fifth?

Yeah. That was a door. Unlocked, no less. Leading out to the catwalk and the ground below via an old set of iron stairs.

CHAPTER TWENTY-THREE

"Robert." Jill was shaking, leaning against the desk to catch her breath. "I actually trusted him to search the room."

"Which should be an indication maybe he's hiding something for someone in particular." I waited for her to get it together and put things into perspective. Patterson perspective.

Jill did so rather quickly, standing to pace the office, her heavy black boots scuffing over the green carpet. "At least we have proof Olivia has reasonable doubt." She paused, met my eyes. "I feel like I'm losing it, Fee." She rubbed at her face with one hand. "The old me would have been out there," she jabbed at the windows, "checking the outside of the building for exits. Not in here, relying on two people," she said that like they weren't exactly sentient beings in her estimation, "who have never been trustworthy to have my back."

"I'm sorry, Jill," I said. "I wish things had worked out differently."

"I need to find a way to eliminate both of them." She halted abruptly, eyes huge, mouth open in an "O" of denial. "I didn't mean—"

"Considering my history," I said with a chuckle, "it's a suitable word even if its meaning might not be clear to anyone else." I squeezed her shoulder. "I get it, Jill. And you're right. But it might have to wait until we get this sorted out."

I left her then, to call in a forensic team and check for prints (yes, I'd used a tissue to open the outside door, I wasn't born yesterday) and headed for home. Except, I found myself walking the streets of Reading, headache returned, unable to make my brain slow down enough to consider trying to share what I was thinking with anyone else, not even Crew.

Darkness fell and the streetlights came into brilliant glow, lighting the perfectly maintained downtown of the cutest town in America. I glanced in the shop windows, ignoring the buzzing of my phone, just wanting to be alone for a while. I knew Liz and Jill would fill Crew and my dad in on what had happened, so they didn't need me. When my phone's continual insistence made me look at last, I fired off a quick message to my worried husband.

I'm fine. Give me a bit.

He sent back, *I love you,* and left me alone.

Because he was that kind of awesome.

The tiny park across from town square seemed a good place to finally sit and take a minute. I stared across the way at the towering statue of Captain Reading still maintaining his watch over our little home. The desecration of the front of his trousers might have come to a regular end, but he still sported a bright yellow depiction of what should have resided under those pants some mornings, as if the artist didn't want us to forget for one second what s/he/they thought of our illustrious founder.

I would have joined in with gusto if they'd included a rendition of Joseph Patterson.

One of the lights in the park had gone dark, near the bench where I chose to plant myself and while I should have maybe felt nervous sitting there in the near-black, I had no such thoughts. Self-preservation had never been one of my strong suits and despite the fact Peggy Munroe and her evil grandniece, Ruth Wilkins, were still out there and, supposedly, gunning for my life, it was actually relaxing and calming to sit and do nothing with my feet swinging and my head finally emptying itself of the stress of the last few days as the warm July evening enveloped me in the soft sound of nearby crickets.

It wasn't hard to hear them arguing. Or to be annoyed by their hissing exchange of anger that interrupted my quiet reverie. In fact, I almost stood up and charged toward them to give the fighting couple a piece of my mind but caught myself as I realized I knew these two and their disagreement might have relevance to the death of the man they supposedly both loved.

"I did everything I could, I swear it." Martin seemed desperate Hannah Brown believe him, though from the tone of her voice—they were in as much darkness as I, their shadowy outlines visible just ten feet away—she wasn't buying what he was peddling.

"You were supposed to make him sign the divorce papers," she snarled. Wait, what? "You had one job, Martin."

"I know, my sweet." Desperation dribbled from every syllable. While the truth of the relationship between Gregg's friend/documentarian/slaveboy and his oh-so-loving wife who knew how to put on a crying show came to light despite the darkness around us. "I'm sorry. You know he refused. I tried everything." I heard him swallow it was so loud. "But now that he's…" he tripped over the next word.

"Dead," she snapped. "The bastard is dead."

"Yes, of course." Martin's voice trembled. "Now that Gregg is gone, you're free."

"You know those brat children of his plan to contest the will," she shot back. "Thanks to his brother. My money could be tied up for years, Martin. And it's all your fault."

"I'll talk to Walter." Martin sounded faintly hopeful. "I'm sure I can get him to agree to the terms you were asking for."

"As long as he doesn't dig into Gregg's financials and realize I've been funneling money into private accounts." Hannah sounded about as far from the grieving widow as I was from a damsel in distress. "Take care of it, Martin. Or we're through."

Hannah stalked away into the night, and I let her go, Martin hurrying after her. I could have followed them, asked questions, poked and prodded. Only to have them refuse to talk and annoy me. Nope, they'd given me enough in their little not-so-private conversation to hand to Liz. Along with the possibility of two more suspects in Gregg's murder.

Though, honestly, it sounded more likely it was only one suspect. Martin had shot to the top of my list.

What was it with men falling in love with their friend's wives, exes, girlfriends?

Sigh.

I have no idea how long I sat there, slow, deep breaths filled with mountain air calming me. I'd never actually observed my town at night, not really, watched with detached curiosity as the storefronts went dark, staff leaving for the night, the quiet of a small town shutting down engulfing me in the kind of peace I hadn't felt since Petunia's burned down.

Funny that thought came to mind, along with the heated sensation of tears, tightening of my throat telling me a good weepfest was about to commence. Except, as I inhaled to let it out as quietly as I could, I spotted, in surprise, the hunched form of an approaching figure, crossing the park, heading for the statue.

And observed in the silent darkness as that same

figure huddled in the shadow of Captain Reading's imposing presence. The faint hiss of expelled air was all the evidence I needed, and laughter replaced tears, thankfully. I waited for the artist to finish, for a passing car to go by, the figure taking time to amble instead of hurry. I didn't rise from the bench and follow until whoever it was passed me, my sneakers silent on the path.

There were cameras watching Captain Reading's statue. And, when I glanced at my phone, taking in the 10PM time, that it was still relatively early, to be honest, to be risking sneaking around and painting phalluses on bronze, I wondered at the brazen confidence of the artist.

Only to pause, to stop in the dark at the edge of the park, to watch him—definitely a him—hesitate himself in the light of the streetlamp on the other side of the big maple, turning slightly as though he'd caught the sound of my approach.

I froze, laughter locked in my throat, at the sight of Oliver Watters, fully lit in all his cardiganed glory and looking rather satisfied by his recent success.

CHAPTER TWENTY-FOUR

The old historian didn't notice I was following him, smothering a giggle behind both hands so I didn't give away my stealthy position until he reached the door to his shop. He had the glass entry pulled partway open, catching my reflection behind him before he turned to face me down with a scowl tinged with enough nervous anger he knew I'd caught him *in flagrante* graffiti *delicto*.

Before he could splutter out any kind of attempt at deflection, I poked him in his narrow chest, grinning openly, then gestured for him to precede me inside the dark shop. Oliver grunted, sighed and finally shrugged at my expression before turning and marching inside, leaving me to catch the heavy door before it struck me.

I listened to the bells overhead stop their annoying jangle as I let the entry swing shut, thudding into place as Oliver huffed his way to the back of the shop. Only the faint light at the counter illuminated the crowded space filled with old furniture, books and knick-knacks that had been here as long as I could remember. Made me wonder if he ever sold anything, including the three books of Reading history he proudly displayed on the glass counter, the rough and obviously homemade covers needing a good photo manipulation.

"You're wondering why." His low voice surprised me, the lack of anger in it. When Oliver turned to face me, his thin hands tucking his dark brown cardigan around him, the leather elbow patches worn shiny from age, the anger he'd displayed at getting caught had faded to resignation. "I take it you plan to inform Sheriff Wagner."

I shook my head, bemused now. The old historian and I had never really gotten along. His terrible attitude and abrasive nature typically set my teeth on edge. Honestly, from what I knew, most people in town found the man obnoxious and, if he had any friends at all, he kept that knowledge to himself. Though, the fact he was a town councilor and had been for some time said something about his connection to Reading.

Then again, maybe he held the position simply because no one else wanted the job.

"I couldn't care less," I said, meaning it, though the answer to this particular puzzle felt immensely satisfying. I loved having questions filled in neat and tidy. "I have no intention of sharing, Oliver. Though yes, I have to admit. I'm curious about your motives."

He hesitated before shrugging those narrow shoulders, the single bright security light casting odd shadows through his thinning hair, over the shiny scalp beneath, making his eyes dark pits, his nose more beaklike than ever.

"Captain Reading is a myth," he said then, abrupt and with a trace of his old pomposity showing before he shook off his attempt at returning to his arrogant ways. "Not the man himself, but the so-called legend." Oliver grunted as he heaved himself up onto the stool behind the counter. "And don't get me started on that Joseph Patterson. The town of Reading was already here and doing just fine before those two vagabonds decided to lie their way into pretending they were anything but a pair of swindling con artists." He snorted. "Imagine the hubris of a fake privateer carving a compass into the harbor rock." Gasp. "He didn't even aim it in the right direction." Oliver seemed greatly amused by that while I did my best not to choke on that truth.

That compass had come to represent the Reading hoard to me as much as anything else. Crew wore it on his wrist, as his father had. I processed this reveal, wanting to fight against the historian's steady confidence but knowing I'd lose.

Oliver wasn't done anyway, anger snapping back into place as he jabbed a finger at the row of books on the counter. "Have you not read my definitive history of our town, Fiona Fleming?"

Um. Oops. "You're saying Captain Reading wasn't?"

Oliver snorted and looked away, sniffing softly as if the previous dislodged something needed retrieval. I winced and thought of Robert while the historian spoke again, firm conviction in his voice.

"According to merchantman and privateer records," he said, "no one with that name commanded any kind of ship, let alone a brigantine. Nor was there a vessel named the *Darkling Dragon*." He glared like he expected me to challenge him while I felt my whole body go numb and then tingly. "Maybe if you had actually taken a moment to read my historical records—all thoroughly researched, thank you very much—you would have known not to pursue this ridiculous wild goose chase."

But the doubloons! "You're saying Captain Reading and Joseph Patterson came to Reading, lied about who they were—"

"And sweet-talked their way into our town's society." Oliver nodded abruptly, reaching for the middle book which he opened to a page near the front. "At the time, Reading was named Lewisville, after the true founder. That family bought Reading's story and it was their oldest daughter—a homely spinster from all accounts—who he seduced and married."

I sagged against the counter, not sure if I should laugh or cry. "Why didn't you just tell me?" I stared down at the books, kicking myself. I'd had these in my possession at Petunia's, had agreed to sell them for him. In fact, I'd been handed a bill shortly after my B&B burned to the ground by the very man sitting in front of me for the loss of his product.

"Would you have listened?" He dropped the book to the counter. "No one in Reading listens."

"I guess they don't want to," I said, understanding. "Human nature. We want to be special, don't we?"

Oliver stared at me, animosity fading. "We can't all be special, Miss Fleming."

"And Alistair Markham?" I wondered about Crew's grandfather, how he'd gotten things so wrong.

The historian grunted something unkind before both hands slapped down on the glass countertop. "That old fool," he said. "I tried to tell him, too. And your Grandmother Iris. Whatever the pair of them were up to, though, you can bet they had no desire to share with me."

Was that bitter resentment and a hint of jealousy I heard in his voice? So, if he would ever be honest with himself—not likely after all this time—he felt left out, didn't he? There was nothing I could do about that. Or was there?

"Oliver," I said, reaching for my phone, cuing up the photos of the doubloons Gregg found, "there has to be a treasure. Otherwise, where did these come from?"

He took my offering, studied the images a

moment, eyes widening until a disdainful smile told me he'd proven his point and I'd given him what he needed to do it. His fingers widened the image before he turned it back toward me and let me see what he'd focused in on. I did while he spoke, all that full-of-himself attitude returning.

"While these coins might be real," he said, "there is no way they came on board the *Darkling Dragon* or as part of any Reading hoard." He pointed, jabbing at the screen, while I shook my head and frowned. I had no idea what he wanted me to see. I shouldn't have worried. Oliver sighed so heavily and with such drama, I shot him an annoyed expression while he crossed his arms over his chest and looked down that beak nose at me. "The date, Miss Fleming," he said. "On the coin. What is the date?"

"1794," I said. Then stopped. Inhaled. Said a very naughty word, while Oliver chuckled.

"That's correct," he said. "And considering the fact the so-called Captain Reading arrived in our town in 1739…"

I looked up from the image, heart constricting, a very sick feeling in the pit of my stomach. "There's no way this coin could be part of his hoard," I said.

"Unless he was also some kind of time traveler," Oliver said. "You're welcome."

CHAPTER TWENTY-FIVE

I wanted to argue, was going to show him the photo of the coin from Grandmother Iris's music box and decided against it. "There's no record of Captain Reading leaving town, then? Maybe making a few privateer voyages after the fact?" I was reaching for straws that never existed and I knew it. But damn it, defeat? Tasted like old dust and bitterness.

"You know the answer to that," Oliver said, snarky enough I could have choked him. "Nor could he have gone to sea at well over one hundred years old, unless he was also an alien." That amused him to no end. "Honestly, you really believed the treasure existed and no one found it after all this time?"

"There's a map," I said.

"I had a look at that map of yours," he responded

while I protested with a silent glare. Oliver winked slowly, leaning forward over the glass. "You think I didn't know that day here in my own store, what you thought you'd found?" He chuckled again, the light behind him making him appear as some evil goblin huddling behind his counter, in the market for my soul. "It's a fake, Miss Fleming. I studied it carefully when I retrieved it from Peggy Munroe's possessions. Someone went to a great deal of trouble to create a map to something that never existed."

Okay, now I was going to have full-on heart failure and I had no idea if I could trust Oliver to call 9-1-1. "What?" Wow, Fleming, how articulate.

The old historian seemed to recognize he'd taken me about as far down the road to reality as he could at the moment without putting my life at risk and backed off, shaking his head, the wisps of his white hair trembling over his shining scalp as if tasting the air. "I'm sorry. I truly am. But I have always personally preferred the facts, Miss Fleming. You have them now. The question is, what are you going to do with them?"

I stared at him a long moment before shaking off my stunned acceptance. Because there was no argument I could present. Sure, I'd do my own research, but Oliver had no reason to lie to me. In fact, he took such pleasure in crushing my dreams it was pretty clear he was telling the truth as he knew it.

Never mind he had no problem spreading terrible rumors about Fiona Doyle I knew were false. Or did I? At this point, could I believe anything I thought I knew?

Discouraging and disheartening in light of everything that came before.

So, if that map wasn't Captain Reading's guide to his treasure, where did it come from? And who created it? What did it point to on the Patterson property and what was I going to do about it?

I swallowed hard, past the sour taste in the back of my throat, and pulled myself together, pocketing my phone. "I do have one question," I said. "How did you manage to avoid getting caught all this time? The cameras…" I trailed off while Oliver shifted uncomfortably on his stool.

"Denver," he finally blurted his grandson's name and I inhaled in understanding.

"Your tech wizard grandchild can't say no to you, apparently," I said.

Oliver shrugged, looked slightly embarrassed. "We'd only just found each other," he said. "I told him everything, about the fake captain, and he agreed to help me circumvent the cameras." He grinned then, suddenly, the expression altering his face from sullen old goat to gleeful teenager who'd pulled the prank of the century under everyone's noses. "You have to admit, it's been hilarious."

I giggled, couldn't help it, needed the release of stress and found myself laughing out loud a moment later, struggling for breath while Oliver laughed with me, wiping at tears that I caught streaming down my face. Because he was right. It was the funniest thing ever.

When I finally exhaled my last snorting chuckle, Oliver handed me a tissue which I took with a smile of thanks. He beamed back at me, and I wondered if, from now on, I'd have a different outlook when it came to the old historian.

He certainly seemed altered by our exchange of amusement, wriggling like an excited puppy on his stool. "Denver's a good boy," he said. "Rigged some kind of loop that runs every night, tapes a new version once a week automatically so the season change doesn't interfere." Oliver jerked a thumb behind him, at the narrow door behind his back. "I have the gear here, but I have no idea how it works."

A sudden surge of inspiration hit me. "Is Denver in town?"

Oliver shook his head then, sagging a bit. It was clear he was attached to his grandson, missed him. "He and Alice are out on some kind of case of hers." He sounded like he didn't approve.

Right. Alice Moore, our local transplanted medium and paranormal debunker, was running her own investigation service, though hers had less to do with the living and more to do with the long dead. But, from what I'd heard from Dad and a few others she'd been running into her own rash of murders fresher than anyone hunting ghosts should have been forced to deal with. I'd lost track of the pair of them, shame on me. Not that life hadn't been super busy, and I had lots of excuses. Still, it would be nice to reconnect and catch up on what had been happening on their end.

"Can you put me in touch with Denver?" Because, if I wasn't mistaken, the camera angle? Took a very clear shot of town hall.

"Of course," Oliver said. "Why?"

"Do you know if he keeps the real footage or not?" Please, let him keep it.

Oliver seemed confused then shrugged. "You'll have to ask him."

I nodded, a bit hopeful. "Can you have him call me?" I scribbled my cell number on the back of one of Oliver's business cards. He scowled at the use of his stationary but nodded.

I left Oliver then, heading for home, mind spinning as much as it had been when I took my walk earlier that night. Except, of course, I had entirely new things to mull over. But I wasn't going to do so alone.

Instead, I texted Crew, Dad and Liz and told them to meet me at the annex, bypassing the house I shared with my husband, entering the foyer as the two investigative men in my life arrived out front and joined me. Liz, in the meantime, was descending the stairs from the room she was using, joining us in the sitting room while I paced the length of the space and told them what Oliver told me.

"But my grandfather—" I hated the stricken look on Crew's face, the way he rubbed at the tattoo on his wrist. "My dad."

My own father looked sullen, angry, but nodded abruptly. "I already knew about this," he said. "I never believed Oliver, Fee. But I should have listened."

Crew stared at Dad like he'd suffered the worst betrayal ever. "Why would my grandfather devote so much time and effort to a lie?"

"And," Liz said, voice quieter but face set in her typical cool professionalism, "if the doubloons aren't from the treasure we've been seeking, whose are they and where did they come from?"

I stopped in my tracks. "That's an excellent question," I said, kicking myself I hadn't gotten far enough into my own thought process to ask it. "Did Gregg plant them? Bring them with him to seed the lakebed?" Was that his real game, pretending treasures were real? "But if so, why bother? And if he was working for Blackstone, what possible purpose would they have for pretending the Reading hoard was real?"

"I should note," Liz said, "I've been digging into the Tortuga crew, and I've uncovered some uncomfortable truths about Anja Härle." She settled deeper into the cushions of the sofa, feet beneath her, pajamas that same dark blue as her suits, ponytail about as perfect as she usually wore it. Even ready for bed she looked like an FBI agent. "Most notably, that she took a great deal of effort to hide the fact when she was a new divemaster, she lost a student in what should have been a routine dive. And while it was never proven to be her fault, Anja went to great lengths—including changing her last name—to sidestep her history."

Crew whistled low. "Sounds suspicious," he said.

"Why hide if it wasn't an accident?"

"She claimed it was," Liz said. "However, it couldn't be proven either way. Though, I should point out the young man had an altercation with Anja on several occasions while he dove with her, and the cause of death was decompression sickness brought on by rapid ascent." Liz met Crew's eyes, then mine again. "Apparently she claimed he refused to listen to her during the dive and that all attempts she made to stop his ascent failed, that he panicked and overpowered her."

"Plausible," Crew said. "If he was bigger and stronger than her."

"And yet," Liz said, "according to the dive shop manager, the young man had been diving for several weeks and had never shown signs of panic in the past."

"I've seen experienced divers lose it out of the blue," Crew said. "Still."

Silence fell while we all chewed that over.

"Since Gregg seemed to like to hold things over people," I said at last, "could he have known about Anja's past? Been using it against her?"

Crew nodded. "If MC didn't know, if Anja was hiding it because she was guilty, and Gregg could prove it…"

"He did know." We all turned, shocked, to find Anja in the doorway. Tears streamed down her cheeks, her long hair tangled around her, bangs heavy over her eyes, hands trembling as she swiped in angry motions at the moisture on her face. Half furious, half guilty, at least that's how it looked to me.

"Who you were," Liz said, "or that you killed that young man?"

Anja's whole body jerked, and she chopped at the air in a violent motion of rejection before stumbling a little. Dad rose, helped her sit down, while the young woman sobbed a moment. When she inhaled a shaking breath, she accepted the tissue Liz offered in her calm and focused way.

"I didn't kill him," she said, voice trembling. "It happened exactly the way I told my boss, all those years ago." Anja inhaled, squaring her thin shoulders, head back, defiant if sad. "He started hitting on me from day one, moment one, and I told my boss I wasn't going to put up with it. He wouldn't stop, was putting other divers in danger because he was forcing all of my attention on keeping him from... being inappropriate."

Yikes. "And your boss wouldn't help?"

Anja shrugged, tearing the tissue apart in long, thin strips, voice falling to a dull acceptance. "Sometimes you just have to put up with it. And I did." She tossed her hair over her shoulder, met my eyes, perhaps sensing my sympathy. Because yes, I was sympathetic. If she was telling the truth. "That day, I smelled the beer on his breath. I knew he'd had too much to drink. And from the way his pupils were dilated, I suspected he was on something else. Maybe cocaine." She shrugged then, helpless, hopeless. "I was so young, just certified. I didn't know how to handle it, didn't handle it well." She sat back, exhaling long and slow. "I tried to convince him not to dive, told my boss he shouldn't be in the water, but no one listened. And so, I went down with him."

"What depth did he lose it?" Crew's own sympathy wasn't hard to read.

She nodded to him as if in gratitude for listening and thought about it a moment. "I think we were at sixty feet. He was pushing his depth, wasn't on the right mix for any deeper, but he seemed disoriented and swam away from me. I chased him, managed to get him turned around. But then he panicked." She stared into the distance like she was reliving it, likely did on a regular basis. "I saw it in his eyes, couldn't stop him. By the time I reached him, he'd had a seizure. Spit out his mouthpiece and drowned."

I cleared my throat in the silence that followed. "Anja," I said. "That's exactly how Gregg died."

She met my gaze with her own full of fear and sorrow. "I know," she whispered. "But I swear, I had nothing to do with it." She shuddered, hugging a throw pillow as if it could protect her from the past. "I've lived with this for years, had nightmares about it. It wasn't my fault, but it was, ultimately. I was his divemaster." Her lower lip trembled, more tears threatening. "I could never, ever, do that to someone on purpose. Not ever. I can barely live with the accident. Murder?" Anja swallowed heavily as if the very thought made her want to throw up. "Never."

"So, what was Gregg using against you?" Liz's turn to shift the conversation.

Anja settled again, clearly had lots of experience

shunting aside the memory of the dead diver. "He never actually told me himself, had Martin do it." Hmmm. That was odd. "Fee, you saw the end of that argument, in the dive shack." I remembered, let her continue. "Martin claimed Gregg had evidence I'd been negligent, showed me a fabricated statement from a diver I worked with. Said he could come up with a few other sets of testimony that would ruin me and probably put me in jail." She looked miserable enough I believed her. "I know this makes me sound guilty. Anyway, Martin said Gregg wanted me to leave Tortuga Divers and join another team. To do for him with them what Chantal was doing with MC."

"Scooping treasure hunts," I said. "He just gets more delightful, doesn't he?" Meanwhile, why leave such an important conversation to Martin? Smelled fishy, but I kept that to myself as the young diver responded.

Anja's nose wrinkled. "You have no idea."

And now, with his death, I guess I never would.

CHAPTER TWENTY-SIX

Morning sunlight streamed into the kitchen at home as the phone rang. I scooped Petunia's breakfast dessert—no judging—of chopped strawberries and banana on her plate, crouching to hand it to her, cell tucked between my shoulder and jaw as I fought off a yawn. I hadn't slept much last night but who was counting?

"Fee." I recognized Alice's voice on the other end of the line. "I hear the treasure hunt isn't going as planned. I'm so sorry." She hesitated before rushing on. "And about the dead people, of course."

I loved that about Alice. Just as awkward about death as I was. Though, since she claimed (and I had no reason to doubt her) to be a medium who could actually sense real ghosts, dealing with the dead wasn't the same for her as it was for me. Maybe didn't feel so final…? I'd always meant to ask and never got around to it because, frankly, doing so might mean I had to actually face the fact the apparition I'd seen of Manuel Cortez had been a real live—forgive the term—ghost and not just a creation of her boyfriend Denver's amazing holographic system.

It had been two Halloweens ago and the memory still gave me the willies.

"Thanks, Alice," I said. "How are things in your world?" Not to deflect or anything, but yeah.

"Fine, thank you." She sounded authentic enough, so I didn't push when she failed to elaborate. "We're staying busy. Oliver mentioned you needed to talk?"

"I was hoping to speak to Denver." Wince. Though Alice didn't take it personally.

"Of course, hang on." I heard her mutter, the sound of the phone thudding against something and then her boyfriend's soft, gruff voice came through loud and clear.

"I won't apologize for helping my grandfather," he said.

I laughed, patted my pug who gulped the last bite of her fruit and licked her lips in anticipation of more. "I wouldn't dream of asking you to," I said. "I'm hoping you can help me with something else."

He exhaled deeply into the receiver. "Sorry to be defensive," he said. "You know I can't say no to him."

I got it, I really did. With his grandmother's death, another despicable human being or not, the loss of Sadie Hatch had left Denver without family. That was until we uncovered Oliver Watters was his grandfather. I hardly blamed the disconnected young man for his devotion, though the old historian was a bit of a lost cause as far as I was concerned.

Fee. No judging. Besides, I'd seen a new side of Oliver last night, right? Changed my opinion about him. Hadn't it?

Grumble.

"If I can help, I will," Denver said.

I filled him in on Geoffrey's death, mentioned from what I guessed the murderer had escaped out the back of the building. "I know you're showing footage you want the powers that be to see," I said, "but does that mean you're recording the real deal along with rewriting history?"

He grunted softly. "I am," he said. "But it automatically erases itself after a week and repeats the cycle."

"We're well within the week," I said. "Any way you could get that footage to me?" I knew Jill had to be thinking the same thing. Only problem was, she'd be getting doctored deets instead of what really unfolded.

"I'd have to come back to Reading," he said, already sounding resistant. "Alice and I are in the middle of a case. I can't leave."

"You do realize if Sheriff Wagner starts reviewing footage from the camera, she'll figure out pretty quickly someone's been tampering," I said. I hated to bully him, but. Come on already.

Before Denver could protest further, Alice's voice took over.

"Of course, he'll come back and get you what you need." There was a scraping sound, muffled voices, then Alice again. "He'll be home later this afternoon. Do you need us for anything else, Fee?"

"No, all good," I said. Before blurting, "Do you have a minute?"

"Of course." She paused, silent, and I seized on the quiet to dump everything that happened on a brand-new pair of ears.

Crew emerged from the bathroom while I was wrapping up, hair damp from the shower, towel around his waist. He raised an eyebrow at me, and I winked suggestively back, but held my focus on Alice as he disappeared into the bedroom.

"Sounds like you have your hands full," Alice said with the perfect amount of sympathy. "I was so sorry to hear about Petunia's. I'm not sure if I told you that."

"Thanks," I said, hip against the counter, pug on my feet. "For listening, mostly." The spinning in my head that had been going on since yesterday—since Gregg's arrival—had diminished to a manageable pirouette. "It really helped."

"My pleasure," she said. "Maybe we can work together sometime." Alice inhaled sharply then giggled. "Again, I mean."

"I think I'll pass on the paranormal," I said, "but

if you ever need me, don't hesitate."

She seemed like she wanted to say more, but signed off instead, promising to visit when she made it back to Reading in a few weeks. I let her go, knowing it was selfish. She obviously had something she wanted to run by me like I'd just dumped my cases on her. And if I really was a good friend? I'd call her back and make her go through it. Instead, I set aside my phone and joined my husband in our room, arriving just in time to watch him tug a t-shirt over his head and run both hands through his black waves.

"Getting long again," he grinned at me when I took my turn, fingers sliding over the softness of his hair. "Maybe I'll shave it this time. Grow a beard." He dodged my attempt to poke him in the ribs.

"Don't you dare," I said. "I love you just the way you are."

There was nothing more satisfying than a Crew Turner kiss.

We spent the rest of the morning researching the doubloons and I had to finally admit Oliver had been 100% right and not just about the fact they couldn't possibly have been part of the treasure thanks to their age. I hung up the phone from a rather short-tempered woman in the United Kingdom's National Archives who informed me in no uncertain terms she was not, in fact, missing anything and no, dear, no such captain existed as she told the rather unpleasant man who'd written the terribly edited book he'd insisted on sending her a copy of.

Okay then.

When Crew received a call from Dad, I didn't argue about him leaving me behind, harnessing up my pug for her walk instead and heading for the annex. Head down, thoughts far away, I missed the approaching car and jumped more than I should have when it pulled to a halt next to me. Since I'd almost been run over last December in a murder attempt perpetuated by Ruth and Peggy, maybe I shouldn't have judged my reaction to the incident. Anyone would be gun shy after something like that, right?

Thing was, while it might not have been either of those horrific woman who threatened me, I certainly wasn't safe, if the expression on Robert's face was any indicator. Surely, he would have loved to plough me down with his sedan if the expression he fixed me with told me his state of mind.

He was out of the still-running vehicle and in my face before I could stop walking or catch my breath, rocking me back on my heels. "Give it back," he snarled, index finger jabbing me in the shoulder.

Petunia growled. She rarely reacted with anger, but her dislike of Robert had become legendary. Maybe she remembered him kicking her into the water and leaving her to drown. Or maybe the cumulative hurts she'd endured had been gathered into a seed of canine logic that tied Robert to everything. Or, more likely, she simply sensed his animosity and, in light of the past, was eager to protect the both of us from him. Whatever her reason, her reaction snapped me out of the shock of his assault and woke my protective redhead.

I slapped his hand away, shaking with anger and the course of adrenaline now controlling me. "How dare you," I snapped back. "Don't touch me."

He seemed shocked by his own behavior before that darkness I'd come to recognize in him surfaced in those dead and empty eyes. "You stole it from me," he said, voice now flat and more frightening for the lack of anything in it, including the anger he'd originally leveled on me. "I want it back."

The hairpin. Grandmother Iris's pin. "It was never yours to begin with," I said, mimicking his level nothingness. "It belonged to our grandmother, Robert, and you know it. You stole it first." There was a twitch, like guilt. Justified, I raised my chin, maybe unable to look down my nose at him, but doing my best. "So back off."

He did, to my surprise, after a long, hesitant moment when I wasn't sure if he was going to attack me, burst into tears or... who knew what? Something was horribly broken inside Robert Carlisle and there was no healing it. He drove off then, squealing his tires, ineffectual and leaving me cold, if only because I honestly had no idea what he was capable of anymore.

It was an uncomfortable moment before I was able to continue my walk, Petunia subdued beside me. I was halfway to the annex when I spotted Martin crossing the street and heading for the back door through the parking lot. Grateful for the distraction, I hurried our pace as much as I could, catching up with him before he could slip in the back, my pug huffing in my arms when I was forced to heave her into my embrace to make the last dash to reach him in time.

Martin didn't look happy to see me, but his tears had dried up at least. "I don't have anything to say to you," he said.

I really wanted to ask why Gregg had him blackmail Anja but figured I'd have to go about it in a way that had him on my side first. My second question seemed more likely to get his attention and hold it if only to defend his dead boss's honor, what little he'd had. "I just want to know if Gregg would have tried to fake a treasure find." That got his attention. The documentarian looked shocked enough his headshake of denial had to be real. I filled him in on the fake doubloons while Martin listened, hands on his hips, frown deepening into a concerned scowl.

"That's not Gregg's way of doing business," he said. Swallowed and looked away. "Wasn't." He pulled himself under control again and went on. "There was no glory in pretending to find a treasure."

Right. And Gregg was all glory hound. "The coins are real, Martin, but they can't be from the Reading hoard. The dates are wrong." He seemed surprised by that revelation. "Any idea where they came from if Gregg didn't fake the find?"

Martin seemed perplexed, finally tossed his

hands. "I have no idea," he said.

"And your relationship with Hannah?" Okay, so I had three questions, and went there, right on the heels of the previous conversation, hoping to catch him off guard.

What do you know? It worked. Martin's shoulders sagged somewhat, and he glanced back toward the door to the annex kitchen before sighing deeply, one hand rubbing the back of his neck.

"I admit it," he whispered. "I'm in love with her. I can't help myself." Martin licked his lips, expression filled with grief and despair and guilt. "She was going to leave Gregg for me. We had it all planned out. I even had the divorce papers ready for him to sign."

"I know." Let him wonder how I knew. "Hannah's been busy, Martin. I know all about the money." Well, I didn't, but I'd heard enough last night to pretend I did.

It was enough. "I had nothing to do with that," he said in a rush, suddenly pale. "I just wanted Hannah."

"Did Gregg know she was stealing from him?" I waited a heartbeat before hitting him with the next question. "Did he know she was cheating with you?"

Martin shook his head at the first question, paused then shook again at the second. "I don't know. I don't think so. He never hinted he did." Martin's face twisted, self-hate so evident I suddenly worried about him. "How could this happen? How did I let myself betray him like that? We've been friends for years. I'm a horrible person." Martin started crying all over again, hopeless and helpless.

I wasn't about to argue with his assessment, though. Harsh? Maybe. I was done with these people.

"I saw you messing with MC's tanks," I said. "I know you said you thought they were Gregg's. Did you really?" I did my best to keep any kind of anger out of my voice, but it was growing inside me again and I just wanted answers. "Did you do something to your boss's air, Martin?"

"No." He didn't argue past that one word, not with his body language or volume or a show of rage. Just that simple statement of denial.

"And Anja?" I watched him flinch, look away. "Gregg tasked you with blackmailing her, but why? I'd think it would be something he'd want to handle personally."

No response. Damn it. He didn't get to go quiet like that.

To my surprise, though, he did respond at last, feet shuffling, a small boy caught in a lie he could no longer defend. "It wasn't Gregg blackmailing her," he said in a gush of guilt. "It was me."

"Chantal too?" Was Gregg—choke—innocent?

Martin belied that, shaking his head. "That's where I got the idea," he said. "I found out about Anja's past by accident when I was researching for Gregg. When I knew Hannah was going to leave him, I figured I'd take advantage of the setup he'd created. It worked for him for years. Why not for me?" Defensive, then defeated.

Fine, whatever. So, he was as despicable as his

boss, if pathetic about it where Gregg had been arrogant. But that didn't answer everything. I whipped out my phone, frustration growing, shoved the images of the doubloons in his face. He looked closely at them while I took slow, deep breaths to control my anger. I seriously needed management classes for my redheaded temper.

"I know these," he said, frowning again, pointing at details on the coins and showing me despite the fact I had no idea what he was talking about. "These are from a previous hunt." He met my eyes, his own concerned. "From Gregg's private collection. I'd know them anywhere. There were a number in this batch, all kept by those who were part of the discovery."

"Including who?" I took my phone back, temper in check now that I wasn't being stonewalled. Ah, so maybe that was the answer to my anger issues. Actually dealing with reasonable people who gave me the information I needed when I asked for it and didn't lie about it.

He paused to think about it. "I don't remember exactly. We've been on so many hunts. But I can find out." Martin gestured for the door to the annex, expression open. "If you'll let me, I can show you."

That's how I found myself sitting next to him, hunched over his laptop, reviewing footage of dives. Martin had hours of Gregg being Gregg and it wasn't long before I was sick of the sight of the man all over again, not to mention his attitude. Dead or not, there was no love lost.

Jill's arrival in the sitting room where we'd made ourselves comfortable immediately followed Martin's soft exclamation of discovery. Her appearance instantly shifted his mood from helpful to anxious. He sat, still and trembling slightly, next to me, hands fisted in his lap.

"I have a few more questions for you, Mr. Faller," the sheriff said, nodding to me. "If you don't mind."

Martin stood and joined her, leaving me alone with the footage he'd been looking for and to my own devices. I could have scoured his computer for evidence he'd killed Gregg. Instead, trusting he'd been playing straight with me, I chose to review the clips he'd cued up and, within moments of screening the last three, knew who the murderer was.

CHAPTER TWENTY-SEVEN

I'm still not sure how I had the restraint to wait for Jill to wrap up with Martin before hauling her aside to tell her what I discovered. Showed her the footage of the person in question holding out the doubloons Gregg thought were a new find. Reading's sheriff instantly got on the radio when Daisy confirmed the suspect had checked out of the annex that morning, putting out a BOLO on the missing murderer.

I planned to head for home, instead deposited my pug in her favorite place—at Mom's feet in the annex kitchen—and ran home for my car.

"Be careful, sweetheart." My mother knew better than to tell me not to do what I planned next. She'd raised me to be this independent, after all. "I'll send your father to meet you."

My car made a fast trip to the yacht club, and I barely had it in park before I leaped out and ran for the diving shed. There was one other car in the lot, though I didn't recognize it, and chose instead to dive headfirst as was my way into the wrap-up details of the investigation.

Turned out Gregg's air tanks weren't the only ones I wanted the forensics team to have a closer look at.

I was in such a hurry, so sure I knew exactly what I was doing, I didn't hesitate as I barreled straight into the dive shed, not noticing until it was far too late, I wasn't alone. Nor that the tall, angry woman at the back of the shed holding the gun on MC? Decided to cover me with it, too.

"You just couldn't mind your own business." Hannah Brown's hand shook, but her finger was on the trigger of the pistol she held, and I had no doubt she knew how to shoot the thing. "This had nothing to do with you or your stupid treasure. Why couldn't you just stay out of it?"

I glanced sideways at MC who met my eyes, hers full of fear. "There are others coming, Hannah," I said, trying for reasonable and kind of making it because I'd had lots of practice with crazy people in the past three years, hadn't I? "You won't get away with this."

She shook her head, tears long gone, seemingly more annoyed by my interruption than scared, despite her trembling hands. "I know what this looks like," she said. "But I didn't kill my husband."

"I know," I said, turning away from the widow, and focusing on the dive team leader whose eyes widened suddenly in surprise. "MC did." I slowly spun back to Hannah. "But not before you and Martin tried to kill her, first."

If the Tortuga diver had planned to deny it, her choice died with that reveal.

"How did you know?" She shifted a bit, face hard and dark now, hands at her sides. Less afraid of the gun than she should have been, as far as I was concerned.

"About Gregg's murder? Or the fact his wife and best friend wanted you dead?" I shrugged, wishing I was wrong. I'd liked MC. She was friends with Liz. This wasn't going to end well. "The coins." MC twitched and I nodded. "You know the coins I mean."

"The greedy bastard," she snarled. "I knew if he saw them, he'd go for them."

"And with his tank compromised," I said, "the deeper he went—"

MC's sharp bark of a laugh cut me off. "I always told him taking risks would kill him one day."

"You asked about them," I said. "The coins. When the doc would release them from evidence. But not so we could examine them."

MC's face told me everything, even as she spoke. "I needed to get them back," she said. "Make them disappear." She coughed softly, almost an apology. "I didn't think this through. I acted on impulse." Her glare at Hannah told me her part had been a crime of passion. But there were more pieces to this puzzle.

"You carry the coins with you?" Who did that?

MC's weak grin joined her shrug. "As a reminder of why I do what I do."

I guess I was no better keeping the one I had in a music box. Hardly secure, was it? "What I don't understand," I said to Hannah this time, "is why you wanted MC dead."

The former Mrs. Brown waved the gun at me as if to emphasize her words. The heat of the July day had raised the temperature inside the shack, the humidity slicking sweat over my whole body under my shorts and t-shirt. Or was it fear finally coming to life as she used her deadly weapon in such a casual manner? "She found out I was siphoning funds," she said. "She was blackmailing me."

MC's scowl deepened, her whole body tense. "You know, it wasn't the fact Gregg was scooping my finds that pushed me over the edge." She glared the kind of hate at Hannah that told me jealousy lived inside her, devoured her, had fueled the unthinkable. "He could have had the treasure. But bringing you here? With him? Rubbing my face in it?" She shook her head in two sharp jerks. "That I couldn't tolerate."

"He never loved you!" Hannah's desperation should have been MC's. She was the one holding the gun. But Gregg's widow seemed like the one with the fears to face, not the dive leader. From what I could tell of MC's expression? She not only had a clear conscience, she was happy to confront the woman before her, gun or no gun.

And I had to get myself caught in the middle of that kind of crazy. Go me.

"He loved me," MC said, almost serene. "He said he regretted marrying you. You know, we were lovers all along. All these years." She hugged herself then. "He didn't have to bribe Chantal. I would have had him as my partner. In work and in life." MC's entire body shifted back to focused intent while Hannah seemed to crumble under her words as though the weight of them was all it took to break her. "And then he goes and does the unthinkable." She grunted as though struck. "The bastard deserved to die for what he did to me."

"Hannah was planning to divorce him." I don't know why I blurted that little detail, but it got MC's attention. I might as well have punched her in the face, she seemed so shocked. When her head whipped around, blue-green eyes gaping, staring at Hannah, the other woman nodded.

"You could have had him." Her hand still shook, but that finger on the trigger never wavered. "I was done."

MC choked on a sob, looked away, down, hot tears hitting the dried-out wood of the floor of the shed. Her shoulders shook a moment before she tensed yet again, dashing at the moisture with the back of one hand, grim line of her lips a terrible sign.

She looked like a woman who had nothing left to lose.

"You figured you'd use Hannah and Martin's attempt to kill you against them." I did my best to distract MC whose herky-jerky response at least refocused her attention on me. And that was a terrible idea. She looked about ready to murder again, and I was closest to her. Not very discerning, that deadly look in her eyes.

She swallowed hard, though, and spoke. "They tampered with my air." She shrugged. "Easy enough to switch my tanks to his. Three enemies with one action." MC's face crumpled briefly before going blank. "36% mix guaranteed a convulsive grand mal seizure. And once the tests came back from forensics, they'd find Martin's fingerprints on the valve. Only Martin's." MC's tone had dropped to dull, empty. "I was prepared to hand over what I knew about Hannah's embezzlement. That would ensure all three of them got what they deserved." MC inhaled slowly, exhaled. "I followed him down." Now she was lost, no longer with us in the hot and stifling shed, gone below, underwater, with Gregg and memory. "I seeded the first coin the day before, pulled it from another dive so he wouldn't recognize it. Just in case." She wiped at her mouth with one hand, staring at the floor even though she looked right through it. "But the three he found, those were from our first dive. I wanted him to know it was me." She looked up. "He understood. I'm sure of it. Tried to surface, but it was too late." MC's voice finally shook, emotion rising as Gregg had tried to. "I watched him, stayed with him. I owed him that."

Okay, I thought she was crazy before, but now? Wow. Just wow. MC's whole body trembled before she gasped in air as though she'd forgotten to breathe. "When he was done convulsing, I inflated his BCD and let him go."

"You're sick." Whoops. I'd forgotten all about the woman with the gun in the literal heat of the moment. But Hannah hadn't gone anywhere, nor had her revolver or that pointy finger on the trigger. "You deserve to die for what you did."

MC stared back, calculating now, empty flatness gone and exchanged for watchful planning. I knew that look. I'd faced a few murderers who'd thought they could get away with it. I wasn't sure what MC thought she could do against a gun, but whatever she was thinking? Yeah, I wanted no part of it.

Hannah might have known what end of that weapon to point at us, how to pull the trigger, but there was no promise she'd hit her intended target and not me in the process.

MC was moving before I finished my mental attempt to weigh all the possible variables, leaping for Hannah who screamed in defiance and fired. The bullet went wide, the zing of it too close for comfort, scent of expended gunpowder flooding the small space with the acrid bitterness of residue.

No time to think about anything, not when MC had Hannah pinned down, the taller, slimmer woman's back hitting the exit door, slamming it open and exposing her to the water below the dock.

Now, a normal person would have maybe made a

rapid exit and called for backup, leaving the two—one a confirmed murderer, the other a thief, cheater and attempted murderer—to finish each other off. But I'd never been accused of the normal label everyone seemed so fond of.

I'd continue to leave that to others.

Instead, Fleming nature fully intact, I dove for the two of them just as MC, shrieking and clawing at her opponent, shoved the pair of them off the end of the dock and into the icy lake.

Carrying you-know-who along with them.

—she sobbed in my arms, dripping and cold, screaming his name while his hand, so pale, grasping for the sky, sank beneath the water—

No, not now. I didn't have time for flashbacks of Victor French's death—

—sinking under the water, Doreen Douglas on top of me, inhaling the lake as the compass under the dock filled my view and mocked me with the lie it offered—

I had to pull myself together. MC had Hannah's head under the surface, the other woman thrashing but the fight rapidly going out of her, and they were ten feet away, my own frenzied battle with memory obviously carrying me out of range. It took two or three seconds (that felt like weeks) to wrangle my arms and legs into any kind of swim stroke that didn't resemble the terrified thrashing of a rank beginner. And another two or three seconds (surely it had been months at this point? Forever?) to reach MC. Grasp her by the back of her shirt. Jerk her free of Hannah.

Who rose to the surface, bobbing lifelessly, while MC fought me off.

I pushed the Tortuga leader away, didn't care she was swimming for the dock, flipped Hannah's body over. Sure, she was despicable, just as much as her dead husband, but she was a human being and I would not have another nightmare on my conscience when I went near water, thanks.

I heard the siren in the distance, vaguely recognized the sound of voices on the dock. But none of them mattered, not while I cradled Hannah's silent body in my arms, another face superimposed over hers in flashes that made me want to sob.

Not Victor, oddly. Vivian.

And then, despite everything, her chest heaving, choking for air, Hannah Brown's eyes opened, and I knew I'd at least gotten this much right.

CHAPTER TWENTY-EIGHT

Chantal and Anja stood together, bags at their sides, in the entry of the annex, not quite guilty but not all that comfortable meeting my eyes, either.

"I'm sorry the treasure turned out to be a fake," the older diver said while her younger counterpart nodded, hands stuffed deep into the pockets of her shorts. Chantal turned to her friend as if for support before shrugging. "Thanks for talking your sheriff into cutting us loose."

"Betraying your boss to another treasure hunter isn't illegal, as far as I know," I said, knowing I wasn't keeping friends I'd thought I'd made but not able to help myself. Loyalty and honesty? Yeah, cornerstones of the Fleming way of being. They could blame my parents if they wanted.

Chantal flinched but didn't argue. I shifted focus to Anja who, at least, was innocent if her story was to be believed. Still, I couldn't bring myself to completely let her off the hook. If she was innocent of that young man's death, why did she change her name instead of fighting for herself?

Then again, what would I have done, young and alone, faced with a sullied reputation brought on by a guy who put both of them in danger?

"What will happen to Hannah and Martin?" Anja shouldered her bag while Chantal extended the handle on her rollie with a solid and final click.

"Who knows," I said. "Maybe prison, if Liz has anything to say about it." MC's guilt aside, I knew the FBI agent wouldn't let the pair of embezzling liars get away with it if she had the choice. "I'm sure whatever happens, they'll get what they deserve."

Ominous much, Fleming?

They both left without another word, loading their bags into the Tortuga truck and driving off. My heart broke as they did, not for the lost friendships—okay, so maybe a little because I really liked them and now, I felt like an idiot for trusting all over again—but for the fact the treasure I'd been hunting all this time wasn't real.

And that for some reason she'd taken to her grave with her, the old bat, Grandmother Iris had been leading me on a multi-year wild hoard chase.

I turned back to the main desk and the computer, settling in to take care of some paperwork. Crew still hadn't forgiven me for what he called my little stunt.

Putting myself in danger, his favorite. Easier to hide out here in the annex than face his disappointment and fearful anger while replaying the scene over and over in my mind.

He'd pulled up in a spray of gravel, not even closing the driver's side door behind him as he raced to me where I sat on the picnic table with a blanket wrapped around me, scowling sourly at the ambulance and the EMTs who were becoming far too familiar.

"Fee." He hugged me, kissed my forehead, then grasped my upper arms in both hands, turning his head to meet Dr. Aberstock's eyes. "Is she okay?"

The doc grinned and nodded. "Perfectly fine." He patted my shoulder, gesturing at the EMTs they weren't needed after all. Phew, dodged that bullet along with the one Hannah fired off earlier.

Problem was, I'd bobbed and weaved out of the path of the wrong projectile. The moment Dr. Aberstock gave me the bill of health nod, Crew spun back on me and, with his voice shaking and that vein in his forehead throbbing, the tic under his eye bounding in time with his pulse, he shook me just a little, both big hands grasping me firmly.

"Fiona Fleming," he growled, low enough it was just us, but loud enough I couldn't miss a single word, "I've had enough. The next time you put yourself in danger like this, I'll…" He trailed off, jaw jumping.

In that moment I had two choices. I could have been sweet and loving and caring and understanding, because that would have been the wifey thing to do, right? Or I could be sarcastic and go for humor in exactly the wrong moment and in the wrong way that meant clashing wills with the man I loved.

I know you know which one I chose. "What?" I cocked an eyebrow, redhead temper at full capacity. "You'll kill me?"

It kind of devolved from there, and I'll spare the details because honestly, I didn't want to remember. We'd whispered/shouted for another couple of passes before Crew stormed off and left me—*left* me, *imagine*—to drive home alone.

As I brought up the spreadsheet to enter in this month's data, I forced myself to stop beating myself up over the mess I'd made of my marriage only to pause, anxiety returning as I thought about the bodyguard who had vanished on me, without a trace. Not that I was blaming Darius for abandoning me. Hadn't I given the poor guy the third degree for trying to protect me? For all I knew, Malcolm had needed him for another job. Or maybe he had a line on Peggy and Ruth and was chasing them down.

And in a long list of them, one more—or something horrible had happened to the hulking man in black and I hadn't done a thing to help.

To be fair, I'd made a second stop at The Orange shortly after Dr. Aberstock cleared me and sent me on my way. Again, no Malcolm—a fact that seemed to worry his boys, despite their usual bravado—and not a trace of Darius.

Yup, nervous for both of them.

I'd mentioned it to Dad, at least, and my father knew me well enough to take it seriously. He'd hugged me and headed for the office, leaving Mom to her baking.

"Malcolm Murray can take care of himself," my gruff and stoic dad said on his way out before pausing, a frown on his face, "but let me see what I can find out."

It didn't take long to update the file since Daisy was really good at staying on top of things, bless her. And so, a short time later, the afternoon sun beating down on me, I walked home, Petunia huffing along next to me, not at all pleased initially I'd dragged her away from my mother's cookie baking, though the pug forgave me almost immediately, as was her way, the instant food was out of nose shot.

Home was quiet, Crew nowhere to be found. Maybe he was thinking the same thing I did and, as the urge to cry battled with the need to have him here to hug me and make everything okay again warred with my independent stubborn reaction to him trying to coddle me all over again, I sank into the sofa cushions and did my best not to relive yet again the fight we'd had just a short two hours ago.

Because I was always successful at not lingering over hurts like an aching tooth.

My husband hadn't abandoned me, the real sticking point of my petulance. He'd left to cool off. I knew better. I was, after all, the mistress of pushing Crew Turner's buttons. Guilt had finally won, enough I texted and was ignored.

Okay then. Ignored it was.

Which led to me glaring at my phone like it was to blame before retrieving the butterfly pin Crew liberated for me from the coffee table and toying with it a moment. Robert had been pissed it went missing. Good. Let him suffer for once. I couldn't care less if Rose gave him a hard time for it or not. The pin belonged to Grandmother Iris, which meant it now belonged to me. I snarled at the missing gems, positive Rose damaged the delicate clip on purpose. That would be just like her to abuse something so precious. I held it up, frowning at it. Maybe I could find a jeweler to fix it? Surely the gems weren't real, and it would cost me more than the thing was worth. But the history of it was the real measure of value, so how could I not take steps to restore it?

Sunlight streamed into the space, washing over my hands as I turned the pin sideways to check the settings, the empty spaces in the wing. Allowing light to shine through, onto the glass top of the table.

Making an odd pattern that caught my breath.

I'd seen it before. Seen that pattern, hadn't I? Until it struck me that the map was a lie, the pin itself, whether part of the mystery my grandmother left me or not, also part of that untruth and I didn't care. Couldn't care less.

That's why I dug out the map, spread it on the coffee table and, with the pin in my hand, folded the map back the way Daisy had contorted it until the red line paired with the compass showed.

Three lines that made no sense suddenly did. And

matched perfectly the missing spaces in the butterfly clip, completing an arrow as the butterfly's wing formed an obvious point.

But what did it mean?

Silly Fiona. It meant it was time to yet again practice my breaking and entering skills and see what the Pattersons were hiding on their mountain.

CHAPTER TWENTY-NINE

Liz sat next to me in the middle of the small powerboat, her gaze focused on the approaching line of land in the distance. Dad had cut the engine and was letting momentum carry us in, lights out, the Patterson's dock rapidly approaching.

Crew's silence wasn't about me, or so my father said when I called him with what I'd found and my worries my husband might be in danger (no, I didn't mention I was actually more concerned he was giving me the silent treatment). He'd gone out of town suddenly on a case, something I wished he'd shared with me and reinforced my certainty he was, in fact, choosing to put distance and quiet between us. I knew he processed best when he had space, but it didn't always work for me.

We'd be having a conversation about how our marriage was going to survive our disparate ways of communicating, he could be sure of that.

For now, I had Dad as my partner in crime, though it surprised me when he called Liz in to help. Even more when the FBI agent gave a rapid yes and met us at the yacht club dressed in tight black everything.

"If anyone asks," she said, stepping into the boat Dad borrowed (I didn't ask from who and didn't want to know what borrowed meant to my father who seemed lackadaisical with the law these days), "I'm off duty for the next few days."

Like that would save her job if she was caught with us. I had no doubt the Patterson family in general—their matriarch in particular—would not only press charges if we were discovered, they would ensure Liz lost her job with the FBI under any means necessary.

She didn't seem that concerned, however, as calm and collected as ever while I shivered next to her and worried about her in her stead. Not to mention Dad and me. After all, I was sure Blackstone had supplied the security bullies who'd kept me from sneaking close enough to witness Alicia and Jared's wedding back in the fall. There was no reason to think that same security force patrolled the Patterson property, but they'd been carrying some pretty impressive weaponry and, if (my favorite word of all time) they were present and if (so delicious, isn't it?) they spotted us and if (the very epitome of worrywart doubtypants in two simple letters) they were so inclined with no reason to believe otherwise to salve my growing anxiety, there was a chance we could end up being shot at.

How was that for a lovely and convoluted exploration of my possible impending mortality while riding in silence in the darkness toward the only place in Reading I had never been welcome ever?

But wait, that wasn't true. I'd been on their dock as a child, evidenced by my recurring memories of the death of Victor French. As Dad steered the silent speedboat toward the bank and away from the main dock—empty of other vessels—I wondered if it was Vivian's brother's death that created the rift between the Patterson family and mine.

No. I braced myself as the hull thudded into the grassy shore, Dad hopping out to secure it before offering his hand to me. Things started long before now, with Fiona Doyle.

The dock was far from the main house, at least, as was the arrow's tip the butterfly had created. Dad had plotted out the location the best he could, his phone coming to life a moment as he checked his GPS. I glanced at the overlay of the current topography with the map he'd scanned into his cell, shaking my head at how far technology had taken us, even more that my father was better at using it than I was.

Weren't most millennial's parents technophobes? So I'd been told. Yeah, not John Fleming. Lucky me.

I followed him as he headed inland, Liz at my

back, keeping my head down and watching my step. The grassy meadow gave way to rocky outcroppings as this part of the mountain made itself known quickly. The main house, easily a mile away, glowed in the distance, lights from the windows making it a glaring obstacle. Every time I looked at it I lost some of my night vision and, invariably, stumbled thanks to my obsessive glances toward the stronghold of the beast.

Imagination running away with you, Fleming?

It wasn't like we were dealing with supervillains or something. I almost snorted at my own nonsensical reaction to being here, on Patterson property, in the middle of the night, chasing down the clue my grandmother left me on a map it was now very likely she fabricated with assistance from my husband's grandfather in an effort to make me chase down something she thought I needed to see.

Right. And I was being ridiculous. Thanks a lot, Grandmother Iris.

It didn't take long to find the location, Dad gesturing for the two of us to join him. I'd worried we'd have a hard time finding what we were looking for, had no idea if we'd be able to pinpoint the spot we'd been guided to. We didn't exactly have information or a sign saying, "Here it is!" waving in our faces, did we?

Apparently, we did. Because Dad was standing over a long, flat rock on which was carved a quartet of butterflies.

Oh. My. God.

Liz crouched next to it, slid her fingers under it, lifted. It came away after a moment, Dad joining in, grunting softly while I fell to my knees and examined the metal chest beneath. A treasure chest? Was this the hoard after all? Had we somehow misinterpreted the map, was Oliver wrong?

Dad pried the large chest out of the ground, and I shook my head at my own folly. This was more like a toolbox, not an old-fashioned container to hold jewels and gold pilfered by a pirate.

I reached for the heavy lock keeping it shut, but my father was already standing, lifting one end, Liz reaching for the other. They didn't seem to struggle with the weight, so I let them carry it, wondering at the faint thudding sounds that came from inside as my father stumbled and almost dropped the front end. He caught it in time, though, hurrying on through the dark toward the shore and the boat and escape.

I was positive we were going to get caught at that point. So sure we'd made a massive error and likely set off some kind of alarm taking the chest. Right now, deep inside the Patterson mansion, a red light flashed a warning and black-outfitted super soldiers were heading our way.

That's why I was in shock, I think, when I settled into my original seat, hands resting on the chest Dad and Liz loaded into the boat before Dad pushed the bow off from shore and hopped on with us. The current from Minute River caught us quickly, as my father said it would, carrying us around the outside edge of the Patterson property, close enough to shore if someone had come looking, we'd have been spotted, but silent as we drifted past, unseen and utterly silent until we cleared the edge of their property.

Dad gave the thumbs up but didn't fire up the engine for another five minutes, only then turning us around the outside edge of the lake and heading for the yacht club. Liz's eyes caught the light in the distance, glistening, faint smile one of satisfaction while I continued to shiver, and not from the cold.

Did we really just get away with it? But what was it we actually got away with?

It felt like a mutual agreement, though none of us actually spoke to make such a pact, that not one word passed between the three of us until Dad pulled up in front of the office. And only then did he sigh, deep and long, hopping out to retrieve the chest. I followed him to his desk, Liz locking the door behind us before joining us at the far end of the narrow space. Dad had deposited the metal box on the wooden surface of his workspace, and we all stood back a moment and examined it as though afraid to do anything else.

"Well," my father said at last, making me jump from the break in the quiet, "we'd best find out what all the fuss was over." And, with that, he reached into the top drawer of his desk and pulled out a pair of pliers. Only my dad would have pliers in his top desk drawer.

He made quick work of the old lock, snapping

the rusting casing open, using the business end to release the mechanism and open the hasp. Liz took it from him as he freed it from the chest, holding it in the palm of her hand while my father took a deep breath and opened the box.

The lid didn't want to lift, protesting with a squeal of unhappy and warped metal, but Dad was determined and, after a brief struggle with the right corner, it let go its refusal to accede. Which meant the top practically flung itself wide when the pressure Dad used to pry it loose no longer met resistance.

I'm not sure what I was expecting to find, though privately, in the very far reaches of my mind, I guess I was hoping for gold. Instead, I peered down into what looked like ashes, with a few white sticks, charred on the edges, stirred up from within. The scent of ancient barbeque overdone hit me a moment later, my mind unable to make the connection, though it was obvious to me, as Liz gasped and Dad took a half step back, one hand over his mouth, they both knew exactly what was in the box.

Took me another heartbeat to connect the old smell of cooked meat trapped within despite the passage of time, paired with the outline of a jawbone to the contents.

"Dear god," Liz whispered. She turned to Dad, her shock palpable. Sure, she was a seasoned FBI agent, but even she hadn't been prepared for this, right? "Do you have any idea who it is?"

My father didn't answer. He didn't seem able, tears now streaming down his face. He turned away while I choked on my own, heart pounding so loudly in my ears I barely heard myself answer her.

"It can only be one person," I said. "Fiona Doyle."

CHAPTER THIRTY

Things couldn't get any worse, could they? Surely not.

Enter Dr. Lloyd Aberstock and so much worse I could barely breathe.

"I'm afraid, from preliminary examination, there is more than one set of skeletal remains in this mess." He stood over the box Dad had dropped on the surgical table, the morgue already quiet but now feeling like a tomb as he spoke. His normally jovial tone was gone, grim sorrow replacing it. "I can't identify the victim without a DNA test, I'm afraid. But there is enough bone matter remaining that whoever tried to burn these," he gestured into the box with his gloved hands trailing bits of ash, "failed in their attempt to disguise this poor woman's identity."

"You're sure she was female?" Dad's voice couldn't have been any flatter, empty of all emotion. I guess he'd released what he needed to at the office before bundling all of us up and calling the doc on our way to the hospital, practically ordering the older man to meet us there.

"The width of the pelvic bone is a dead giveaway, I'm afraid." Dr. Aberstock winced. "Apologies for the unfortunate use of language. But it's these bones that concern me the most." He held up a tiny one that looked like the remains of a chicken wing. "From an infant. I'd say newborn." He set the bone gently aside on a strip of heavy paper he'd unrolled, laying it out next to the few others he'd already excavated from the ashes. "A tragedy, this."

Dad left us then, turning around and marching out through the swinging doors without saying another word. Liz held me back when I tried to follow.

"Let him have a minute," she said, compassion in her face if not her regularly scheduled FBI tone of voice. "I take it Fiona Doyle was pregnant?"

I nodded, swallowed hard against the need to sob and throw up at the same time. "That was the rumor."

"Until we know for certain this is, indeed, Miss Doyle, it remains just that." Dr. Aberstock seemed offended by the leap in logic. "A rumor."

Fair enough. I wiped my mouth with the cuff of my jacket, pulling back on my overwhelm enough to keep from falling completely apart.

"Siobhan was wrong, then," I said. "She thought Fiona was alive." I met the doc's eyes. "If this is her."

He sagged a little, shrugged. "Fine." Dr. Aberstock went back to sifting through the ashes. "Speculate."

"I'll wait on the lab," Liz said.

"And you'll be explaining where you found these remains how, Agent Michaud?" The doc looked back and forth between us over the round rims of his glasses, fluffy white eyebrows arched, cheeks pink. Why did he have to look so much like Santa Claus pawing through the acrid remains of a dead woman and her baby as though some gristly present he planned to deliver to an unsuspecting child? I'd never think about Christmas the same way again.

Liz looked suddenly uncomfortable. "I know," she said, glancing at me, then. "Fee, honestly, I figured we'd find nothing. Or something ridiculous. Not this." Her right hand rose and fell, thudding against her thigh. "I have to report this. But that means also reporting where we found the box." Any concern washed out of her expression the moment she said it, jaw tight, eyes narrowed. "I'll just accept the consequences."

"I can report it," I said, touching her hand, feeling her tense from the contact. "You don't have to be involved, Liz." I met Dr. Aberstock's eyes, and he nodded.

"As far as I'm concerned," he said, "you met us here, Agent Michaud, after Fiona found these remains. Alone?" He was obviously trying to protect Dad, too.

"No." My father had returned in silence, striding then to the table, crossing his arms over his big chest, glaring at the box like it broke his heart. "I found it. Fee and Liz had nothing to do with it."

We both started to protest but my father just grunted and refused to respond which, in John Flemingspeak, meant the case was closed, and nothing would make him change his damned fool mind.

Grunt. Flemings.

"I want to know how Grandmother Iris knew about the body." Sigh. Bodies. "And why didn't she just tell us they were there? Why the stupid treasure hunt?" Sick sense of humor, Grandmother. Sick.

With no answers forthcoming, I lasted about five more minutes. Until the doc lifted out a perfectly preserved skull no bigger than a grapefruit.

I just couldn't take it anymore. With tears partially blinding me and my grief over the woman I'd been named for welling up inside in a bubble of pending sobs, I spun and marched out. And kept walking.

The morgue connected to the main hospital through a narrow hallway just past Dr. Aberstock's tiny office. I took the corridor, rounding the corner into the tall glass and stone entry of the hospital's main foyer. My feet kept moving, past the bank of elevators with their shining stainless-steel doors, the gift shop, the few people shuffling their way to the coffee shop for a snack while the bored attendant behind the counter looked like she was second-guessing her employment options.

I wasn't really seeing any of them, paying attention to my surroundings. Instead, I followed the colored lines on the floor, guiding me by coded stripes through the hospital halls, half expecting to be stopped at some point, only to be ignored as staff did their thing and let me do mine.

Maybe I looked like I'd just lost someone important to me and they didn't want to disturb me. Well, they would have been right. The fact I'd never met her? Didn't matter. It felt as if a part of me had been discovered in that metal box, desecrated by someone who'd attempted to hide what they'd done with fire and a burial no one would ever uncover.

But we had. I paused near the end of a hallway, looking up, realizing I was lost and had no idea what part of the hospital I'd ended up. Didn't matter. I leaned against the wall, staring without focus at the hand sanitation dispenser bolted to the gap between the doorjamb and the clear plastic slot for patient files. We'd found her, and her baby, thanks to Grandmother Iris. Had she discovered the resting place and carved the butterflies into the stone? But why? Why not bring the bodies out herself? Why not tell Dad when he became sheriff? Why the subterfuge and the trickery and the endless line of mysteries?

If my grandmother knew, why didn't she just say something?

That question's answer would have to wait.

Because, as I sighed and shook off the lethargy of my quiet wandering, I looked up at a hint of movement ahead, the dark hall further on home, it looked like, to offices.

And spotted the familiar young man in the suit exiting one of the doorways. He paused at the exit, turning back just as a second person emerged. In a flash of memory, I made a connection, and, knowing how important this could be because there were other mysteries than the death of Fiona Doyle, I tucked myself into the partially open door beside the hand sanitizer and listened.

"The next shipment better not be light on product," the first young man's voice carried faintly, enough in the quiet of the hall to reach me legibly. He'd cleaned up his accent a bit, no longer sounded like a smartass kid, but it was him, all right. Pitch Conway might have gotten a good haircut and a nice suit, but he was still the drug-dealing punk I remembered, under all that. Never mind he was Alicia's little brother.

"I'm doing my best." Why was I not surprised Pitch's partner was none other than Barry Clement? The doc's assistant sounded nervous. "We're moving too much product through this one location. Can't they slow down a little? I haven't come this far to get caught."

"You have your instructions." Pitch sounded almost pleasant in contrast. "See to it you deliver, Barry. You know what happens when the bosses aren't happy."

I didn't see Barry's reaction to that, but the threat was obvious. The tapping of footfalls drew near, the sound of another set retreating further down the hall telling me I only had to wait a moment and I'd be alone again.

Yeah. Wasn't big on waiting. Though, I didn't know if it was Barry or Pitch I grabbed and yanked into the dark office with me, the assistant or the drug dealer who yelped in surprise and staggered to do my bidding as I flicked on the light, prepared for anything.

Anything, that was, expect for the initial stunned expression on Alicia's brother's face that flipped almost instantly to a big grin.

"Fee Fleming!" He hugged me hard and tight. "Thank god. We have to talk."

Um. Okay. "Pitch," I said. Stopped as I tried to sort out my thoughts. But he was way ahead of me.

"I know, I know. Here." He tugged me toward the desk and the two chairs on the closest side. I sat with him while he ran both hands through that nice haircut, the harsh lighting showing the faint pockmarks of old acne scars on his cheeks, healthy living not quite able to completely erase the premature lines around his mouth and on his forehead. He was maybe twenty-three, but he looked a decade older and not in a good way. "I'm glad you found me. I was trying to figure out a way to get to you without anyone finding out. This is perfect." Pitch practically rubbed his hands together, a quick flicker of fear in his eyes.

"What are you doing here?" There, a coherent question. Go me.

He sat back, that playful kid he'd been long gone from the haunted expression now taking over his face. "I'm helping Barry Clement steal drugs and filter them through the hospital for the black market and I have been for months."

So, Dr. Aberstock had been right. "Blackstone."

Pitch grunted a laugh, but there was zero humor in it. "Leave it to you to connect the dots," he said. "Man, my bosses hate your guts, you know that?"

Did they now? Happy to oblige. "Why are you helping them?"

It hit me even as the words left my mouth, the answer to my question so obvious and glaring I almost hugged him.

"Alicia," he whispered. "I'm scared of them, of Blackstone. But I'm more terrified for my sister."

"What does she have to do with this?" Were the Pattersons part of the drug trafficking? I was already in a shaken state and found my brain wasn't taking on new information like it should, thoughts shunting from one to another before I could pull them together.

Pitch's phone buzzed and he checked it, paling out while I sat there and gaped at him. "I have to go." He stood abruptly, tucking the cell back into his interior pocket. He paused one moment at the door, hand shaking where it settled on the handle. "I'll be in touch, Fee," he said. "If anyone can help Alicia, it's you."

And then, he was gone, and I didn't even try to stop him.

Good thing, actually, because when I got a call of my own, my whole attention shifted one more time.

"Fee," Daisy said, sounding excited and a little shaken, "I need to see you right away."

"The annex?" I rose from the chair Pitch had sat me in, only to have Daisy change the plan.

"John and Lucy's," she said. "Bring your dad and Liz. Fee, it's important. I think we have a way to find out what's going on."

She didn't have to tell me twice.

CHAPTER THIRTY-ONE

Vivian was the last to arrive, hardly surprising, though she looked like she hadn't been to bed yet or never slept and likely didn't because maybe she was a perfect alien who'd taken a human body and rest was for the weak.

Punch-drunk? Likely. It *was* the middle of the night, on its way to the beginning of morning. And honestly, if we didn't want to attract suspicion, we should have waited for at least dawn to gather instead of piling into my parent's house with the lights blazing—the only one on the block—all our cars parked willy nilly despite the town parking ban because hey.

Middle of the night, yo.

Conspicuous or not, no one seemed like waiting

was something they intended to suggest. Even Dr. Aberstock had joined us, Jill in her pajama bottoms with one of Matt's oversized hoodies draped over her, hands tucked into the long cuffs. I tried to reach Pamela and Fleur but was forced to instead leave a message. I'd greeted Emile Reis when I'd entered, he and Daisy already sitting with Mom on the sofa, my mother acting like these kinds of gatherings happened all the time while offering each arriving guest tea, coffee and some cake.

Mom and cake. At least that much was right with the world.

I waited for Vivian to take a delicate seat next to my mother, waving off the offer of refreshments with a real smile, before I stood and usurped my bestie's attempt to run this little meeting of the minds.

"Before you tell us what you found out, Day," I said by way of apology, "Dad and Liz and I have our own discovery to share." I nodded to the doc who shrugged. He'd already given me permission to speculate, right?

It was Dad who told everyone about the discovery of the butterfly clip's missing gems, Liz who explained our sneaky intrusion on the Patterson's land, my father again taking his turn, uncovering the butterfly stone and the metal chest underneath. No one spoke or even twitched as Liz then finished off with our escape and subsequent opening of what had become a coffin.

But it was Dr. Aberstock who filled in the rest,

confirming a woman and an infant had both died of causes still to be determined, identities unknown and that some attempt had been made to burn their remains.

"I have no other information," he said. "Fee, I know you believe her to be Fiona Doyle and her rumored offspring with Teddy Patterson. But without proof, we shouldn't jump to conclusions just yet."

"Agreed," Dad said, gruff and a little angry.

"That out of the way," I said, "I had a little encounter of my own you should know about."

Dr. Aberstock wasn't surprised by Barry's involvement in the drug trafficking operation, but he seemed put off by mention of Pitch Conway.

"I had no idea," he said, tugging at his lower lip with his thumb and index finger, other arm crossed over his round belly. "We're then assuming he's telling the truth he's only working for Blackstone because of Alicia?"

The kid was a drug dealer when I met him. But he also set himself up to save his sister three years ago. "I have no other information," I said with a slow wink. "We shouldn't jump to conclusions just yet."

The doc laughed and poked at me with one finger. "Far too clever, dear girl."

I wasn't sure I agreed with him and sat on the armrest of the sofa next to Vivian while waving at Daisy. "Okay, Day," I said. "Hit us."

She inhaled, glanced at Emile who smiled and

nodded encouragement, before speaking. "I went digging into the company Dad's shares came from." She squeezed her boyfriend's hand a moment, beaming a trademark Daisy Bruce full wattage at him. It was pretty obvious from the way he stared back at her the two of them had zero doubts where they belonged. Almost made me cry. Day deserved that kind of happiness. "Vivian, your father left you shares in the same company."

The mayor nodded, her elegant upsweep shining in the living room light. "Pierre Noir," she said. "What of it? The company has no assets I could ascertain and certainly no value." Vivian glanced at me. "Wait, our fathers left us shares in the same company? Why?" Now we had her attention.

"Were you aware your father and Donald Bruce were friends?" Dad leaned forward, helping himself to the small pile of cookies beside the plate of cake. Mom was so engrossed she didn't even try to stop him, and I knew for a fact that was his fourth and she had him on a diet.

Vivian's frown and headshake were all the answer we needed.

"With Emile's help, I was able to trace the company back to a familiar corporation." She beamed that amazing smile at all of us, giggling suddenly. "I'm such a silly goose. Emile had to point it out to me. Vivian, do you know what Pierre Noir means in French?"

Gut. Punch. Even as Vivian gasped.

"Blackstone," she whispered.

Okay then. Well played, gentlemen.

"This is excellent news," Emile spoke, that faint French accent of his as yummy as ever. "It turns out that my beautiful flower and you, Vivian," he nodded to her, "are the primary owners of the founding base corporation—the first numbered listing in the chain that has become impossible to chase down from the outside—that formed the backbone of Blackstone." His slow smile lit his face, his pale eyes. "A door into that corporation if you like. Set up and controlled by no other than Donald Bruce and Ranier French."

"And left to their daughters in case something ever happened to them." Daisy hugged herself suddenly, that smile internal as much as it was external. Because no matter what happened from here, she knew the truth at last. Her father didn't just love her. He trusted her with a secret he knew she'd eventually be responsible for exposing.

Wow. I thought my dad played his love close and stoic.

"Gotcha." Liz looked positively delighted, in a satisfied and vengeful kind of crushing her enemies underfoot with a maniacal laugh kind of way. I'd have to remember that one. It suited her, but I could pull it off under the right circumstances.

Winning made me giddy.

"Any idea how they managed it?" Dad looked a bit awestruck, but at least he was still thinking. Me? My brain kind of shut off in gleeful anticipation of Liz and the FBI tearing Blackstone apart from the inside. While wishing Crew was here to be in on the massive news.

Emile shook his head. "For all we know, they were part of the original board of directors that set up Blackstone decades ago. Almost forty years, in fact." He squeezed Daisy's hand. "Sorry, my flower. This is your story to tell."

Sweet. She blushed, shook her head, free hand around his bicep as she gazed up into his eyes and my heart constricted because no way was Daisy Bruce not marrying this man and that meant...

I was going to lose my best friend, wasn't I?

Fiona Fleming. You stop that right now.

"You know what this means." Liz stood, began to pace. "If they structured it properly, there's an excellent chance that Daisy and Vivian are the primary owners of Blackstone." She laughed out loud. "Oh my god. My boss is going to lose her mind." She spun and tossed her hands. "They can't stop you from asking for any and all information you want about the entire corporation."

"Wait a sec," I said. "Does that mean if Blackstone is involved in criminal activity, Day and Viv are liable?" Well, that would suck.

But Liz was shaking her head. "I can promise you right now, no contest, both will have full immunity if they agree to hand over information in the apprehension and prosecution of illegal acts performed by employees of Blackstone."

That sounded official enough I bought it. And, from the nod Vivian gave, followed by Daisy's when Emile smiled at her, they thought the same.

"Agent Michaud," Vivian said, icy cool, "I believe I speak for both myself and my partner in Pierre Noir when I ask the FBI to conduct an investigation into whatever has been done to use our corporation and all subsidiaries for illegal gains."

"Well said," Daisy dimpled.

CHAPTER THIRTY-TWO

I hated to burst the bubble of happy, but there were so many questions left. Including a dead body we had, as yet, to tie to a murder suspect.

"Can Geoffrey's death be linked to any of this?" I glanced at Jill who looked lost on our company suddenly, like a little girl wearing daddy's clothes and pretending she fit in so she wouldn't be sent to bed and miss the grown-up stuff. Yup, got all of that from the near terrified expression she let loose before smothering it with her best attempt at pulling a Liz. Didn't make it to cool confident, but at least didn't look like she was going to throw up.

"I don't know," Jill said, voice soft and low. "I'm working on it, but my hands have been tied."

"Council," Vivian growled. "It's not your fault,

Jill. Clearly, there is Patterson interest behind keeping Geoffrey's killer a secret."

"Like that's going to stop you." I met Jill's eyes with mine, poured all of my confidence for her into my gaze, hoped she got the message. "Doc, any idea what killed him yet?"

Dr. Aberstock nodded. "In fact, I was preparing my final report for the sheriff when your earlier discovery distracted me." He scratched at his white beard a moment, as though pondering what he'd uncovered. "As I'd suspected, he died of suffocation. There was sufficient petechial hemorrhaging as well as elevated carbon dioxide in his blood and foam in his lungs, all indicators he was asphyxiated. I'm still waiting on forensics to identify the object used to block his airways, but whatever it was left no fibers, though I did note a trace scent similar to the gloves I use. It's possible whoever killed him did so by sealing his nose and mouth with some kind of latex."

"He'd have to have known his attacker pretty well to let them get that close to him," Dad said.

"Agreed," the doc said. "Bruising was minimal, however. I did find a small puncture mark on the back of his neck, but I have, as yet, to identify if a drug was injected into his system to incapacitate him." He shrugged. "Apologies, but the lab is a bit slow."

Well, we'd sent them evidence for not one but two murders, so fair enough. And we weren't the only town they serviced. Just the most prolifically deadly.

Maybe that needed to replace our cutest town in America tagline. I was sure Vivian wouldn't go for it, but hey, didn't hurt to try, right?

I needed sleep.

We wrapped up, everyone heading for their prospective homes. I cornered Dad, asked about Crew, but he shrugged it off, head down with Liz who was clearly eager to get started.

"Just call him, Fee," Dad said. "He'll want to know what's going on."

Argh. No help there. I made it home, feeling out of sorts that Petunia was still alone, waiting for me by the door. Several attempts to call Crew went to voicemail and the three texts I sent were ignored.

Either he was mad at me and not talking to me (probably), was busy or asleep or his phone was dead or off (possible), or he was DEAD IN A DITCH, murdered, kidnapped, being tortured and I'd never see him again and our last words to each other would be the fight we had (panic).

I didn't sleep well, called him again as soon as the sun came up. "Please," I said, knowing my voice was shaking, "Crew, just call me. I need to know you're all right."

When my phone rang a few minutes later, I dove for it, though I'm sure Dr. Aberstock didn't deserve the resigned sound of my voice when I answered a call that should have been from Crew.

"I've found something interesting," he said. "But I'd like to show you if you can come to the morgue?"

"What about Dad?" Grumpy? Me?

"He's rather busy with Liz, I'm afraid, and they have the sheriff on their team at the moment." Dr. Aberstock seemed suddenly hesitant. "I'm sorry, Fee. It can wait. Blackstone is more important."

Grumble, guilt. "I'll see you in twenty minutes." I hung up, looked down at Petunia who shifted her fat pug body to her other hip, licking her lips, big eyes staring up at me like she knew I was about to leave her. "Sorry, girl," I said. "Duty calls."

As I pulled into the parking lot, choosing a spot near the morgue door, far from the main area, I noted three men, all of whom I knew, in a heated conversation near the dumpster at the far end of the lot. They must have seen me pull in and, as I climbed out, they parted ways. But not before I noted the angry expression on Barry's face, the tight tension on Pitch's. And, to round out their trifecta of hmmm, Christopher Jenkins, looking sullen and ready to come apart at the seams, hustled past me to his own car.

He was the only one in range, so I went for it, following him, hearing the beep as he disarmed his alarm.

"I'm sorry about your father, Christopher." He stopped and spun to face me, rage replacing that sullen expression. That made me hesitate, but not for long. I was a Fleming, after all. "I'm sure they'll find whoever killed him."

"Even if it's your husband?" He fired that at me as if it were a weapon, but it had no impact. I already knew Crew hadn't killed Geoffrey. And neither had

Olivia. But now that I'd seen Christopher with Barry and Pitch... well, I was beginning to wonder if Geoffrey's death had something to do with Blackstone and the drug smuggling after all.

"Where were you when your father was killed?" Kind of a nasty thing to ask someone who's just lost their parent, but you know what? He was a jerk and made no attempt to act otherwise, so he could just suck it up.

"With my mother," he snapped back. "You can ask her."

"Because your mother would never alibi you to protect you," I said.

Christopher muttered something distinctly rude under his breath before jerking open the door of his car. "You have no idea what's going on in this town," he said. "And I'm not going to be the one to fill you in."

"No need," I said with the faintest smile, knowing I was baiting him and that it was likely a terrible idea but hating to let him go without a nice dig for him to linger over. "I'm far more informed than you think. And if you're involved in the smuggling, Christopher?" I grasped the door of his car and leaned in a little while he stared up at me, eyes wide. "Well. Your mother won't be able to save you from me." With that, knowing I was blowing smoke and not caring, I slammed the door and backed off.

It took him a bit to drive away, fumbling for keys and to start his car and by the time he did leave I was convinced he was either a) guilty as sin and ridiculously bad at hiding it or b) in way over his head. My guess was the latter.

Dr. Aberstock was waiting for me in the morgue when I arrived, Barry nowhere in sight. "Where's your assistant? I just saw him come in."

The doc shook his head, frowning. "Barry has the day off."

Okay then. "What did you find?"

I was expecting him to whip out a file on Geoffrey or even pull the body out of the cooler. Instead, he handed me a piece of paper. Blackstone stationary. With Alicia's name at the top of it.

I gaped at it while he shook his head.

"I'm sorry," he said, "but it looks like our young friend is in a bit of trouble."

Tell me about it. The memo went into detail, connecting Alicia, blaming her, for the drug misappropriations, using White Valley Lodge as a drop-off point. "This is a setup document. Something they can hand to the police when they come knocking." A scapegoat plan.

"I found it at the bottom of Barry's trashcan," he said. "I'm not above snooping." He gestured at the small station near the door. "But that's all I found, I'm afraid."

Wait. "His desk is cleared out?"

The doc nodded. "He hasn't been to work in days."

Interesting.

I thanked Dr. Aberstock for the document, chest

tight as I sat in my car, trying to decide what to do with it. If I handed it over to Jill or Liz, they would have to enter it into evidence. But if I didn't, I couldn't express to them my belief this was a ploy to control Jared or Alicia or even Pitch. Whatever the case, it was like having a hot potato in my lap. I kept lifting it, reading it, setting it down, feeling the discomfort of it in my presence as though it burned me every time I let it go.

My phone rang, making me jump. Again, not Crew, though the person calling was a welcome contact.

"Tell me everything," Pamela said, gruff and deep.

I did. And, as I did, I heard Fleur, too, whispering a question, that uncomfortable echo of being on speakerphone making me nervous.

"You're welcome," Pamela said when I was done. "I'm glad that information helped. Fee, as for the bodies…" she trailed off. "Don't be so sure you know who that woman might have been."

"What do you mean?"

"Just keep an open mind." Pamela hesitated, Fleur whispering again. "We have to go. I'll drop in to see you this afternoon. I might be able to shed some light on just who the dead woman was and who killed her."

She hung up before I could stop her. And that was an unsatisfying call.

The next one came on its heels, another welcome voice.

"Hey, Fee." Denver sounded tired, crunching something between his teeth as he spoke. Okay, a welcome voice until he decided to eat while he talked to me. "I looked over the footage at the time you mentioned. I only saw one person, but it's kind of hard to make out who it is. I'm sending you a screenshot. Hope it helps."

And then he, too, hung up and I almost screamed in frustration at the people around me and their terrible phone manners.

Until the image uploaded, and I got a good look at the person in question and realized I knew who the murderer was.

CHAPTER THIRTY-THREE

"Going somewhere?" I didn't wait for Barry Clement to invite me in, pushing my way into his small apartment the moment he answered the door, taking in the luggage in his tiny living room, his unsettled state. He had to have been unsettled to not check to see who was knocking.

He scowled, backing away, shaking his head. "I don't have to answer your questions," he said.

"Perhaps," Jill said, sauntering in behind me, "but you would be advised to answer mine, Mr. Clement."

Surprised? You shouldn't be. Of course, I brought Jill with me. No way I was going to give Crew any reason to be angry with me again, especially not over chasing down a murderer alone. I might have been headstrong and a busybody, but I was learning.

Honestly, it was kind of nice to feel safe. She and I had done this before, back in December, arresting Ian Rudge for murder. Thea Isaac's death had led to Jill being made sheriff, so I'd had an ulterior motive to bring her along. This time, though? All about appeasing my worrywart husband.

Now, if only I could stop worrying about him and his continuing silence, we'd be all set.

Barry's dark expression turned to sudden fear, his whole body convulsing in a single surge of denial. He stumbled back, tripping against his big suitcase, almost falling and catching himself in the nick by the arm of the sofa. I'd expected him to react badly to our appearance, but the sheer terror on his face, the tears welling in his eyes, the way his hands shook as he held them out in front of him as though to ward us off, all powerful indicators I'd underestimated the hold Blackstone had over him.

"I'm in over my head." He choked on a sob. "Have been since day one, don't you see that?" Barry's hand swept over his mouth, the back of his neck, while Jill closed the distance between them, not so subtly placing herself between me and the shaking coroner's assistant. Barry didn't seem to notice or care, sagging into the cushions of his couch, head in his hands, still shaking. "Why did I come to this miserable little town?"

"Why don't you tell us?" She, at least, was able to muster empathy, though whether manufactured for the moment or genuine I had no idea. Nor did I care.

I did, though, give her space to ask her questions, since he looked up in response to her tone, his desperate and consuming fear easing enough he could answer.

And answer he did. "Blackstone," he said, a near wail. "They were paying my scholarship, told me if I didn't take the job and a leave from school, they'd..." he swallowed hard. "They'd ruin me."

More blackmail. "How?" Jill sat next to him, shaking her head at me when I tried to approach. Look at me obeying and listening and everything. I held my ground while Barry spoke to Jill, ignoring me.

"I have a record," he said. "Blackstone's lawyers had it expunged. At least, that's what they told me when they recruited me."

"Who specifically, Barry?" Jill had her phone out, but he laughed a harsh denial.

"I have no idea," he snapped at her, clearly at his breaking point, one knee bouncing violently, hands clenching at the fabric of his jeans like he was trying to tear off his own skin. "It doesn't matter. A pair of their lawyers showed up in my dorm one night." I couldn't help but wonder if one of them was my cheating snake of an ex, Ryan Richards. "Told me they knew about my drug addiction." He hesitated, glanced at me. "I lied on my entrance paper to get into medical school. If the college found out, I'd have been expelled." He returned his attention to Jill, desperate now. For what, understanding? Compassion? Wasn't getting any from me, but the sheriff was doing a bang-up acting job. That was if Jill was acting. She had a bigger capacity for kindness than I did. "They said they'd dealt with my record and I owed them. Showed me paperwork that they could use against me if I didn't do what they wanted." Beads of sweat joined forces and trickled down his temple, shaking hands wiping it away only to tug at denim again. "I saw no harm in what they asked me for. Working as a coroner's assistant was a great opportunity."

"Until they started asking for more than just you filling a position," Jill said.

Barry jerked like he'd been dealt a blow. "Small things at first," he whispered, going suddenly still, as though the adrenaline that drove his trembling shut off like a faucet tap. "Mislaying paperwork from the lab. Delaying reporting findings to Dr. Aberstock." He seemed truly guilty about the latter. "Then, they asked me to find a way to start funneling prescriptions through the hospital."

"How long, Barry?" Jill's tone hadn't changed. Maybe she was feeling sorry for him.

He shrugged, collapsed a little. "Two years."

Wow. The doc had only caught on nine or so months ago. Barry had been doing a hell of a job. Too bad he didn't learn to apply that kind of dedication to being a good person.

"And your association with Pitch Conway?" I should have stayed out of it, but I couldn't help myself.

Barry's rage was sudden and brilliant and, before

Jill could react, he was on his feet and launching himself at me, screaming, "This is all your fault, Fiona Fleming!"

I'd faced down murderers with criminal intent before, and while I'd come out of such interactions in one piece, for the most part, I'd typically taken a solid hit or two prior to either being rescued or managing to fight off my foe. Thing was, I'd never really been prepared for this sort of conflict. I'd only started taking self-defense lessons from Jill in earnest about a year ago, boxing, kettlebells, even some judo. As a result, I was much stronger than I'd ever been, and tied to my every-other-day runs with Crew, I was actually in the best shape of my life.

Barry, on the other hand? Barely had a couple of inches on me, was clearly neglecting his physical health if his lack of strength was any indication and certainly wasn't a match for the woman I'd become.

I didn't think because I'd been trained not to. The moment he came within striking distance, my right leg rose, hands fisting loosely in front of me, heel thudding with solid and audible impact into Barry's gut, just below the ribcage, dead center. I watched him crumple to the ground, howling in agony, stepping back, my own rush of adrenaline reaching my system a few seconds after it was needed.

Jill had him cuffed and back on the sofa a minute later while he panted and sobbed, and I did my best not to let the rush of hormonal excitement make me grin too broadly at my success. The sheriff nodded, her own eyes sparkling, and I knew she was proud of me even as she returned her attention to Barry.

All fight had gone out of him, all attempt to hide. He looked like a man defeated long ago and only now admitting it to himself. How long had he borne those dark circles under his eyes, the sallow complexion of one not quite completely healthy, the thinning hair, the sunken cheeks under sharp bones? Even his lips, dry and patchy, added to that impression I had he'd begun to rot from the inside out. Was he ill? Or was it just the darkness he carried inside him getting the best of him?

"Barry," Jill said, phone recording from its spot on her knee, "why did you kill Geoffrey Jenkins?"

Not even a flicker of denial crossed his face. "He called me to his office," he said, monotone of a broken man almost—almost!—arousing my pity at last. "Told me I had to up the transfers." His lower lip trembled. "That was the first time I realized he wasn't just part of it. He was running it." Barry slumped once more, that faint effort at feeling sorry for himself clearly draining him. "He said they were almost done with that part of the business and my services would no longer be needed here in Reading. I thought that meant they'd let me go back to school." Okay, there was a genuine sob. "But no, no. He said they wanted me to set up in a new hospital, a different part of the country." Now he met Jill's eyes, panic on his flaccid face. "All I could see was my life winding out in front of me, an endless line of hospitals, of thefts, of being the scapegoat for Blackstone. It could only end two ways." He finally turned to me, blank stare unnerving. "Either I'd end up in prison, or dead. So, I decided to do something about it."

"You killed him," Jill said.

Barry nodded. "I left, went back to the morgue. Filled a syringe with ketamine. Fast-acting, he wouldn't feel a thing. And I went back to town hall. He didn't suspect me, was as arrogant as ever. I knew about the balcony, the catwalk, the stairs. He'd made me leave that way twice before when he didn't want it known I'd been with him." His hand twitched in his lap as if reliving the deed. "I walked around behind him while he went on and on about how I owed Blackstone for saving me from being expelled." Barry giggled then, a lifeless sound of exhaustion and a soul that had truly given up. "I stabbed him in the neck, held him the minute or so it took for him to pass out, then held one of the gloves I'd put on over his mouth and nose and waited for him to die."

Dear. God.

Jill swallowed, looking ill but forging on. "Barry, you said Geoffrey was running the drug operation."

He jerked a little, refocusing on her, exiting the murder scene in a twitch. "You're all fools, you know," he said without emotion. "So much you don't know. So many things tied together in a ball of string you've been chasing and chasing even though the truth is right there." Barry jabbed a finger at me, the chain of the cuffs rattling. "In front of you." Again that jab, at Jill this time. "Blackstone doesn't work for the Pattersons or vice versa. The Pattersons *are*

Blackstone."

I didn't respond. He thought he knew more than us, maybe was shocked to discover I wasn't surprised. "We know," I said. "We're already inside, Barry. And we're taking them down." Let him chew on that.

He actually looked hopeful a moment, turned to Jill who nodded, grim and determined. But his expression flat-lined again quickly as though hope had no place in the heart of a man like Barry Clement.

"They'll kill me," he said. "Kill all of us."

"You said there are more connections we haven't made." I prodded for details. But Barry had finally had it, I guess because he fell silent and refused to say another word.

Aside, that was, from, "I want a lawyer."

Okay then.

CHAPTER THIRTY-FOUR

Home was an empty place without Crew, never mind Petunia's relocation to the annex so I could pace and think without stepping on her as she followed my every step with her relentless pug logic. If she stayed on my heels, I couldn't leave her behind.

I'd fired off a series of long texts to my absent husband, filling him in on everything we'd learned, before shooting one to Liz.

I'm worried. He's not answering.

She messaged me back immediately. *Me too. I'm already on it.*

Should I have been more relieved that she believed me or terrified she was worried, too?

Where's Darius? That was from Malcolm, the first

I'd heard from him in days.

Excellent question, I sent back.

Silence for a moment while renewed concern for my bodyguard kick-started guilt I'd forgotten to worry about him, too.

Meet us at the lake house.

Fifteen minutes later I was hugging Siobhan Doyle, then Malcolm Murray himself, guided into their gorgeous home overlooking Cutter Lake. I couldn't help but stare out into the water, where only days ago I'd found yet another dead body   well, it found me, but there you go—while my hopes for the Reading hoard were dashed.

"We've been in Ireland," Siobhan said, taking my hand and guiding me to sit. "Closing my affairs so I can relocate to Reading permanently." She glanced at her husband, face pinched. "Darius would never leave you, dearie. What happened?"

I told them both everything, from the treasure hunt, the murder of Gregg Brown, the subsequent death of Geoffrey Jenkins. That all roads seemed to lead to Blackstone and the Pattersons. And hesitated in the last moment, before informing them as gently as I could about the contents of the box we'd discovered on the mountain.

"Butterflies were Fiona's favorite," Siobhan said, without emotion. "She said she shared that love with Iris, spoke so kindly and lovingly of your grandmother." And then she cried, both hands over her face, Malcolm gently cradling her against him.

He should have looked sad. Instead, for some

reason, he seemed, well. Rather guilty. And I made a weird connection only my Fleming brain could leap to.

"Malcolm," I said, "is your crime family connected to Blackstone?"

"Yes," he said. "Corporate takeover of organized crime." He barked a laugh, Irish accent thickening as he lost control of his emotions. "Imagine that, lass. Businessmen more corrupt than admitted criminals. Poetic, somehow."

Yikes. "That means—"

He nodded. "With the information you've shared, that means the Pattersons own my family." Malcolm inhaled slowly, exhaled. "They own me, dear Fee."

He may have sounded rather calm saying it, but I could see the rage in his eyes, see the way his jaw jumped, his rigid body contained and coiling for action. I'd always been a little scared of Malcolm, at least until I discovered he was my godfather. It was then I knew he'd do anything for me, had likely stepped in when I didn't know he was protecting me, before openly doing so by assigning me his favorite bodyguard. That fear of him? It was back. Because there was murder in his eyes.

Siobhan had stopped crying, reaching out to pat his cheek. Her touch caught him, held him, her gaze diffusing him somewhat, though when she turned to look at me, her lined skin still damp with her tears, she was somehow even scarier than her true love.

"Tell us what you want us to do." She didn't seem like the type to take orders, but Malcolm nodded with her while I exhaled slowly in relief they weren't going to run off and get themselves killed trying to end the Patterson family. Because organized crime and Hollywood expectations and all that.

"We're waiting on Liz to tear open Blackstone," I said. "In the meantime, I need you to keep business as usual." They both looked rebellious but finally relented. "I'm so sorry. I wish I had better news."

"I was so sure my darling girl was alive." Siobhan trembled but seemed on her way to recovery. I worried since she'd suffered a massive stroke not so long ago, the trauma of finding out Fiona was dead might trigger another. Wait, was that even possible? Whatever, I didn't want to risk it.

Malcolm seemed suddenly concerned with her health as well, patting her hand, kissing her cheek. "We'll go see the doc, my love," he said. "See our wee one and her babe for ourselves."

Siobhan touched his cheek with shaking fingers, and I suddenly knew I was no longer in the room for either of them. "Oh, my dear," she whispered back. "Can we?"

That was my signal to leave. So, I did, driving home with my heart in my throat, multi-layered emotions threatening to level me. Tears flowed and I went hunting for a tissue, checking everywhere. When I flipped down the driver's visor on the off chance, a piece of paper fluttered free and landed in my lap.

I gaped down at it, had to slam on the brakes to keep from hitting the back of the white car in front of me. Pulled over to the side of the road and examined the last piece of the map with shaking fingers as I flipped it over.

And read the small, yellow sticky note attached to the underside.

Doing my best to be honest, Miss F, like you want. But this belongs to you. D.

I gently peeled the note from the map piece and kissed it. Darius. He'd stolen it from Rosebert for me, clearly. Snuck it into my car for me to find. And, in that moment, I realized it wasn't the butterfly pin Robert had confronted me about.

It was the missing piece of the map.

So, when had Darius liberated it from my cousin? Before he vanished, obviously.

Oh my god. Did the Pattersons find out? Was Darius's the next body I was going to find?

That terror was overwritten by a single word inked into the back of the piece in bold, block letters. Familiar letters written, if I could prove it or not, with a heavy, black fountain pen that had been destroyed in the fire when Petunia's burned, the same pen Grandmother Iris cherished for as long as I could remember.

SISTERHOOD.

That word changed my direction and my focus and reminded me there was one person left in town who would be willing—if not able, depending on her illness—to tell me just what Grandmother Iris had been up to. Because it was clear this was never about the hoard. That was simply a disguise, a means to catch and hold my interest, to keep me searching and hunting for clues and truth. This was a message from my grandmother about the Pattersons.

Sisterhood. I knew exactly who she was referring to. And, as I pulled into the circular driveway of the French mansion after a brief but necessary detour home, I ran their names through my mind. Iris Fleming. Marie Patterson. Doreen Douglas. Peggy Munroe, if not by consensus. And Martha French.

The old lady had tried to tell me before, but her dementia and interruptions prevented it. This time? I wasn't taking Vivian's no for an answer.

CHAPTER THIRTY-FIVE

It wasn't Vivian I had to contend with when the maid opened the front door to greet me. Instead, it was the hurried and tactical clickity-clack approach of Rachelle. The mayor's previously estranged mother had made an appearance in Reading long after she'd decided living in Montpelier or wherever it was she'd taken her share of Ranier's fortune, wasn't suiting her needs any longer. Perhaps because she missed her daughter, though I doubted very much it was her loving relationship with Vivian that had brought her home. If anything, the tall woman, aging not nearly as well as her child though with the same face, weathered by deep-seated narcissism and with that fraudulent smile she clearly assumed was working on everyone around her tugging at her overly augmented lips, was here to make Vivian's life miserable.

"Why, Fiona, dear," Rachelle gushed at me, a bit out of breath from hurrying to find out who was at the door. And they called me a busybody. "How lovely to see you." Her smile instantly flashed to a pout of concern so dissembling I almost laughed in her face at the absurdity of it. "What a dreadful time you've had of things in the last little while." She grasped my hand and practically jerked me into the white marble foyer, the maid just having enough time to dodge before my entry ran the girl over. "However are you holding up, you poor thing. Just horrific." And in those wide eyes, those manicured fingertips pressed to her chest, in that expectant look as she waited with—I kid you *not*—bated breath for my answer, I knew it wasn't concern driving Rachelle's questions, but morbid curiosity.

I considered my response options, torn between gory details in an attempt to yuck her into retreat (which, I discarded, knowing she would just ask for more), or a blasé brushoff that might backfire into her asking me to leave.

Fortunately, I didn't have to make the choice between the two. Clara French's appearance at the double doors to the sitting room caught Rachelle's attention, the sudden and sullen drop of her expression more than enough of a distraction to give me the opening I needed.

"Clara," I said, a bit too enthusiastic, but the intensity of the energy in the room, the heightened fakery making me as jittery as three cups of espresso.

"How nice to see you."

The old auntie must have realized I was looking for rescue, because she swiftly joined us, one hand on Rachelle's arm. "Fiona, dear," her blue eyes crinkled around the corners. "You're looking for Vivian? She's upstairs, but she can join you presently."

Rachelle's lips were already parting, clear offer to join our conversation pending. But Clara was faster, tugging on the other woman with firm conviction and a long-suffering smile.

"We should leave the girls to their catch-up, Rachelle," she said. "Come along. You can help me make Martha her tea."

Rachelle's enthusiasm died instantly at the same moment she pulled her elbow free of Clara's grasp. Her blonde hair tossed as she spun, high heels tapping on the stone floor. "I'd rather die," she shot over her shoulder before disappearing deeper into the house.

Clara let her go, smile never wavering, though the iron glint in her eyes spoke a million curses. "It is lovely to see you, Fee," she said, linking arms with me. I joined her on the walk to the sitting room. "Apologies for Rachelle. Her visit has been... trying. But we're establishing our pecking order." Clara nodded once, soft giggle escaping, and I couldn't help but laugh with her.

She might have looked the part of the sweet old auntie, but I would never again doubt the rod of pure steel that clearly ran through her middle.

Martha didn't move when I joined her, Vivian's

grandmother huddled low in her armchair, heavy drapes drawn, the beautifully crocheted blanket over her knees draped to the floor around her. She'd lost volume since I'd seen her last, as though her entire body had begun to retreat into itself. Her once thick, white curls seemed thin, pale pink scalp showing where the roller lines hadn't quite been brushed out. Paper-like skin sagged from her cheeks and jowls, tugging at the corners of her closed eyes, thin blue veins a visible network under the powdery white flesh.

I almost left right then and there. She'd lost that bit of robustness I remembered from our first meeting. I hadn't noticed she'd been failing so very badly when I saw her in December. Maybe she'd taken a turn in the past six months or so. I knew she'd been suffering from dementia for many years, but it seemed like her body was finally going the way of her failing mind.

Soft footfalls interrupted, Vivian's high-heeled strides muffled in the thick carpet of the big room, towering ceiling devouring the majority of the sound. She joined me without a word, looking down at her sleeping grandmother with pinched concern I once would have mistaken for disdain.

I'd learned a lot about my old friend turned enemy turned friend again in the last six months. All of which I liked and, to my guilt and regret, wished I'd known a long time ago.

"You wanted to see me." Not a question.

But I shook my head at the beautiful blonde next

to me, pointed at Martha as I sank into the seat next to her while holding out the stolen map piece. Vivian accepted it, eyes widening, gaze snapping to me a moment after she read the single word on the back of the page.

"I have to talk to her, Viv," I said.

She looked like she wanted to reject the idea, but it was Clara who touched her cheek and nodded.

"She's been talking about Iris ever since she saw Fee again." Vivian's aunt smiled at me. "Says she has secrets she can share only with her sister."

I waited for the mayor to acquiesce and, when she did, even held off as Clara sat next to her mother-in-law and gently touched her shoulder.

"Mum," she said, that faint British accent of hers adding a lilt to her voice. "Fiona is here to see you."

Martha stirred instantly, pale eyes opening, watery around the edges, lips smacking a moment as she struggled to pull herself more upright. Clara instantly helped, Vivian adjusting the blanket as it slipped from the movement, hands swift and gentle. Martha ignored them both, her eyes locking on me and, as they did, she beamed the kind of smile that reached inside me and warmed my weary heart.

"Iris," she said, clapping her hands with great enthusiasm before lunging forward to grasp mine. She might have looked frail, but there was nothing wrong with her grip. "You're here. Finally. Is it done?" She didn't wait for me to answer, sitting back, hands clasping in her lap, eyes twinkling. "It took so much to keep Peggy's snooping out of things," she said, one index finger tapping the end of her own nose as she laughed. "But you were right to trust me. I took care of her. She knows nothing of what's really going on."

Which meant Martha did. I almost stopped breathing. "That's perfect," I said. "Thank you, Martha."

She patted my hand, sighed, sorrow replacing her joy. "I just wish there had been another way. Surely, we could have gone to John. That boy of yours, he's far cleverer than you think. But, I know," she waved off my protest despite the fact I didn't try, talking to Grandmother Iris, an old conversation, clearly, one I was now privy to. How remarkable. "You're worried about him. And from what we've learned, you have reason to be. I know why you didn't want to share what I showed you, so dreadful." Martha shivered. "Are the butterflies still there, where the dear ones lie?"

Dear heavens. So, it was Martha who found the bodies? And told Grandmother Iris?

"Yes," I said, choking on the truth.

"You said not to tell," she whispered. "Said it was too dangerous to follow Marie. But I couldn't help it, you see. I needed to know if you were right, if she was up to no good. I didn't mean to find them. But I did. And now we know." She snuffled. "We never really knew her, did we, Iris?"

What a weight to carry with her all these years. "I suppose not."

"Still, I don't know what good this subterfuge will

do." Martha seemed vexed suddenly, impatient, batting at me with both hands. "Aren't they enough evidence?" Her eyes suddenly flooded with tears, and she looked down, the moisture trickling slowly through the folds in her flesh like running a maze to escape. "Can't we just lay them to rest?"

Crap. How did I answer that and get more information from her? "We will," I said at last. "You're sure Peggy's out of it?" Maybe if I rebooted the conversation, I could get more out of her.

Martha snorted. "She's always been the outsider. I still blame Doreen for that mistake, bringing her anywhere near the Sisterhood." She said it like it needed a capital letter to give it weight. "Imagine her challenging Marie for leadership." Her eyes glistened all over again. "Though you two had your own battles for that role, didn't you, dear Iris? I think we all knew who our real leader was, Marie's money or not." She was crying again. "Why did this have to happen? If only we could prove it." Martha wiped at her cheeks, brushing off Clara's attempt to hand her a tissue. "But you're right, Iris, of course. We have laid the groundwork to the truth and, one day, when that clever son of yours finds what you've left, he'll bring her down."

"Who?" Oh, why did I open my mouth? I already knew who.

Martha started at the sound of my voice, blinking, as though torn out of the past and thrown unhappily and unsteadily into the present. She stared at me a long moment before a petulant child appeared in her eyes, pulling at the corners of her mouth. Martha's withered hands picked at the weave of the crocheted blanket suddenly, heels thudding in protest against the base of the chair.

"Nononononononono!" She twisted away from me, angry, furious even, for no apparent reason. Clara instantly tried to soothe her, touching her shoulder, but Martha batted her away. "I SAID NO!"

I sat back in my seat, hand sliding into my pocket for the other items I'd brought with me, knowing it was likely a lost cause but hoping I might get through to her. "Martha," I said, voice firm, trying to channel Grandmother Iris. "Do you remember these?" I held out my hand, the four butterflies in my palm.

She turned to look and froze. So sad and yet incredible to watch her morph once more, from the terrified and lost old woman dying of a dreadful disease to the woman she used to be, years ago. She beamed at me again, hand reaching out in tentative question, and I nodded. Martha took one of the butterflies and clipped it in her hair.

"Thank you for giving it back to me," she said. "I hated to lose it, Iris."

"You're welcome," I said and took a chance. "We don't need it anymore, so you can keep it. Just the doubloon." And held my breath, hoping.

Martha's nose wrinkled, shoulders hitching upward in her sudden glee while she patted at the pin in her hair over and over again. "Let them chase a treasure that never existed," she giggled. Instantly her entire being shifted once more and she grabbed for me, nails digging into my wrist as her intense and focused attention actually freaked me out a bit. "As long as it makes them dig, it served its purpose."

Bingo. "Exactly," I said, brain whirling as I struggled for another way to ask her who she was talking about. Dad? Me? Her son, now long dead? But as I did, as I hesitated, I knew I was too late. She was fading again, drifting back to the disease. I could see it devouring her, taking her over, and, less than thirty seconds later, Martha sank deep into her chair and began to snore.

Vivian drew me up and away from her grandmother, Clara joining us, the mayor's crossed arms and tight expression worrying. Did she blame me for pushing Martha too hard? But no, she seemed less upset and more intent when she spoke at last.

"Has she said anything to you about any of this, Auntie?" Vivian's voice shook just a little, clear indication she was as emotionally tied into this as I was, at least on the inside if able to hide it on the outside.

Clara shook her head, glancing over her shoulder at the snoring old woman. "She would never speak of it, only mentioned Iris and the Sisterhood." She sighed. "I'm sorry, Viv, dear. Fee. I wish I could help. Maybe if she rests a bit, she might be able to tell you more."

Fair enough. I let Vivian escort me out, not much spoken between us. Because there wasn't much to say, outside of what we already knew and speculation. And I wasn't in the mood to make educated guesses right now.

Instead, I drove home, the three remaining butterflies in my pocket. I might regret leaving one behind with Martha, but, on the other hand, at least I knew where to get my hands on it if I needed it and, besides, if it brought her some joy, I felt I owed it to her.

Grandmother Iris. What the hell did you drag me into?

I was almost home when my phone rang. I answered it despite not recognizing the number, though I did vaguely the male voice on the other end when I said hello.

"Miss Fleming. Have you seen Mr. Murray or Ms. Doyle?" One of Malcolm's boys. Another twinge of guilt over losing Darius and now this.

"Aren't you supposed to keep track of them?" I didn't mean to be facetious, but seriously. Wasn't that their job?

"Yes, ma'am." He sounded angry. "But they've both gone missing."

Wait, what? "Since when?"

"Since half an hour ago." Okay, that was panic in his tone now even though I almost eye-rolled. He was freaking out over a half-hour? For all I knew, they'd snuck off for some private time. After all, they'd just found out their daughter was dead for real.

"I just saw them at the lake house," I said. "But that was about an hour ago." Wasn't it? How long had I been at Vivian's? "I'm sorry, I wish I could tell you more." Hesitated, worry waking as I thought of Darius, Crew's silence, and had a sick, sinking feeling take me over. "Call me when you find them."

I hung up, pulled in my driveway. Called Crew. Voicemail. And received a text that got my attention.

Had an epiphany, Vivian sent. *Need to see you. Patterson dock, twenty minutes. Be careful.*

Pretty telling I didn't even hesitate. B&E, anyone?

CHAPTER THIRTY-SIX

I drove this time, instead of taking a boat, parking out of view of the main gate, pulling off near the edge of the Patterson side of the mountain. I was going to be longer than twenty minutes, the hike in to the dock at least that from where I did little to hide my car's presence. Maybe I'd reached the point I didn't care anymore what Marie and her family thought. Getting caught might have been refreshing. But I do know that walk to the fence, the tree-climb to get me over (had experience with this kind of thing, didn't I?) and subsequent walk around the edge of the manicured forest leading to the lakeshore wasn't done in stealth. If anything, I was being deliberately noisy.

Come at me, bro. I was so done.

The fact I made it to the dock without incident actually made me rather sullen and sent my mood plummeting. Had I been looking forward to a confrontation with a group of black-clad men carrying giant guns and wearing mirrored sunglasses to hide the snake-like look of their eyes? You betcha. Instead, as I tromped my way onto the wooden planks, the sky overhead heavy with clouds as another storm brewed, waves rising to choppy threat past the shallower shorefront, I realized why I was so worked up.

Far too familiar, this weather even, standing here on this dock, looking out over the water. I stayed on the top level, avoiding the steps that led down to the water's edge, not sure I was ready for that trip down memory lane. I hugged myself, chilled suddenly by the rising wind, the spate of rain that fell on me in a hurried warning more was to come, and I'd been a fool to make this journey.

I hadn't even wondered why Vivian wanted me to meet her here, hadn't asked. There was no sight of her and the longer I stood there, the more uncomfortable I became, fighting off the phantom image of a young man's hand disappearing slowly under the water in front of me.

Not real. Hadn't been for a very long time. Didn't change the fact the longer I waited, the more I wished I hadn't come at all. In fact, I almost left five minutes in, anger tight in my chest, anger at Vivian for stirring all of this up for me again and not even having the courtesy of showing up. I did a great job of reliving it myself, thanks, without being dragged out to the real deal all over again.

As I spun on my heel to leave, ready to give Vivian a piece of my mind when I saw her again, a low moan reached me, caught my attention, my breath. I stopped, all fury forgotten, Victor's loss, everything, at that sound. There it was again as if someone was injured. Maybe if I'd been somewhere else, wasn't so deep in the memory of what happened all those years ago, maybe if it hadn't been a rainy, gray day like the last one Victor saw, I might have acted more rationally. Instead, not thinking, only reacting, I hurried to the steps and down to the main dock and froze.

At the sight of Vivian French, handcuffed and semi-conscious, lying tucked against the stair risers, hidden from sight until I joined her below.

It took me a second to realize it hadn't been she who'd summoned me here, had it? Far too long, held in shock and stupor that gripped me like the hand of death itself, pinned to the wooden boards by time and memory and understanding I could do nothing about.

Footfalls behind me freed me, but not in time. Though I did have just enough to recognize him before his gun rose and fell, striking me in the temple, the blow making me see stars and darkness. But not before I made out the bitter desperation on Robert's face.

And enough guilt to eat a man alive.

Hard not to groan as pain woke me, impossible not to shed a few tears from the agony in my head. Hands grasped me, gently held me down when I tried to rise. Something soft beneath me, the scent of whoever supported me so familiar, so dear, I whispered his name without opening my eyes to be sure I was right.

"Crew."

His lips brushed mine and I did look then, that darling face above me, a trail of blood running from his right eyebrow to his chin. So much blood, enough to make me gasp and cry all over again from the pain, in my head and my heart, that someone did this to him.

I looked again, the world wavering around me. Why was the ceiling so far away? Wait, I was outside, in the rain, at the dock. What was I doing on what felt like a sofa, in, I realized, a giant and rather palatial—if old-fashioned in décor—room that reminded me enough of Vivian's house I almost guessed we'd been taken there?

Had Crew found me, fought off Robert, rescued Viv and me? But no, as I turned my head, I realized I didn't know this place, bigger even than Vivian's sitting room. And that, to my surprise, there were more people I knew and loved gathered here.

Where was here?

"Sit her up." Was that Vivian's voice? Her hands,

gentle like they had been with her grandmother, tidy and quick, tucking a pillow behind my head as Crew slowly lifted me to an upright position, the aching increasing a moment, dizziness washing over me while I gasped for breath. "Fee." Vivian looked pale while she entered my sphere of vision, darkness closing in around the edges while I panted past the pain. I'd suffered a concussion a few years ago. This felt far too familiar. "Are you okay?"

I nodded, though I wanted to shake my head in denial, then wished I hadn't moved at all. "Where?" I licked my lips, forced my eyelids to part, squinting at Crew, at my parents hovering behind him, Mom terrified, Dad grim, then to Malcolm and Siobhan on the sofa across from us. I blinked, looked to my right, Daisy tucked in next to Vivian, all of my favorite people. Minus Dr. Aberstock, apparently.

"Patterson mansion," Crew said, soft and low. "I've been here since we…" he didn't mention our fight, but I knew what he meant, shaking his head before he licked his lips. "They jumped me when I was heading out of town. Turned out it wasn't a client who called after all."

Who was he talking about? Took another minute to realize we weren't alone in the room, that several of those aforementioned black-clad and mirror-glassed guards were standing statue-like at the two doors.

I sat forward a bit, the pain ebbing and my wits returning, but knowing I was far from okay. Robert. I whispered his name, must have because Vivian grasped my hand, squeezed it. When I glanced at her, she winced, touched the back of her neck, nodded.

"Me too," she said.

The bastard. I'd long joked about committing murder, but this time?

This time, if I got the chance, I was going to kill him and screw the consequences.

"Why are we here?" I touched Crew's cheek where the crusted blood had congealed. He cupped my hand against his face. "What's going on?"

"We don't know," Dad said, gruff voice angry. "They won't tell us anything." He had a deep bruise on his left cheek, had clearly been struck, too. Mom didn't look harmed, at least, or Daisy from what I could tell, and Malcolm and Siobhan were calm and collected enough.

"They can't just keep us here." Right? There were laws and things. Clearly, I was still struggling with reality. "Liz?"

"No sign of her," Crew said, faint relief in his voice. So maybe we had a chance after all.

I almost said as much, except one of the doors opened quietly and we all shifted our attention to it immediately. The woman who entered nodded to the guard who stepped back instantly, giving way to her. Tall, slender, iron-gray hair in a perfect coif, face lined, heavy with makeup. She kept her distance yet, hands folding in front of her pale blue dress.

"Marie," I said. I knew this woman. I'd caught a glimpse of her from behind, while she exited the barn the day of Alicia and Jared's wedding. But, as I got a better look, I realized it couldn't be Marie Patterson. Too young. More my parent's age, this woman, despite her hair color.

What the hell was going on?

The woman paused a long moment, her gaze drifting to Malcolm and Siobhan. Before she lifted both hands and tugged at her hair, pulling free the wig and protective cap beneath to shake out long, red locks.

"Well, Da," she said in perfect generic American English, not a trace of an Irish accent left. "Tell me. Are you proud of your little girl?"

CHAPTER THIRTY-SEVEN

Okay, so I don't know what I was expecting. But after everything that happened? I was absolutely and utterly floored by the fact the tall redhead who took a casual seat, crossing her knees with grace to rival Vivian's, her green eyes locked on mine, was alive.

And well.

And... what?

"Fiona," I whispered. "You're Fiona Doyle."

She laughed, a soft but rich sound, and it carried as every single person in the room stared in complete silence.

"I'm so disappointed," she said when her amusement retreated, though she continued to smile at me as if this were some grand joke, and I was the butt of it. "I was positive you'd figure things out. I suppose I overestimated my namesake." She winked at Dad whose jaw had apparently become unhinged because his mouth hung open. "You did well with her, though, I admit it. Nice to see you, John. Lucy." Her gaze twinkled, freckled nose wrinkling. "I really should have done away with you both when I realized you wouldn't stop looking for me. But nostalgia has more of a hold over me, I suppose. And it really has been fun watching you mourn me all these years."

She laughed again, and this time the evil in her shone through. Pure, unadulterated. I thought I'd run into real darkness before. I'd seen flashes of it from Robert at times, knowing now that deep hate and vitriol had to be sourced from the death of Victor French. And even some of the men and women I'd caught for murder had shown their own flashes of nasty.

But here? Sitting before me in a pale blue designer dress, sat the devil herself.

"A pity, really," she said, focused on me again. "We could have worked well together, given the right circumstances. But you came along far too late for that, Fee, dear. I'd already taken what I wanted and was busy building my empire when you ran away from home, crying over Daddy not wanting you to be a police officer just like him." More laughter. Seriously. My shock was transmuting into disgust and the beginnings of rage.

And I wasn't the only one. "Fiona." Dad finally managed to speak, big hands shaking before he grasped his own knees and squeezed until his knuckles turned white. "We were your friends." So much agony from my father, he sounded lost, almost broken.

Fiona's smile held pity, gaze flattening out. "I learned from the best how to get what I want," she said, not even looking at her parents. "Isn't that right, Mum? Da?" She flicked at an imaginary piece of lint on her skirt. "I was raised by the mob. Are you really that surprised?"

"I suppose I shouldn't be," Malcolm said, voice thick. "Well played, lass."

She ignored her father, green eyes never leaving mine. "You have spunk, my dear. I admire that. But far too often you've interfered with my plans. I thought perhaps I could keep you confused and off the trail. Thanks to that meddling grandmother of yours, however, you've been getting closer and closer the last year or so." Fiona sat forward, almost eager. "The treasure hunt. When you found out it wasn't real, did it hurt?" She sat back then, hands grasping the arms of her chair. "I have no idea what your grandmother was thinking."

"The bodies," I whispered. "The grave."

Fiona started, paled as if slapped. Spun and gestured abruptly to one of the men guarding us. He joined her, leaned in as she hissed a whispered command before he spun and left the room. She seemed to regain some of her composure, but her true nature was showing through that dark amusement of hers at last, the evil surfacing to make its presence known.

"I see," she said. "Well. How disappointing. However, I'll have everything wrapped up here before the lab is able to identify the DNA Dr. Aberstock submitted. If I had known it was from those two, I would have had the evidence destroyed before it even left the morgue." She shrugged, settled back into Fiona Doyle, Demon Queen. "A minor setback."

"The bodies," I said. "Whose?"

Her expression emptied to nothing. "You know who," she said.

"Marie Patterson." Of course. Sisterhood. "And?"

She sniffed, tossed her head. "The child was only necessary to snare Teddy, though I was forced to carry to term." She seemed annoyed by that. "Once I had him under my control and Marie dead, his offspring was no longer needed."

Oh. My. God. "You murdered her."

Fiona's expression didn't change. "Strangled the little wretch in her crib. Satisfying, if I do say so myself."

Evil. I'd called her evil. But there was no name for what she was.

"That grandmother of yours." She chuckled, but this time in anger. "She was a thorn in my side from the moment I set my sights on the Patterson fortune." Fiona glanced at my parents, shrugged. "I don't know how she knew, but she figured it out. She and that writer friend of hers." She nodded to Crew.

"Alistair Markham. Your grandfather. You have no idea how infuriating it was to have you, of all people, become sheriff of Reading. And then, amusing." Fiona's mercurial being flickered from angry to titillated in an instant. "I did everything I could to get you to quit, Crew Turner. Even contemplated having you killed." She tapped her chin thoughtfully with one manicured index finger before sighing deeply. "But you brought so much frustration to Fiona's life, not to mention your own self-torture, I let things be. Now, I get to destroy both of you, and so soon into this love affair of yours." She tsked. "Silly me. I thought killing Marie and taking control of the family would be the end of things, but Iris's nosiness forced me into hiding. And so, you see the result at last." She spread her hands wide. "Fiona Doyle died. And in her place, the reclusive Marie Patterson retreated into her domain. Where I built the empire I deserve."

"You've been masquerading as Marie this whole time." Mom sounded utterly dumbfounded.

"Of course, Lu. Don't be thick." She seemed to take delight in Mom's hurt reaction.

"Who knows about this?" Vivian's voice trembled, just enough I knew she was fighting her own fear but doing a better job of hiding it.

"A choice few." Fiona steepled her hands in front of her, switching crossed legs in a slow and graceful motion. "I was careful, pretended to be ill for many years, emerged once the old guard had been carefully relocated, still with limited exposure to the family." That's why most of the family no longer lived in

Reading. The sheer scope of this entire process had to impress. No, I wasn't admiring her. Wasn't. Still. Wow. Could I have shown that level of commitment? Well, considering I wasn't a lying sociopath, likely not. "It has become necessary to include certain members of the family into the secret. Though, some of them weren't intentional and had to be silenced when their ambitions became their priority."

"Lester Patterson," I said, thinking about Doreen.

Fiona winked at me. "Very good, Fee. He should never have been let in on the truth. I had one of Marie's Sisterhood take care of him."

"And Geoffrey?" But no, his death had been all Barry's desperation.

Fiona shrugged. "You be the judge," she said. "I can tell you, though, if it weren't for Patterson greed, I would never have succeeded." She looked around her, arms wide. "I might have walked into this, but I built so much more." That flat look again. "I took the pathetic attempts they'd made at corporate domination and turned Blackstone into a force to be reckoned with."

"You played us." Dad couldn't seem to get past that fact, his arm sliding around Mom's shoulders. "Played all of us."

Fiona shook her head, false pity behind her smile. "With parents like mine, are you really surprised?" She finally shifted and looked at her mother and father who stared back, faces pale and creased in agony. "My own father turned his back on me.

Didn't you, Da? When I wanted to join the family business, what did you say to me?" Anger was escaping her control, the more she talked, the more vivid its presence until she was shaking with it by the time she jabbed a finger at Malcolm. "Care to tell them what you said to your only child when she came to you with her desire to be just like her dear old da?"

"I said no." He was barely audible.

He might as well have slapped her. She leaped to her feet, rage overwhelming her, entire tall body shaking from it as she screamed in response, spit flying from her mouth.

"YOU SAID I WASN'T GOOD ENOUGH!" If she'd had a gun or another kind of weapon in her possession in that moment, I'm positive both of her parents would have died instantly. Instead, she used the one weapon she did have control of. "You said I would never amount to anything in the business. Women didn't have the balls to do what was necessary." She pulled herself under control as she wound that out, smile returning, red hair wild around her. "So, I ask you again, Da. Did I make you proud after all?"

He didn't respond. She didn't seem to care, retaking her seat while I chewed on the truth of all of this before spitting it out in her face.

"Your daddy hurt your feelings," I said at my most disdainful, "and so you had a temper tantrum and a hissy fit and murdered people so you could show him. Wow, Fiona. You should have stopped talking. I was starting to think you were some brilliant genius. But you're just a spoiled child whose father told you no."

I didn't think before I spoke, realized as the words left my mouth there was a very good chance Fiona's reaction would be to order one of her guards to put a bullet in me.

Instead, face pale, eyes intent and full of madness, she hissed at me. "Everything I've done up to this moment has been carefully planned to the finest detail. I have been pulling your strings, Fiona Fleming," she spun on Dad, "and yours, John," then my husband, "and yours, Crew Turner, for years." One hand sliced through the air.

"Why call Dad about your suspicions about the family?" Seemed like a dumb thing to do.

Superiority worked for her, unfortunately. "I had to lay false trail, of course."

"Marie's murder was premeditated." Dad sounded like he was going to be sick.

"Don't judge yourself too harshly, dear John." Fiona was laughing again, and I wondered if she was actually cracked down the middle. Trouble was, even if she had gone around the bend into Crazytown, she didn't seem to have lost control of her sense of reality. "I won over you and Lu, your mother, Iris, with my Irish charms, oh so easily." She ended that sentence with a healthy accent as if letting out the young woman she'd been for just a moment. "When I realized the Pattersons were easy targets, I seduced Teddy. So simple. The poor man was starved for affection." Okay, gross. "Unfortunate he didn't last much longer than his dearly departed wife, but I needed to maintain the story going around town, the story I seeded."

"That you were pregnant and the two of you ran away together." So, Oliver's lie had been created on purpose.

Fiona didn't reply because there was no need. "You know, I do regret the loss of Geoffrey." She seemed genuinely disappointed. "He discovered my identity himself, so clever. Actually, wanted to help, the dear man. Came up with some rather clever ideas of his own. I'll miss him." She settled in her chair again. "Remind me to do something permanent to Barry Clement before his trial in recompense for my loss."

She really was nuts. "All the sideways steps with Blackstone," I said. "Making it look like conflict. All part of your plan to keep us from finding out the Patterson family controlled the corporation?"

That got her back up. "I control Blackstone," she snapped. "I *am* Blackstone."

Whatever, crazy lady I was named after.

Fiona wasn't done, clearly, settling in visibly to pontificate, her amusement back in place, her composure collected and genteel. "Imagine. A criminal enterprise that encompasses most of the eastern seaboard, including," and here she paused to giggle, "my own father's crime family because, honestly, how could a girl resist such an opportunity?" She shook her head at her own cleverness.

"Grandmother Iris knew, found out about Marie." I prodded Fiona. "The Sisterhood knew."

She tsked at me. "Iris had an inkling, came to try to see Marie many times. I had her sent away, finally created a rift with her using Peggy Munroe's husband. Simple enough to create strife in the so-called Sisterhood without Marie there to keep them in line." Fiona turned a heavy gold ring on one hand, admiring the big diamond set there. "Doreen was easy enough to manipulate. In fact, I was the one who gave her Lester's bank account information, the very paperwork she needed to blackmail him." I'd always wondered where the bank statements came from. Now I knew. "That's what happens to Pattersons who don't toe the line." Fiona returned her gaze to me. "I destroy them. Until the rest do as they are told." She seemed satisfied with the conversation, enough to continue. "As for Martha, she's been lost in dementia for years, long enough I stopped worrying she might be a threat. And Peggy Munroe? Had her own small criminal enterprise keeping her busy." Fiona seemed pleased with that fact. "I own Reading, I have since the night Marie died when I smothered her with her own pillow." Her hands twitched and I wondered if she remembered the action, was reliving it. "I will not let anyone take away what I have built."

Fiona rose then, abrupt and swift, as though suddenly bored with us. She glanced at her watch before gesturing to one of the two remaining bodyguards. He joined her immediately while she spoke with an air of distracted disinterest.

"It's been lovely to catch up," she said, "to finally share all of this with you, my dear Fee." Forget everyone else, apparently, including her parents, and mine. "But I'm afraid your remaining questions will go unanswered. It's almost time."

"For what?" I perked, not liking the sound of that, head still aching but at least feeling like I could stand and maybe fight or something, anything, to wipe that smile from her face.

She didn't answer, leaving the room as silently as she'd arrived and, when the door closed behind her, the two bodyguards resumed positions, rifles in hand, while the silence in the room descended in a smothering crush of defeat.

CHAPTER THIRTY-EIGHT

It was Daisy who broke the silence, huge gray eyes wide and full of confusion. "This was never about the treasure?"

Oh, boy. "Sorry, Day." At least my head was a bit better. I was even able to sit up and not feel like the world was spinning and closing in around the edges in dark patches. "This was about Grandmother Iris knowing something was up with Marie but not having proof and doing her best to lay a trail for us to follow."

"For me to follow." Dad interrupted, shaking his head, frowning and angry. He looked like he wanted to pace but was thinking better of it, considering our babysitters and their threatening weapons. "She hinted over the years things weren't right. And the sudden end of her friendship with Marie..." He wiped at his face with both hands. "Maybe I should have known something was really wrong."

"How could you, John?" Mom patted his knee, her own composure helping not just me, but all of us from the apparent circle of calmer expressions and faint nods that came with her statement. "We already knew the Patterson family was up to no good. Fiona's takeover didn't raise flags because she only amplified the problem. She didn't start it."

Truth in that. Enough Dad seemed willing to stop beating himself up at least and focus on the here and now.

"Why didn't Mom just tell me?" He'd turned his anger on Grandmother Iris. Thing was, I hardly blamed him for that. I was feeling a teensy bit out of sorts with the old lady myself. And in teensy bit I mean heaps of blame and frustration, Fleming style. "Why the elaborate plan?"

"And," Crew said, voice shaking with his own emotional turmoil, though the hand that held mine showed nothing of it, steady and strong, "why did my grandfather get involved?"

"Because he loved her, silly." Fiona had returned, none of us noticing as she rejoined us, sitting in the chair she'd vacated, contented smile returned. "The old fool. He came looking for the treasure of his ancestor." She clearly found that hilarious, eyes sparkling as she taunted my husband with a flick of her fingers in his direction. "I was here, in the house, when he came to interview Marie about it. I heard all the stories, all the arguments he had that the hoard was real. Trust me, I know a con artist when I hear about one and Captain Reading wasn't very good at lying. Anyone with half a brain would know his story was nothing but bunk." She snorted softly, another finger wiggle making Crew twitch as she dismissed everything his father and grandfather led him to believe. "That ridiculous book of his only found him ridicule. Did you know Iris never let him in on her suspicions? He clung to that fantasy of his until his death. I know. I asked him personally." She winked at Crew who flinched, paled. "I had to know what he knew. I wonder if he realized who I was? Not that it matters. The irony that he loved the old bat and she lied to him, too. All to protect him, like she tried to protect you, John. And dear Fee." She seemed highly amused by that. "How unhappy she would be. I only wish she was still alive and well to see no matter what she did, I still win."

I had no proof, but I was positive, in that moment, Grandmother Iris flipped over in her grave.

Fiona's fingertips tapped on the arms of the chair. "All this despite the fact Marie insisted there was no treasure here." Fiona's forehead creased a moment as she leaned forward, focused on me. "I was curious, I must say. I understood you found a map, a doubloon, other bits and pieces outside that empty collection of half-truths and stories Alistair published." Another quake from my husband but he held it together. "I needed to know Iris's purpose for leading you on such a wild goose chase."

"Which was why you send Gregg Brown to snoop on our hunt," I said.

"Indeed." Fiona paused then. "Unfortunate, how death follows you, my dear. We have that in common, it seems."

I wanted to tell her we had zero in common, but that wasn't true, unfortunately.

"Darius Smith," I said. "My bodyguard." I glanced at Malcolm. "Did you hurt him?"

In other words, was his dead body the next one I was going to find?

"On the contrary," she said, waving one hand in a reassuring gesture. "I had him reassigned back to Chicago. By force, unfortunately. He didn't want to leave. But I own the O'Shea family, and they own him." Another smile pulled at her lips, a sly sideways glance at her father. "Delicious, if you ask me. That particular coup will never get old."

I could imagine. "We're now assuming for some reason Grandmother Iris didn't think she could come out and openly expose what was happening, perhaps didn't know the whole story, and instead set this entire thing up to give us the chance to figure it out."

Dad grunted softly. "Knowing a Fleming would never abandon a mystery."

Dogs with a bone. Sigh. Were that predictable?

"The fact Alistair had no idea," I said, squeezing Crew's hand. "That Grandmother Iris simply used his hunt as a means to an end. You know, what?" I sat up a little straighter, meeting Dad's eyes. "That makes total sense. She must have seized on the treasure at the time, as a means to an end."

He nodded. "She could have just told me."

"And risked putting you in a position where you could do nothing or force you to risk your life over something she couldn't prove." Mom looked at Fiona. "You would have killed John, I'm assuming, if he'd interfered."

Our captor smiled and nodded.

"How she knew about the burial site I have no idea." Fiona sat back again, foot bobbing over her crossed knee, her first show of agitation in this iteration of our conversation. No way was I telling her Martha French was the source. "Clever of her to mark the grave with those ridiculous butterflies of hers." She shrugged. "She'd clearly been adding to her evidence over the years. I do wonder why, if she found the remains, she didn't uncover them and deliver them to the authorities herself. Though I suppose, with her silly Sisterhood broken and Alistair gone Iris had no one to trust with the knowledge she'd uncovered. Not without risking you, John, in the process." Fiona glared at me a moment. "Perhaps it was her pending death and her choice to lure you back that allowed her to finally risk her precious family." She might have been right. Was all of what Grandmother Iris assembled done in anticipation of my return? I found that hard to believe, but at this point, I wasn't underrating the crafty old lady.

"It was a mistake to not properly dispose of the bodies, but to be honest, I forgot they were there."

Fiona's lips twisted. "An error I am correcting right now. All evidence will be eliminated as soon as we're done here."

Panic for Dr. Aberstock punched me solidly in the chest. "Don't hurt him."

I didn't have to say who I was talking about. Fiona's amusement at my quick command wasn't doing much for my confidence.

"Lloyd Aberstock will be dealt with as well," she said. "You aren't in any position to worry about his future anyway, dear Fee." Again she glanced at her watch. "Not long now." She stood, gestured to her guards, the second leaving, only one remaining behind.

"Until what?" My heart rate increased. "You kill us all?"

Fiona beamed a smile at me. "Of course, my dear. You expected another outcome?" I honestly had nothing to say to that. Didn't matter because she was already continuing. "It's unfortunate, really. I've enjoyed my years here, pulling the strings of my empire." She looked around the room, fondness in her expression. "But Reading is no longer secure, and I've outstayed my ability to hide. Besides, the FBI is far too interested in who runs Blackstone, thanks to your Agent Michaud. She's chasing ghosts, by the way." She nodded to Daisy and Vivian in turn. "While you might have found Pierre Noir as a doorway into my holdings, I can assure you, Ranier and Donald weren't nearly as clever as they thought. I've had redundancies built into the entire network for years now. Already I've shunted the majority of my controls to other corporations." She laughed then, a belly laugh of utter delight. "Leaving what remains of the Patterson family holding the cards to the collapsing mess the FBI will ultimately unravel."

Crazy or not, she had my kudos for planning ahead.

"They knew something was going on." Vivian spoke up at last. "My father and Donald."

Fiona's flat stare spoke volumes now. I was getting used to reading her shifts in mood. They'd angered her, made her life difficult. "Both of them, yes," she said. "Demanding meetings with Marie, poking into Patterson business." Fiona's eyes never left Vivian's. "It was an unfortunate day when Ranier brought his children—and their little friends—to the house to confront me."

Vivian flinched. And so did I.

"Victor," she whispered, face so white I thought Vivian might pass out.

Fiona didn't move, but it was almost like she loomed over the mayor, the two of them the only people in the room while tension built between them.

"Nosy, that one," she said. "Far too curious for his own good. Ranier's brat shouldn't have been poking his little nose into other people's business."

"He saw you." I interrupted, partially to relieve the pressure of their mutual focus and partially because I was never very good at keeping my mouth shut.

Fiona didn't look at me, but she did respond.

"Yes. Without my wig, my disguise. It was clear from his shock he recognized me, called me by name, even. And ran off before I could stop him." Her own personal tension eased a bit, smile returning. "Fortunately, I had my own faithful follower in young Robert Carlisle." She sniffed softly, head tossing. "He accepted Marie Patterson, his mother's boss, knew best. Easily manipulated, like Doris." Dad's sister wasn't my favorite person in the world, nothing like him. I could see how she could have been talked into anything. And her son didn't fall far from the family tree. "Simple enough to discover from him, through gifts and special treatment, what weaknesses plagued the young French boy. Convincing Robert just how very special he was and how much it would mean to me to play a practical joke on Victor... well, simplicity itself." Bright happiness woke in her face, Vivian crumbling under Fiona's growing delight. "Robert didn't fail me, nor did the wasp next I'd been told by the groundskeeper he needed to remove from the dock." Fiona watched Vivian carefully as she went on. "So simple to convince him to lure your brother to his death. With the added bonus, of course, that I owned Robert from that moment on." She jabbed a finger at Vivian suddenly, rage showing through the sunny expression she wore. "If Ranier had simply let things alone, his child wouldn't have paid the price. But did he take the warning to heart? No." She chopped sideways with the side of her hand, Vivian flinching though the blow was nowhere close to her physically. Clearly, however, it struck solid and true emotionally. "When I found out he was preparing to move on Blackstone, I took care of him permanently."

Reinforcing to me Grandmother Iris's reasons for keeping Dad out of it. If someone as wealthy and powerful as Ranier French could be targeted, what recourse would my father have had? I suddenly felt terrible for my grandmother, realizing she must have been desperate, in the end, to protect us but unable, like any good Fleming, to just let things go.

I didn't get to dwell on it for too long. The remaining guard perked, touching one ear, then spoke.

"Ms. Doyle," he said. "We're ready."

"Ah, excellent." Fiona clapped her hands together, beacon of light all over again. "I love it when a plan comes together." Her lips pursed then, cloud passing over the sun. "At least, for some of us. Namely, for me." She let her hands drop to her sides. "I'm afraid tragedy is about to befall the rest of you, the kind of horrific event they'll be talking about in Reading for centuries to come." Fiona turned toward the exit, still speaking as her guard stepped aside to let her leave. "So unfortunate a rockslide triggered by blasting for new construction is going to bury Patterson House and everyone inside it." She stopped, met my eyes, sad smile joined by a wink. "But that's a possible consequence to living on a mountain. Isn't it?"

CHAPTER THIRTY-NINE

Before she could make her triumphant exit, the guard perked again, concern flickering over his stoic face while my heart thudded in response to what we'd just heard. I almost missed the black-clad man's sudden whisper to Fiona, her flash of a scowl in the turmoil of my fear.

Instead, I let my mind—threatening to descend into panic and despair—latch onto the word his mouth formed as he leaned toward his boss. *Intruder.*

Had Liz found us?

Fiona spun back toward us, though she only had focus for her parents. Darius, then? Had he somehow raised the cavalry and was rushing to our rescue? Didn't matter. Fiona paused near her mother and father, freezing in place a long moment before bending, swift and precise, to kiss them both on the cheek. Neither attempted to stop her from the act of passionless goodbye, Siobhan staring up at her daughter with contempt.

"You asked if your da was proud," the old woman said, Irish accent thick with her disdain. "That's all you ever wanted, was it, dearie?" Siobhan spit on her daughter's high heel. "You can go to your own grave, Fiona, no daughter of ours, knowing you are nothing but scum to both of us."

I was hoping that rejection might shake her. Instead, Fiona smiled. And slapped her mother so hard across the face blood flowed from Siobhan's lip and down her chin.

Malcolm half rose with a growl of fury, but Dad was faster, lunging for him across the coffee table, the black-clad guard already leveling his gun at the old Irishman.

"No." Fiona waved off the weapon. "No bullets. He'll die in the rockslide like the rest of them."

It had to have been coincidence. Surely no one could have such perfect timing. But, to my shock and, honestly, faint amusement because my brain is weird, the instant of the loss of attention for the rest of the room created the perfect moment for the previously mentioned intruder to make her appearance.

But not Liz, not that formidable FBI agent I hoped would save us in the nick of time. Nope. Instead, as Fiona hovered over her mother's bleeding face, Dad pinning Malcolm's shaking body to the sofa, the guard's gun slowly lowering from its threatening aim in their direction, a whisper of motion caught the corner of my peripheral vision, drawing my attention away from the tableau of familial discord to the soft and swift opening of a panel next to the fireplace.

A secret passage? Apparently, and not my first experience with such, thanks to my adventure on Black Mountain, Blackstone part of that mess too, weren't they? This particular covert entry disgorged the grinning, stooped but oddly threatening form of Peggy Munroe. Not just because of the gun in her hand, aimed at Fiona, in itself a clear and present danger despite the distracted guard. But there was something about her aura, about the way she strode into the room like some supervillain whose master plan to destroy the world had finally reached its moment of truth, that lent her an air of utter and complete terror.

So, she'd tried to kill me twice. Maybe all I was sensing was my own remembered fears. Then again, maybe not.

The gun went off, the sound so loud I was actually floored by the act of Peggy pulling the trigger. I'd expected some kind of conversation, a standoff between her and the guard. No one just walked in and shot someone, did they? Surely there was some kind of honor code among crazy people who thought they were better than everyone else and didn't deserve to be put in jail for their acts against humanity. Somewhere written they had to warn each other and pontificate on those same acts, revealing truths, disgorging their version of events before the good guys rode in and saved the day.

Apparently, Peggy didn't get the memo. And I was wrong, it turned out, where that gun was pointed. I should be forgiven for guessing it was Fiona who Peggy targeted since I was still suffering from a head wound and, from their positions in the space, the guard's location could easily be in the same sightline.

I figured the crazy old lady would shoot the other crazy lady. Instead, the bullet bit through the back of the guard's neck and dropped him instantly to the floor.

He fell behind a chair, disappearing from view, that truth sparing me the sight of bleeding and dying and all that. Not that I was focusing on the fallen man at the moment. Not when two things happened in exactly the same instant to blur the line between someone else's death and dear god, I'm going to die.

First, Fiona spun, mouth agape, to face the woman who killed her guard. And second, the floor under my feet rumbled as the sound of an explosion—far too close for comfort—shook the house down to the bedrock.

Peggy cackled, doing a little jig dance of happiness, the business end of her revolver never wavering despite her antics. Fiona's hands slowly rose in response and for the first time, I saw fear on her face. Nice to see the tables turned for once. Not that Peggy was our saving grace or anything. She'd be happy to see me dead. But with the woman holding us hostage now a hostage herself, we had a much better chance of surviving. Right?

Another explosion, closer this time.

Yeah, right.

"Marie." Peggy stopped her tapping feet.

"What have you done?" Fiona paled, licked her lips. "We're on the wrong side of the bridge, you madwoman." She glanced at the exit, inching toward it, but Peggy fired again, the bullet just missing from what I could tell, a puff of plaster exploding on the far wall from the impact.

"Why, I've set off your little plan early." Peggy ignored all of us, focused on Fiona. "You're blowing the mountain to high heaven, Marie. So that's where I'm sending you." She laughed. "Or, more likely, you're going below, to the hot place. I'll see you there."

This time Fiona lunged for the door, but Peggy was faster, the next bullet blowing a giant hole in the panel, just below the handle. Fiona cried out, hand going to her cheek, where a chunk of flying wood had sliced her skin. Blood dripped from between her fingers, but she was still alive.

Maybe I'd get my supervillain oration after all.

That was if the damned explosions would stop. At this rate, as the whole sofa shook, dust falling from the ceiling in response to the third, we'd all be dead under a massive slide of rock before Peggy could get out her litany of evil.

"Your guards were no match for me," the old

lady said. "Or Ruth. Turns out she's very good with explosives, years spent working with that useless brother of hers in his construction business." Yikes. "You made your last mistake, Marie. We'll die together here. The last of the Sisterhood." Another cackle. "Just the way it should be."

"I'm not Marie Patterson, you old fool." Fiona's hand fell to her side, the blood flow continuing, a trail now making a stuttering line down the front of her blue dress. "Snap out of your insanity, for god's sake. I'm not here for you. I'll let you live if you just lower the gun."

Maybe Peggy would have listened six months ago. But I could tell there was nothing left of the woman who I knew, not a shred of the old woman who used to spy on me over the fence at Petunia's. No, she was long lost in the past. Unlike Martha French and her dear, dear heart, the Peggy who used to be carried darkness with her, and there was no going back for her.

"I know you didn't want me," she snarled, stalking toward Fiona with the gun leveled. "I know you and Iris conspired to keep me out of the Sisterhood." Her finger twitched against the trigger, visible even from this distance. "I know you never thought I was good enough. Well, Marie. Am I good enough for you now?" She grinned, maniacal and insane, while the irony of her statement stirred a hysterical giggle empty of amusement. Close enough to Fiona's own need from her father, wasn't it, to feel like poetic justice? "We played in these passages, years ago, when we were all girls together. You would never have found them without me. But still you treated me like you never wanted me." Were those tears on her old face? Peggy wiped at them with the cuff of her tattered brown cardigan, pale flowered dress dirty on the hem, and were those cobwebs in her wispy hair? "I gave you a gift, I gave you my friendship. And you cast me off." The gun slashed the air. "You cast us all off." I already knew Peggy didn't take rejection well. But she'd been her own mastermind, once upon a time. "You learned everything from me. Asked me how to build your empire when Teddy proved weak, the family fortune in trouble. I showed you everything, taught you all I knew. And this is how you treat me?" Rage flew from her lips in drops of spittle as she came within five feet of Fiona. So, it had been Peggy who helped Marie begin Blackstone? And the budding criminal enterprise Fiona took over? If Marie's family money was gone, if the family was in trouble, it would explain her descent into criminal activity before Fiona could even get her hands on the Patterson name. "I was the best of the Sisterhood and you rejected me." The gun wavered at last, her old hand shaking as if with palsy, but only for a second. "I made my own empire, without you. And now you'll die, and everyone will know I was the leader." She thumped her narrow chest with her free fist, the sound hollow and painful. "Me. Peggy Munroe. Not the all-mighty Marie Patterson."

"I. Am. Not. Marie. Patterson." Fiona's Irish

accent emerged. Panic rose in her. "Where are my men?" Not a question for Peggy, but one she seemed happy to answer with a giggle of glee.

"Waiting on the other side of the bridge," she said. "Like you ordered them to."

"I did no such..." Fiona's fear was as real as mine, now. "It can't end like this. I've prepared for every eventuality."

So tempting to interrupt, fire off a Flemingism burn to end all burns. But did I dare risk distracting Peggy from her focus? None of my friends or family spoke up, so we all had to be thinking the same thing. Even as a fourth explosion made my ears ring, a shriek escaping me, while the entire house rocked from it.

Peggy's attention flickered, confusion emerging, her hand shaking suddenly, gun descending as she looked around her. Fiona must have seen her moment of weakness, and, in that instant, she wasn't the only one on the move.

Dad. Crew. Fiona. Malcolm. All en route to the crazy old woman and the gun. At the exact instant the ceiling over the far wall fell in.

"Don't!" Peggy's roar of denial made it through the echoing sound of destruction, her focus back, unflinching despite the collapsing house. The men froze, Fiona stumbling to her knees while we coughed and choked on plaster dust. We had to get out of there, had to run, but not with an insane gunwoman standing in our way. I eyed the secret passage, still open, barely accessible now that the crown molding covered the floor in chunks. "The perfect ending, don't you think? Taking you, Iris, Martha, me. Doreen will just have to rot in prison." Another cough. I glanced at Vivian, realized who filled in the gap for her grandmother in Peggy's foggy memory. "You know, Iris knew. She knew there was something wrong with you." Was Peggy waking to the present? "She told me about the fire, sneaking up here and seeing you burning something that looked like a body. Where you buried the remains in an old tool chest." Grandmother Iris had heard that from Martha, clearly did her best to protect her friend. Because it was obvious, she never trusted the woman with the gun. Peggy coughed herself, weapon at the ready despite her slowly draining energy. I could see her failing, knew it was only a matter of moments before she lost control of the gun. Prepped myself to grab my mom and Daisy and Vivian and get the hell out of there. While the old woman went on. "How she used that old fool, Alistair, and his ridiculous treasure book to make a hunt. Not for gold though, Marie." Peggy's last cackle was sad, agonized. "It was a Marie Patterson hunt. Only no one wanted to play." She exhaled deeply, sorrowfully. "And now, the game is over." Her expression flatlined at last. I knew that expression. Held my breath for the curtain call. "So endeth the Sisterhood."

She pulled the trigger.

As a massive explosion rocked the room.

CHAPTER FORTY

I was sure that was it, we were dead, but somehow the rest of the ceiling held, and we were still alive when, gasping and choking on the dust she'd created, Ruth Wilkins staggered through the secret door and into the room.

"We have to go!" She shouted like she'd been partially deafened and perhaps she had. She certainly looked like she'd come too close to an explosion, the side of her face peppered with little cuts, one hand cradled against her as if damaged by flying debris. Ruth had once been an imposing figure to be reckoned with but, as she'd been when I'd seen her last six months ago in my basement apartment at Petunia's, she appeared reduced, shrunken. A broken woman who'd sold her soul to the insanity of the past Peggy Munroe couldn't shed.

Ruth's visible terror wasn't helping my own fear level. I sat forward, Daisy's hand in mine, Mom reaching for me as we moved in unison. Thinking what? We'd get to run when Peggy and her grandniece did, just like that? Were we all keen to obey the shouted words Ruth threw at Peggy? Um, yup. Let me out of there, right now.

"I'm not going anywhere." Peggy didn't even turn to look at the woman who'd made her plan a reality. "None of us are. This is how it ends."

Ruth's shock told me, even now, she didn't believe her great aunt had completely lost her mind. She spun in silence, her eyes meeting mine in a brief instant of panic before she made it one step toward the exit that was the secret door.

In that same moment the ceiling finally gave way, crushing her beneath a large portion of the second floor.

Not that I got to witness her death, because with the collapse came a rush of dust, driving me to the floor for cover, Mom jerked down beside me, Daisy too, Vivian's arms around my bestie as she ducked and covered. I looked up in time to see Crew struggling with Peggy for the gun, jerking it free from the old woman's hands, just as Fiona, face a mask of utter rage, struck my husband on the back of the head with a chunk of plaster.

I don't remember how I reached her. I have no idea how I made it across the room to my namesake before her hands even fell to her sides, the blunt instrument she'd used to bring Crew down dropping to the dust. I registered the blood on her cheek caked in white powder, the look in her green eyes as I hit her bodily from the side, carrying her into the door beside her, the cracking of wood as she struck just where the bullet Peggy fired earlier shattered beneath the handle. Sweat. More blood, more dust.

Dad, staggering, falling to the side as he stumbled over rubble, while Peggy resumed her control of the gun. I hit the floor with Fiona beneath me, flipping to my side, lying next to the woman I'd been named after as we stared up into the grinning face now peeking at us through the fog of plaster in the air.

A vague sense of déjà vu prodded. But there was no Petunia to interrupt the shot this time, no faithful pug to distract. My only saving grace in the final moment of my life was the wavering decision on Peggy's face as she tried in her madness to decide: Marie or Iris?

The ground was shaking. I heard the rumble as I saw Peggy make her decision, felt the earth give way, the shock on the old woman's face as the wall beside her—beside me, with Fiona between me and impending death—disintegrated, ceiling collapsing in time with the destruction—and enveloped the world in crushing darkness.

CHAPTER FORTY-ONE

I coughed into the black, chest tight, something heavy digging into my right leg. I tried to shift position, to free myself and screamed from the instant pain.

"Fee." Someone choked out my name, warm touch on my fingertips. I coughed a sob, feeling consciousness fade before it came back in a rush of agony. "Sweetheart, I'm here. Fee. I'm here."

"Crew!" I wanted to hug him. Why couldn't I hug him? I tried to reach him again, new levels of torment taking my breath.

"Fee, don't try to move." He sounded like he was crying, doing his best not to, but failing. "Please, my love. Stay still."

So hard. I panted into the dark, biting my lower

lip as hard as I could to keep from screaming. Pitch black and heavy, the air thick. I couldn't breathe properly, panic seizing me, struggle at the verge of conscious thought.

"Fee." There he was again, that touch, were those his fingertips on mine? I held to that barest connection like the embrace I couldn't have, his voice and that spark of current between our two bodies something to cling to.

Enough to keep me from losing my mind.

"Fee." Oh my god, that was Dad. "You're okay?"

"Something's on my leg." I wanted to sob. "Dad, are you hurt?"

"I think my ribs are broken." A soft cough, but that gravel voice never wavered. He sounded close. He'd been near me when everything went to hell. "Lu, she's okay. She's awake."

"Fiona." Mom's voice was barely audible but sounded like she was crying, too. "Oh, sweetie, be brave. It's okay."

Was she talking to me or herself?

"Day? Viv?" I couldn't seem to speak above a harsh whisper anymore.

No one spoke. And panic returned.

"I'm here." Malcolm. Okay, focus on Malcolm. "Siobhan." He sniffed. More tears. Silence.

"Peggy and Fiona?" Something was pressed against my side, and I realized from the give it wasn't part of the house. I'd been with my namesake. Was it her body next to me?

"Here." She did nothing to disguise her Irish

accent. "Though I hope the old lady died in the crush."

"No such luck." Peggy's cackle reached us all. "Is this hell, Marie?"

Sure felt like it.

"There were sirens," Dad said then. "They went quiet a few minutes ago. But I heard voices just before you woke up, Fee."

Rescue. Now, to hold it together until they dug us out.

Took a while. Far too long, in my estimation. I have no idea how long, or how we survived, alternating between sobbing hysterically to release my stress and lying still and quiet and terrified of being trapped there forever. At least Vivian's voice broke through, confirming she was okay, and then Daisy, my dear Day, safe with the mayor beyond where Mom lay trapped.

Safe. All of us safe. A miracle.

It was Mom's idea to sing. She'd always had a lovely voice, a sweet alto. Why she picked a Christmas carol to start off, I had no idea. Maybe it was all she could think of. But as the familiar first notes and words escaped her, I latched onto the faint hope in the sound and did my best to keep up.

I lost track of how many we sang while we lay there in the dark under the weight of Patterson House, waiting to be found, rescued. When Mom faltered, Daisy started a new tune, then Vivian. Even Crew gave it a go leading one, though it was Malcolm's dirty Irish song that made us all laugh and then weep and then sing again.

Light was a shock, bright and vivid, through cracks above me, voices calling out while we sang, and hope blossomed. I wasn't expecting the chunk above my face to shift, the sudden exposure to night sky and rescuers with powerful flashlights, nor the snuffling and excited tongue swipe of the giant black dog who licked at the endless flow of tears—now of gratitude—that streamed down my face.

Likely not for the last time, Moose, that most faithful of Newfoundlanders, had rescued me.

Turned out Ruth Wilkins might have watched her brother lay demo, but she hadn't actually mastered the rulebook when it came to placement. Fortunately for us.

"You're just lucky Peggy made her move the charges," Liz said two days later while I sat, my leg propped up on three pillows, aching despite the painkillers from the gash where a chunk of rebar had punctured to the muscle. I was lucky it didn't go all the way through, the ceiling and wall forming a pocket that protected not just me, but my loved ones, from the rockslide Ruth's sloppy attempt at killing us created. "From what I saw, if she hadn't, the setup the Blackstone mercs lined up would have brought down half the mountain."

"Yeah, really lucky," I said.

"You're alive, aren't you?" She winked at Crew who sat back in the chair he occupied next to me, arms crossed over his chest. He had a bandage over one eye, the only evidence he'd been in the room at all. If anyone was lucky, it was him.

"You said you dug her out of the rubble, too?" I reached out and touched Crew's cheek, and he instantly unwound, taking my fingers in his, kissing them. He'd been incredibly attentive since we'd been allowed access to one another, hardly surprising. I never wanted to let him out of my sight ever again. "I thought she died."

"That old mansion was well built," Liz said. "Everyone made it out. Except the guard Peggy shot."

Fair enough. The house couldn't be blamed for Peggy's aim.

I shivered as I remembered being pulled from the rubble, Moose's soft fur under my hand, Liz at the vanguard of the team carefully excising us from the remains of Patterson House, Bill Saunders himself lifting me to safety while his big dog looked on. It didn't take long, once they found us, to get us all out, though I refused to leave in the ambulance—hello, my old friend EMTs, yes it was me again—until everyone was found.

That meant I got to watch Fiona Doyle being led away in handcuffs, Peggy, too, though that old lady was tied to a stretcher and, ultimately, raved in delirium I stopped listening to the moment she was loaded into the back of a second ambulance.

Emile's panicked arrival and subsequent hug and passionate kiss for my bestie was one-upped, that classic Hollywood ending they seemed to be wrapped up in punctuated by my darling Daisy firmly pushing her true love away from her and staring up into his pale eyes.

"Emile Reis," she said in her clear voice, "I love you. Will you marry me?"

Jill appeared at my door, interrupting that gorgeous memory, small wave of greeting hesitant and expression taut with guilt. I gestured for her to join us, patting at the tears arisen by remembering the expression on Emile's face, his enthusiastic agreement to Daisy's proposal, how we'd all wept, even my stoic dad, for our happy ending that shouldn't have been. I pulled her down on the bed next to me despite the pain her jostling generated and proceeded to tell her and Liz—with Crew's help—everything that happened.

Not that they didn't know most of it. We'd all dumped so much on them that night, as the spotlights combed the wreckage and rescue crews did their best to ensure they pulled all of us out safely. It had been an odd moment, spotting Robert standing at the edge of the rubble, that sullen darkness on his face, staring at what used to be Patterson House. But satisfying, I have to say, to watch Vivian take Jill's hand, blood from a cut on her cheek caked with dust and Grace Fiore suit torn and filthy but her expression set and determined and lead her to Robert's side.

Where, clearly and audibly, she spoke in that icy voice of hers no one could deny. "Sheriff Wagner," Reading's mayor said, "you are to place Robert Carlisle under immediate arrest for the murder of Victor French."

My cousin's expression didn't change. No attempt to deny it, just that steady black consuming him as he met Vivian's eyes. And lost, looking away.

It should have been satisfying to watch Jill cuff him and lead him to her truck, with Rose shrieking at her to release him, background noise barely audible once they were out of sight. Vivian returned to us, Mom hugging her, Daisy. Dad. Crew. Then me, joined by Malcolm and, thankfully safe and sound, Siobhan.

They'd allowed us a few minutes to take a last look at what could have been our final resting place before Liz shunted us forcibly off to the hospital where, to my relief—and a huge hug behind it—Dr. Aberstock greeted us in person, alive and well.

"Was there ever any doubt?" He really had to ask, didn't he?

CHAPTER FORTY-TWO

Pamela seemed content to sip coffee and listen to me fill in the gaps for her big exposé on Fiona Doyle and Blackstone. From what I'd heard, the *Boston Globe* had offered her a job again, though she hadn't told me either way if she was staying in Reading or heading out. Fleur's silent watchfulness and faint, continual mocking smile seemed to tell me she had her own hopes for Pamela's future.

My worries about the Pattersons I actually cared about—a shortlist that encompassed Pamela's wife, Aundrea, Jared and Alicia—were unfounded. They hadn't been in the house and, it turned out, the country when everything went down. Though, from what Fiona set up, they were prepped to take part in the fall of the Patterson clan.

"She threatened all of us," Pamela told me, setting her coffee aside as I wrapped up. "Not directly. I never got to meet the infamous Marie. I think she knew better than to let me see her face." She shrugged. "But she leveraged Aundrea against me, the kids against you. I know Alicia was told if she didn't toe the family line, she'd lose Jared."

She'd told me as much. "Did they know about Fiona?" I couldn't bring myself to believe they did. And hadn't she said so? She only trusted Geoffrey.

"I think Aundrea suspected," Pamela said, toying with the plastic lid lip. "She wouldn't tell me anything. And I wasn't allowed to talk to you, could barely contribute to the paper. So, when I'd had enough, I left to find the evidence I needed to get my life back."

"I still think you could have told me I wasn't going to find you floating in Cutter Lake," I grumbled. Bitter, who, me?

Pamela flashed me a wicked grin and a wink. "You should know me better than that by now, Fiona Fleming." She sighed then, sinking back into the plastic chair as chatter of other customers went on around us. I wasn't sure why she chose a public venue to have our conversation. I'd had enough of the stares and whispers of Reading's residents since Patterson House was crushed under Ruth's rockslide. Two weeks later, they were still talking about it. Fiona had been right, I guess, though they'd given up on Petunia's burning down, so this would likely fall to the wayside in short order.

I winced as I flexed my right leg, the ache from my injury still lingering. Dr. Aberstock had said it would be a couple more weeks before the pain was gone, but that didn't mean I couldn't begrudge the fact he was right.

"Thanks for the info," Pamela said. "Liz has been a bit tight-lipped, though she gave me more than I expected."

Whoops. "Just promise me you won't jeopardize her investigation." Turned out Fiona's warning about her secondary plans had given Liz what she needed to find the new home for my namesake's criminal empire. She'd told me despite finding what they needed to bring Fiona—and Blackstone—down, it would be years before they followed all the trails, tracked down all the players now scattering to the winds, and cleaned up the mess she'd left behind.

Better Liz than me.

"I hear you visited Robert," Pamela said, eyes narrowing, fishing, as always, for more info. It was in her nature, as it was in mine, so I didn't give her a hard time for it.

"Just wanted to make sure he's where he's supposed to be." I broke eye contact and took a sip of coffee, not wanting her to see I hadn't told the whole truth. I wanted reassurance, yes, he really was in a jail cell, and not in Reading, either. The state troopers had carted him off and I'd had to go to Southern State Correctional Facility to see him.

Part of me just wanted to know he was really going to pay for what he'd done to Victor. And part of me wanted answers to questions I wasn't sure would come out in court.

"Come to gloat?" He hadn't been friendly, but he hadn't rejected my visit, either. Robert had lost that heavy darkness, his boastful bravado. He looked shrunken and old in his orange jumpsuit, mustache joined by the scruff of a new beard I guess he'd been too lazy to shave. But he was still Robert, and he had a lot to answer for.

"I came to ask where you got the piece of the map." I wasn't sure he was going to answer, but he seemed open enough when he shrugged.

"Mom," he said. "She stole it and the hairclip from Grandmother Iris's room when she was there for the funeral." He didn't seem to care he just called his own mother a thief. "I didn't think the treasure was real, by the way." Nice attempt at a return to confidence that didn't last. A haunted look passed across his features, tongue licking his lips in an audible swipe. "Victor," he said. "You're going to ask about Victor next." I didn't respond, waited for him to go on. Robert sat on his hands on the bench seat across from me, chin dropping to his chest. "He was my friend." He coughed softly, jaw jumping, while I refused in no uncertain terms to allow even a scrap of compassion or empathy or whatever cousins or distant relatives of those two emotions might try to weasel their way into my heart. Because no. Absolutely not. Some things were unforgivable. "I've had to live with what I did. We were kids." He looked up, met my eyes, while I gave him a wall of silence. "I was a kid. I didn't mean to kill him."

He could tell himself whatever lies he needed to

get himself through twenty-five to life, but I wasn't buying it.

"Doesn't excuse the rest of it, though, does it?" There was a laundry list of crimes Liz presented to the state troopers, all to do with the Pattersons, all delivered, bless her heart (and I meant that in the most Southern way possible despite being from Vermont) by none other than Fiona Doyle.

Robert hadn't answered. And I'd walked away, struggling to feel good about any of it. We'd won, but some of us had lost so much, could we really ever call it a victory?

"You've heard they're broke now, right?" I started out of the memory as Fleur spoke up, resentful justification in her voice. Like she thought they deserved everything they got. Because she was talking about the Patterson clan, wasn't she?

Pamela squirmed in her seat, unhappy suddenly. "Apparently."

"Emile is in process of buying up their remaining assets and property." Daisy told me as much, hesitant about it herself. "Including the mountain." What was left of it. Every time I looked across the lake at the remains of Patterson House, I cringed a little. So close, Fleming. So. Freaking. Close.

Maybe, like a cat, I had a set number of lives. If so, I had to be reaching my limit. I glanced down at the pug sitting on my foot, her happy grin and panting enthusiasm as she waited for treats that weren't forthcoming giving me hope. Since our return from the hospital, she'd rallied and acted now, more than ever, like the pug I'd adopted three years ago.

Maybe she had nine lives, too.

"I heard," Pamela said, returning me to the conversation I'd almost forgotten about. "So, Daisy's staying in Reading?"

"At least part-time," I said. "Emile wants to rebuild the mansion for her." Talk about a fantasy love affair. Those two made a prince/princess story look like a cheap tabloid romance. Nice to know I wouldn't be losing my bestie anytime soon.

"And you?" Pamela's nosiness wasn't going anywhere. "What has Fiona Fleming decided to do with the rest of her life?" She grinned over her coffee cup. "We could always use another reporter."

I shook my head at that, unable to stop the rueful smile in response. "Sorry. Dad has his heart set on Fleming Investigations." I'd already had my heart-to-heart with Mom and Daisy about leaving the annex to them, and neither seemed all that surprised. Though, I admit, Mom looked relieved and grateful when Daisy then informed us she wasn't leaving Reading.

Poor Mom. She must have thought she was losing both partners in the blink of an eye.

"You were mine first." Pamela set her empty cup aside, stretching as sunlight beamed in the glass front of Sammy's and bathed us in warmth. It felt good to be outside. Felt like I'd been hiding, hibernating in Crew's house the last two weeks.

"Have that fight with Dad," I said.

Pamela laughed. "Go up against a Fleming?" She leaned in and hugged me, to my surprise, rare show of affection returned as I embraced her back. "Not a chance." She rose then, Fleur instantly at her side. Which again made me wonder about Aundrea, their marriage. I had, as yet, to talk to her directly, she and her son, his wife, avoiding me.

Well, I'd get to it. When the time was right.

I had time, thankfully. And it was a beautiful day.

With a smile for my pug, I headed out into the street with a wincing limp for additional company, to enjoy the gorgeous weather in the cutest town in America.

CHAPTER FORTY-THREE

I passed the statue of Captain Reading, pausing to look up at the attempt Olivia had made to make the old scoundrel and liar look impressively heroic and saluted his grim visage. I couldn't help the soft inner sigh of regret and disappointment over the treasure, but it was satisfying to know that mystery was solved, once and for all.

And not just that one. Warmed a girl's busybody heart, it did, having the answers I needed to sleep at night.

I set out again, Petunia happily waddling beside me, with a strange thought. Maybe now that all the mysteries in my life were solved, I could get to the most important one. That being the man I married, my darling Crew, who, despite my love for him, still surprised me at times. As my steps carried me past the office, I glanced in the door, spotting my darling and his former partner talking near the entrance.

Of course, we stopped in, my limp going magically away as we did. I hated Crew to know I was still in pain, though I was positive he saw past my fakery. Didn't say anything about it, though, despite knowing how protective he was of me. Like I said, the man was still a mystery.

Maybe that was the best part of being married. Figuring each other out.

Crew hugged me instantly, scar over his eyebrow giving him a deliciously dangerous look I wasn't complaining about. Liz embraced me in turn, then Dad, who joined us from the bowels of Fleming Investigations with a beaming smile on his face. My father didn't complain when I hugged him, despite knowing even the gentlest of embraces had to hurt. He'd cracked four ribs when the house came down. Mom had come out unscathed, mine the only serious injury. My father set one hand on Crew's shoulder, the other on Liz's, while the two of them shrugged at me as he spoke.

"And then there were four." Dad winked. "Fee, I know we're partners, but I figured you'd be all for hiring our newest investigator."

I gaped at Liz who giggled. Like, girl giggled, so uncharacteristic for her I continued gaping while she pulled herself back into Agent Michaud mode.

"Not full-time yet," she said. "I'm wrapping up with the Bureau over the next month or so. But once that's done, I'm all yours."

"Dad." I choked on that word. "I trust you have a plan to keep all of us gainfully employed." I knew he'd been taking jobs outside Reading, but honestly, we were four grown adults, two of us in the same household, looking for one small business to support us. Yes, I had reserves thanks to the success of my bed and breakfast. But that wasn't going to last a lifetime.

Dad just smiled. "Trust your old man," he said.

"If you say so." I didn't mean to kill the buzz, but I wasn't sure if he knew and only remembered just then. "Did Malcolm come to see you?"

My father hesitated, then nodded. "He and Siobhan are setting up here permanently like they wanted, and Malcolm claims he's going legit."

Darius's return to Reading had been quiet and full of guilt. He had, as yet, to say anything to me, keeping his head down, refusing to meet my eyes, back working for his old boss now that I didn't need protecting anymore. Though I'd been told in no uncertain terms my former bodyguard was now on the bottom of the pile, the lowest of the low, and it would take a lot for him to recover his position, if ever.

I'd tried to thank him for the map piece, pivotal in solving the Patterson/Fiona mystery, but no such luck. Never mind his silence and hangdog acceptance of the punishment Malcolm had forced on him for being dragged physically from his post and basically held at gunpoint (okay, I was guessing, but knowing

Darius, it would have taken as much to keep him away.) We'd be having a talk about that guilt of his. Just as soon as Malcolm forgave Darius for leaving me. Which might be never.

Retired crime bosses and their codes of weird honor. Seriously.

Liz grinned like she'd believe it when she saw it. "The O'Shea family is in disarray with the collapse of Blackstone so it's the perfect time for Malcolm to cut himself loose," she said. "I guess Fiona's agreed to a plea bargain, is turning everything over to the federal prosecutor for a reduced sentence." She held up both hands as I tried to protest. "She's getting life, Fee. Don't worry. But in a minimum-security prison, rather than multiple life sentences in supermax."

Still. Grunt.

"It's been a productive week," Dad said. "Barry Clement plead guilty to murder."

"Any sign of Pitch?" Alicia's brother was a survivor. I'd be surprised if he got himself caught.

Liz's headshake told me I was right. "And all of the Pattersons who could, scattered. Including Geoffrey's son, that journalist, what was his name?"

"Christopher." Well, good riddance. I was kind of pissed he'd gotten away with whatever it was he'd gotten away with. I knew he had to be tied to the drug ring, especially after our last conversation. But there were more than enough charges to go around and maybe a few Pattersons slipping through the cracks didn't matter so much. Now that the family was broke, maybe they'd become less reprehensible.

Because they were all just as guilty, as far as I was concerned.

"Our cute little town is almost brand new," Crew said. Sighed. "Why couldn't this have happened when I was sheriff?"

I laughed, hugged my husband. "Like you would have made it a month without something substantially criminal to sink your teeth into."

He looked offended before winking slowly.

Smartass husband. I knew him better than I gave myself credit for.

"Jill has her hands full tying up the loose ends," Dad said. "I told her we're here to help."

At least the sheriff was going to be able to hire some new deputies at last, hopefully much better than the one now sitting in prison. The fact Rose still held her position rankled. I was going to make it my priority to uncover the evidence I needed to put the other half of Rosebert behind bars. Or, at least, make her life miserable and get her fired.

I'd settle for either.

The door opened, entry chime warning us we weren't alone, and we all turned to find the perfectly put together Vivian French joining us. No hesitation in hugs this time, either, even Liz giving the mayor a solid embrace, one Vivian seemed happy to return. And, to my surprise, when she pulled free of the agent's arms, she was smiling.

A real, genuine smile. Which she turned on me.

"I thought you all should be the first to know," she said, the iciness gone from her tone, showing us the real Vivian French, likely for the first time. "I've spoken to Olivia. It's my decision at this time to step down as mayor of Reading. I've asked her and the council in the interim to allow her to resume her position until an election can be held. They've agreed."

Wow. "Viv, are you sure?" She might not have pushed tourism like Olivia, but she'd carried us through the worst of this disaster. And our new/old friendship made me loyal enough to want her happiness.

I shouldn't have worried. She shrugged delicately, that easy elegance of hers going nowhere, even if her cold veneer was long gone. Or was it? She arched an eyebrow, tone dropping back to chill judgment, as she answered me.

"I've had enough politics, thank you," she said. "It's time I returned to more important matters." She sniffed softly. "As the Queen of Wheat."

I choked on a laugh, embarrassed and yet unable to stop the giggle that escaped. "How long have you known?" Ack, that nickname.

Vivian just winked.

Strolling through the dusk-wrapped streets of my hometown with my handsome husband at my side, my panting pug between us, was just about as close to heaven as I'd ever get. His fingers twined naturally with mine like we'd always been in love, holding hands the connection I craved the most since our time under the mess that had become of Patterson House. Sure, I loved his hugs, always would. But the memory of him keeping me together with that simple touch would stay with me the rest of my life.

We talked about nothing and everything, Dad's plans for Fleming Investigations—he was still keeping a lot to himself, though we'd cornered him into a staff meeting in a few days when Liz could return to join us—my retirement from tourism, his from law enforcement. His grandfather, my grandmother.

Life. Death. And new beginnings.

Why our footsteps carried us to the empty green space that had been Petunia's, I didn't know, but we both paused at the same time, my (our) eager pug snuffling at the sidewalk as if remembering there should be something there for her, sitting abruptly, head cocked to one side, ears raised as she whined softly over not finding what she was looking for.

Tears welled, the back of my throat scratchy and tight, as Crew drew me against him, cheek pressed to the top of my head, big hand rubbing a soft circle over the small of my back. We just stood there a long time, Petunia finally meowing her pug protest at the confusion of the situation and sinking to sit on my feet.

"I've been meaning to mention this," my darling husband said, voice husky, deep, as darkness fell, the streetlights flickering on. "I miss Petunia's. So many memories." I looked up at him, nodded, unable to trust my own voice. "But you'd be wasted, Fee, going backward. You deserve the chance to do what you love." He touched the tip of my nose with one finger. "My beautiful, nosy busybody."

I laughed, couldn't help it. Nodded again.

Crew kissed me softly but deeply, slow and lingering, then hugged me tight while he turned to look at the empty place where my heart had come to live.

"Seems a shame to leave it vacant," he said. "Especially when we're going to need somewhere to raise a family."

Tears, so many tears. A house. A home. For us. For the children we both wanted, here in Reading. Where Petunia's used to stand.

I kissed him, hugged him and nodded against his wide chest.

Grandmother Iris would have approved.

The Reading
Reader Gazette

VOLUME 1   ISSUE 1   JULY 14, 2021   WWW.RRGAZETTE.COM

News Briefs

1. **Captain Reading Day cancelled until further notice:** With regret, we are cancelling our previously scheduled celebration. All citizens are asked to return their Captain Reading official merchandise to town hall immediately. Thank you for your cooperation.

2. **Parking Violations:** Your town council would like to remind you that parking restrictions continue year round. Any Reading resident caught street parking will be reprimanded and their car impounded. While we realize parking has become a major issue for our town, the sheriff's department is authorized to remove your car without notice. They ask you to please park responsibly and with our town's continuing prosperity in mind. Let's keep Reading's streets safe!

3. **Stolen fire hydrants:** Could anyone with information please come forward regarding the missing fire hydrant on Main Street. While you were kind enough to cap the outlet, we would really like our hydrant back, no questions asked. Thanks you, Reading FD

4. **Park Hours:** It has come to the attention of town council that our downtown park has become a preferred area for activity unbecoming Reading residents, mostly of the teenage variety. Please note the Reading Sheriff's Department will be conducting regular patrols in and around the park and tickets for lewd behavior will be written.

Winner of this week's Fire Hall 50/50 draw: Marie Patterson. Clearly someone's idea of a sick joke.

Please send any pending community notices to: pamela@rrgazette.com before 4PM.

Diving and Drugs Death Duo

MC Tortuga, 34, of Tampa, FL, and Barry Clement, 28, of Montpellier, VT, named in two separate homicides

Treasure hunt no match for black market gold

By Pamela Shard

In a stunning week in Reading history, two murderers have been brought to justice in a duet homicide of revenge, blackmail and town politics.

The death of noted treasure hunter, Gregg Brown, 38, of Portsmouth, ME, came swiftly when his oxygen tanks were tampered with, causing a grand mal seizure underwater, ending in his death.

"Mr. Brown drowned when he ejected his mouthpiece in Cutter Lake during the seizure," says local coroner, Dr. Lloyd Aberstock. "Hell of a way to go."

While treasure hunting comes with a degree of risk, no one knew how risky looking for the alleged hoard of Captain Reading might end up. Certainly not local residents Fiona Fleming and Crew Turner.

"It's a tragic loss of life," Mr. Turner said. "It should never have happened." As an experienced diver, Mr. Turner seemed shaken by the death.

Though it's understood his murderer, MC Tortuga, leader of the dive team hired to look for Captain Reading's hoard, feared for her own life, instead of alerting local authorities, she took matters into her own hands and will now pay the consequences of her actions.

Even more shocking was the death of local accountant and Patterson family member, Geoffrey Jenkins, 49, of Reading, VT. As part of a criminal prescription drug trafficking ring run through our local hospital, Barry Clement claims to have taken his orders from Mr. Jenkins, as part of the mysterious corporate conglomerate, Blackstone. Now known to be owned and run by the formerly missing and presumed dead Fiona Doyle, disappeared over thirty years ago, Mr. Clement claims he was forced to misappropriate drugs for the black market and that Mr. Jenkins threatened him, leading to the attack that ended his life.

With the destruction of Patterson House in a planned demolition that almost took the lives of many Reading residents--including Fiona Fleming and her family, many details about the

AUTHOR NOTES

Well, here we are. At the end. At last. No shame, I cried a lot writing this book. And editing it. Because despite the fact I know I'll be back to Reading before we know it, I'll miss Fee's voice in the interim.

She's been no end of delight for me, our darling Fiona Fleming. When I set out to write this series, I really didn't know what to think, where she'd take me, if I'd learn to love her like I do all of my characters.

For those of you who have read the Hayle Coven Novels and have made yourselves at home in Wilding Springs, coffee with Syd, Sassafras in your lap looking for pats, Ethpeal cackling her fuzzy socked way across the kitchen... feels like family.

I didn't expect Fee to feel the same, but she does. I miss Petunia's like it was my own B&B that burned to the ground, miss the kitchen, Lucy making cupcakes and cookies, Daisy and her flowered dresses, the sitting room, the carriage house. I miss Fee's apartment and the third floor bathroom, the Green Room and the beautiful foyer lit by the sun. I miss feeling Grandmother Iris's presence in that dear old space and I know all I have to do to visit it again is go back. And.

I'm moving forward, instead. And so are Fee and Crew. When you see them next, it will be two months after this book has finished, and we will have taken a fun and murderous journey with Alice Moore that will hopefully bring you as much joy as Fee's.

For now, I'm off to a Florida plantation house rising from the swamp, to help Alice investigate a ghostly presence who may or may not be a murderer...

You, my dear reader, are welcome to join me. Or, do as I will eventually, and go back to the beginning and remember all the reasons we love Fee so very much.

There are those who made this series possible who need mention, and I do that now with the absolute and utter gratitude of one who knows she could never do this without support:

Christina, you brought Fee to life with the most amazing covers I could have asked for. I can't wait to share what we're creating for Alice.

Kirstin, I will always say yes because you do. Thank you for making this journey so much easier for me.

And, for this book in particular, no small mention, I want to express my deep thanks and adoration for the amazing women and men who assisted me in the creation of this book's first murder. To Marie, Chantal, Anja, Walter, John and Mark, thank you. I enjoyed turning you into murderers, despicable human beings and victims, while taking your advice on how to commit the ideal underwater crime. My diver friends, *gracias*.

Best,
Patti

A lot has changed since I wrote my last author's note for Fee's series. Including the beginning of her second one! Find *Patent Pending and Death* available now and happy reading in Reading, still the cutest town in America!

ABOUT THE AUTHOR

Everything you need to know about me is in this one statement: I've wanted to be a writer since I was a little girl, and now I'm doing it. How cool is that, being able to follow your dream and make it reality? I've tried everything from university to college, graduating the second with a journalism diploma (I sucked at telling real stories), am an enthusiastic member of an all-girl improv troupe (if you've never tried it, I highly recommend making things up as you go along as often as possible) and I get to teach and perform with an amazing group of women I adore. I've even been in a Celtic girl band (some of our stuff is on YouTube!) and was an independent film maker (go check out the Lovely Witches Club at www.lovelywitchesclub.com). My life has been one creative thing after another—all leading me here, to writing books for a living.

Now with multiple series in happy publication, I live on beautiful and magical Prince Edward Island (I know you've heard of Anne of Green Gables) with my multitude of pets.

I love-love-love hearing from you! You can reach me (and I promise I'll message back) at patti@pattilarsen.com. And if you're eager for your next dose of Patti Larsen books (usually about one release a month) come join my mailing list! All the best up and coming, giveaways, contests and, of course, my observations on the world (aren't you just dying to know what I think about everything?) all in one place: https://bit.ly/PattiLarsenEmail.

Last—but not least!—I hope you enjoyed what you read! Your happiness is my happiness. And I'd love to hear just what you thought. A review where you found this book would mean the world to me—reviews feed writers more than you will ever know. So, loved it (or not so much), your honest review would make my day. Thank you!

Made in United States
North Haven, CT
29 August 2024

56708162R00193